amelia unabridged

amelia

unabridged

ashley schumacher

WEDNESDAY
BOOKS
NEW YORK

First published in the United States by Wednesday Books, an imprint of St. Martin's Publishing Group

www.wednesdaybooks.com

Library of Congress Cataloging-in-Publication Data

Names: Schumacher, Ashley, author.
Title: Amelia unabridged / Ashley Schumacher.
Description: First edition. | New York, NY : Wednesday Books, 2021. |
Identifiers: LCCN 2020037487 | ISBN 9781250253026 (hardcover) |
    ISBN 9781250253033 (ebook)
Subjects: CYAC: Grief—Fiction. | Fans (Persons)—Fiction. |
    Friendship—Fiction. | Love—Fiction.
Classification: LCC PZ7.1.S3365545 Am 2021 | DDC [Fic]—dc23
LC record available at https://lccn.loc.gov/2020037487

Our books may be purchased in bulk for promotional, educational, or business use. Please contact your local bookseller or the Macmillan Corporate and Premium Sales Department at 1-800-221-7945, extension 5442, or by email at MacmillanSpecialMarkets@macmillan.com.

First Edition: 2021

10 9 8 7 6 5 4 3 2 1

For Edward. You're simply the best.

"What will we do?" Emmeline asked, watching as the storm clouds gathered into menacing darkness.

"We'll do the only thing we can," Ainsley answered. "Endure."

prologue

Everyone has a story about the first time they read the Orman Chronicles. This is mine.

The day my father left us, it was sunny. I remember thinking it was odd, because in books tragedy always strikes during a storm, lightning and thunder magnifying the worst that could happen. But my father didn't care about the perfect, cloudless sky, or how he was leaving with our only car, marooning us in our grief.

Even then, I couldn't help but imagine us on an island. The sofas in our small living room became piles of uneven sea stones. My father's crossed arms and defiant stance became a crumbling, abandoned lighthouse that stood uncaring against the angry waves of my mother.

Through the front window blinds, I could see his reason sitting in our peeling green van, a woman—*girl*—who wasn't even ten years older than me. Her freshly twenty-one appeal was somewhat dulled by her habit of worriedly gnawing on her index finger as our eyes connected over the dashboard.

I recognized her, I dimly realized. A cheerleader from

the Saturday afternoon college football games my father had dragged me to for the past three months.

I let the broken bit of blind fall back into place with a quiet shudder as my mother pleaded with Dad to stay. My stomach twisted into a hundred cruel shapes and my mind forgot all about the island, the lighthouse, everything.

"For Amelia," my mother begged, mascara dripping down her face in a way I thought only happened in movies. "You can't leave her, Willy. She's your daughter. Tell him, Amelia!" She roughly jerked me by the shoulder to face them. "Tell. Him."

I stared at them. Mom with her self-dyed red hair sticking up in all directions. Dad, trying to look stoic and resigned, his polo collar smudged from the self-tanner that had turned his pale skin orange.

I turned back to the window.

"Let him go," I said. "What do I care?"

I wasn't sure if the ceramic pot holding the succulent I grew from a seed in elementary school fell when Mom whirled away from me, or if she knocked it off the table on purpose.

When the green van finally barreled away, tires jumping over the cracked drive, my mother went to her bedroom and slammed the door. I stood there, listening to the kitchen faucet drip in tune with her sobs, before my feet carried me out the front door, down the driveway, and block after block, until I found myself in front of Downtown Books.

I never came here unless I had a gift card. I couldn't afford to pay the price on a book's bar code, only on a yellowing discount sticker at a used bookstore. I spent my babysitting money on new school supplies and the occasional hot lunch, instead of my usual cheese and mustard sandwich, never on books from here.

But, that day, I let myself stand there and gaze through the window for as long as I liked. I could stay all night, I thought, watching customers drift around the low shelves like sailboats bobbing on the horizon. I didn't have to go home to a Dadless but Momful house, didn't have to clean up the shattered pottery and succulent leaves still scattered across the floor.

My reflection in the bookstore window looked haunted, my bright yellow Harry Potter shirt washing out my pale white skin and blue eyes. My long hair—caught somewhere between blonde and brown—wasn't helping. I wondered if emotions could suck the color right out of you. I wondered if hatred and bewilderment could make you anemic.

I don't know how long I would have stood there, outside looking in, if not for Jenna Williams.

The glass door to the bookstore wasn't even fully open before she poked her head out and said, "You're Amelia, right? You can't just stand there. It's creepy. What are you doing? Come inside if you want to look."

"I don't know," I said.

Even in my daze, part of me felt like I should be curtseying or something. Jenna Williams—reigning valedictorian from fifth grade onward, *always* impeccably dressed, the first of our grade to wear eyeliner, noted tennis enthusiast—was the closest thing to royalty in the freshman class, though she never held court. She had a few girls from the tennis club she hung out with, but nobody ever managed to get closer than arm's length. It made her all the more appealing, really, than the girls that collected doting admirers and disciples. Jenna was less obtainable. She was never unfriendly, but she was a supernova in a galaxy of new stars and we all knew it, even the teachers.

We had been classmates since kindergarten, but I was surprised she knew my name.

Maybe it was because of the star thing, but I heard myself tell her, "My dad left today."

She sighed, berry lips bright against her suntanned skin, and said, "Like *left* left? That sucks. Do you want to talk about it?"

I would have been less surprised if the stone lion sitting outside the fancy restaurant across the street had opened its massive jaws and made the same offer, but I managed to mumble, "No, thank you."

"Good," Jenna said. "There are too many books and not enough time as it is."

"I don't know," I said again, nervous. If she was a star in the galaxy, I was one of those astronauts that gets disconnected from their ship and floats through space until they run out of oxygen.

"There's nothing in the world a good book can't cure," she said. "Come on, pick one or two. My treat."

And so, in the bright artificial light of the bookstore, we browsed side by side like this was how we spent every Friday evening. She wasn't a supernova and I wasn't a deserted daughter, and despite the part of my brain incessantly remembering my mother's crying and the sound I imagined the cheerleader's teeth made against the flesh of her finger, I was content. Or maybe resigned.

When we brought my book and Jenna's four to the register, the bookseller smiled at my choice, *The Forest Between the Sea and the Sky*, the first of the Orman Chronicles, by N. E. Endsley.

"This book is *so good*," she enthused. She had a pair of reading glasses on her nose and another pair forgotten atop her head. "The author isn't much older than you, probably. Only sixteen or so. Ain't that something? You'll have to let me know what you think."

I finished the book in one sitting, under the glowing bulb of Jenna's crème-colored bedside lamp. I spent the night at her house, though it was less of an invite and more of an edict. When we left the bookstore, I was taken in the Williamses' very nice car to their very nice house, and it was as if I had always been there and always would be.

"Jenna never brings friends over," her dad boomed cheerfully.

It was a short drive from the store to their home, but long enough for Mrs. Williams to smile at me with her eyes in the rearview mirror.

When I borrowed Jenna's cell phone to call my mother and let her know where I was, she didn't answer. I left the numbers for the Williamses' house and Jenna's cell and told her to call me back. She never did.

I was worried she'd be furious when they dropped me off the next morning, but she was still in her room. If it weren't for the acidic smell of microwave instant pasta, I wouldn't have known she was even there.

But Orman had already taken root in my heart and was under my arm, begging to be reread—begging me to forget the dripping faucet and empty driveway and football games and to run away to a world with problems much greater and more fantastical than my own.

Come away, come away, it whispered.

I went gladly.

The story follows two sisters, Emmeline and Ainsley, as they discover a hidden realm, adjacent to our world, full of old prophecies and whispering forests. Emmeline has always been the quieter, meeker of the sisters, but when a drop of her blood soaks into the forest floor, the Old Laws bind her as ruler of the realm, making outgoing, take-charge Ainsley incredibly jealous.

Things only get worse when Ainsley finds out that *she*, not Emmeline, is the ruler that has been foretold in Orman for centuries, and their rivalry rages, with an entire world hanging in the balance.

But just as the tension between them is about to snap, they're yanked back into the modern world, with televisions and air-conditioning and green vans that leave and never come back. The Old Laws, it turns out, do not take kindly to outsiders— even prophesied outsiders—staying in Orman forever.

The story ends with Emmeline and Ainsley on the carpet of their bedroom floor, staring at each other in fury and confusion, not knowing why or how they have been exiled from Orman—or if they will ever return.

A few months later, on an uncharacteristically cold Texas night in December, I gave the book to Jenna. It was the same night she told me her parents had begun to make dinner reservations for four without thinking.

"Welcome to the family," she deadpanned, like it wasn't the best thing in the world. "You, too, are now required to spend your free time sitting through Dad's corny jokes and Mom's complaints about work between bites of overly salted chips and salsa."

After my emotions quieted to somewhere between elation at being engulfed into a complete and whole family and despair that my own would not miss me, I took *The Forest Between the Sea and the Sky* from my backpack and set it on the pillow beside her.

"Read this," I said. "It's perfect."

"Nothing's perfect," Jenna said.

"This is."

Jenna stayed up reading long after I pretended to fall asleep. In the hazy quiet, I fretted that the book would not grip her like it had me, and then where would we be? Would she think it was too childish? Would she think *I* was too childish and not want to be friends anymore?

But if there was someone I should have trusted, it was Jenna.

"Ainsley," she told me without preamble when I opened my eyes the next morning. "I side with Ainsley. You?"

"Emmeline." I smiled, sitting up in bed and picking a piece of flattened popcorn from last night's movie marathon off my nightshirt. Jenna was already showered and dressed, her curly black hair tucked into a neat bun.

"Are you saying that to be contrary or because you believe it?" she asked.

I rolled my eyes. "That's something Ainsley would say."

Together we spent the morning debating the finer points of Orman, forming theories about how the girls would find their way back—if ever—and speculating about book 2.

Back then, we didn't realize what the Orman Chronicles would become. We couldn't have known, sitting cross-legged on Jenna's unmade bed, that the book and its sequel would turn into major best sellers that got translated into more languages than I knew existed. Orman cultivated a fandom that ran like a twisting golden ribbon across oceans and races and religions, surprising critics, but never readers.

Jenna was right: there is nothing in the world a good book can't cure.

And the Orman Chronicles?

They're the best kind of good.

chapter one

If my life were a book, I would start here, standing in front of the long row of check-in tables at the California Children's Book Festival with something that feels very much like hope blooming in my chest.

And if Jenna were the editor of my book—and she totally would be, because she'd want to make sure I got it right—she would disagree. She would say I should start from when we first met, or six days ago, when we graduated from Crescent High to tearful hugs from her parents and distant pats from my mother. But just this once I'll ignore Jenna's advice and start here, standing in the middle of the atrium, staring upward at the huge, colorful banner suspended above the check-in.

There are at least a dozen author faces in neat, orderly rows, but it's the center photo that makes my fingers tingle with excitement. The focal point—the largest photo of them all, and dead center—is N. E. Endsley, with his sharp cheekbones and dark, layered hair that is two steps of sophistication above boy band hair.

It's a testament to his writing skills that his first book sold so well without the inordinately attractive author photo on the back flap.

"Author of the Orman Chronicles" is all it says beneath his unsmiling photo, but everyone knows the final book is coming. Those of us who paid a prince's ransom—or whose best friend's parents paid the ransom as a high school graduation gift—to be in the room for his special announcement are hoping to hear at least a release date and hopefully—*squee!*—a short excerpt.

I have little time to be excited beyond the sharp pain of glee that makes me feel as if the world could never be this exciting again. It's a kind of morose happiness that I squash down because Jenna has already stridden to one of the tables and is fetching our wristbands.

"Jenna Williams," she is saying to the blue polo behind the table when I near. "And Amelia Griffin. Both VIP passes with access to the N. E. Endsley session."

The man flips through a stapled stack of papers before giving each of us a wristband with VIP embossed along the thin rubber. I twist mine over my hand without looking, but Jenna holds hers up for examination.

"This one has a nick in it," she says. "May I have another?"

The man seems confused for a split second too long—all I can see behind his eyes are endless file cabinets—so before Jenna can unleash her usual speech about presentation and quality, I work the band from my wrist and quickly swap it with her nicked one before she can argue.

"It's fine," I say. "I don't care."

Jenna rolls her eyes and says, "You should," but blessedly we walk away lecture-free and into the long rows of booths and tables stacked high with swag and books.

———

When the Williamses had asked us what we wanted for graduation, over dinner in late February, Jenna had barely looked up from her plate of enchiladas.

"There's a book festival the week after graduation," she said. "It's only a couple of days. We could fit it in before Ireland."

I had jerked my head toward her, surprised.

"Have you been looking at my computer again? How did you know about the festival?"

Jenna rolled her eyes. "As if you're the only one with an internet alert out for anything related to N. E. Endsley."

There was no doubt that she had chosen this for my benefit. Later, when she dropped me off at my house after a car ride full of my squeals about meeting N. E. Endsley, I leaned over to hug her good-bye and whispered, "You don't like internet alerts."

"What?" Her voice was casual.

"You don't like internet alerts or subscription newsletters because they take up too much time and clutter your computer."

Jenna looked out the window to hide her smile. "When did I say that?"

"You didn't." I grinned. "I just know. And when *did* you look at my computer?"

She turned to face me, indignant. "I've told you before you ought to lock it when you walk away from it in the library!"

"Yeah," I deadpanned. "Wouldn't want the riffraff seeing my search history of book festivals and—"

"And llama memes when you're supposed to be studying?"

"Don't judge." I shoved her shoulder and turned it into another awkward car hug. "Besides, if I hadn't left it open, you would have asked for something sensible for graduation. Like textbook covers or . . . I don't even know what, instead of the best, best, *best* thing on the planet."

"I don't think textbook covers are a thing in college, Amelia." Her voice was even, but I could feel her smile.

"Whatever. You know what I mean." My nose was lodged against her hair. She smelled like shampoo and her fruity, too-sweet perfume.

"Thanks, Jenna," I whispered, and found myself oddly choked up.

"I'll enjoy it, too, you know," she whispered back. "But you're welcome. Happy graduation. Is this hug over yet?"

"Almost. Your perfume is trying to kill me."

The same perfume brings me back to the festival, to the pulsing hustle of book lovers swarming around us, which is no match for my enthusiasm.

"Look at it," I urge Jenna, jogging alongside her fast walk to thrust my wrist in her face. "Look! This band means that, in only three hours, we get to see N. E. Endsley. *Endsley*, Jenna."

Jenna does not pause, unfazed by my attempts at distraction.

"Amelia." She says my name with a mix of exasperation and affection, but more of the latter than usual. "There are other events before his session, and we should enjoy some other panels and booths, too, okay?"

"Whatever you say, JenJen." I say the pet name her first and last boyfriend gave her under my breath, thinking she won't hear it in the din.

"Do *not* call me that."

Her dark, curly strands bounce toward me all at once, and her eyes narrow, but a corner of her lips is restraining a smile.

"Oh, come on, JenJen. Lighten up. It's a perfectly good name for a girlfriend . . . or a poodle."

"Shove off," she says, laughing. She steers us into a booth of T-shirts in all the colors of the rainbow with catchy book phrases printed on their fronts: I READ PAST MY BEDTIME or I'M A BOOK DRAGON, NOT A BOOKWORM. Most can also be purchased as posters, and I push us toward the rolled-up plastic tubes near the back of the booth.

"This is why boyfriends are useless," Jenna mutters. "They distract you from schoolwork and they make up stupid names that your so-called friends never let you live down."

"Chin up, JenJen," I say, extracting one of the poster tubes from its brethren. "What do you think of this one for our dorm room?"

The top of the poster is decorated with little cartoon people attempting and failing to ski, skateboard, and surf, the message below reading, "If at first you don't succeed, read a book instead."

"That hardly seems conducive to an encouraging study environment," Jenna says. "Besides, I don't appreciate the implication that one cannot be a reader *and* an athlete."

"Killjoy." I *thwap* her on the shoulder with the tube.

"Child." She grabs the poster from me and hits me lightly atop my head, before heading to the register and sliding her father's credit card across the counter.

"You didn't have to buy it," I say afterward.

She shrugs. "Dad said, and I quote, 'It's your graduation present. Go crazy. But don't tell your mother.'"

"Your poor mom," I say. "She's going to want to throttle you when the credit card bill comes in. Meanwhile, you'll be far away in Ireland, collecting plants and being nerdy."

"Specimens," Jenna corrects.

"Whatever." I sidestep a woman in a long skirt pushing a dolly full of boxes like it's a race car. "She'll want to give you one of your own lectures and you won't be there to hear it."

"I'll just blame it on you and she can give *you* an earful."

We move into a slim, unoccupied space between booths so Jenna can pull up the festival schedule on her phone.

It suddenly strikes me as very adult, our solitary trip to California. Jenna and I are in charge of the events we attend, where we eat lunch, what swag we buy. I keep waiting for somebody to accuse us of being unaccompanied minors, to escort us from the premises and call our parents, but we're eighteen. We're enrolled in Missoula for the fall. We *are* adults. Sort of.

I am vitalized and cowed by this realization, and I want to remember this moment of watching my friend lead the way on our first long-distance solo trip. While Jenna scrolls, I wrestle my trusty digital camera from my backpack and remove the lens cover. I look through the viewfinder and snap one picture—it's my rule—and then let the camera hang from its strap around my neck.

"If we book it, we could make it to ballroom C for the 'It's Only a Flesh Wound: Violence in Fantasy' panel," I say, grinning. "Get it? *Book* it?"

My laugh echoes in the small space, but Jenna only snorts and keeps scrolling. I practically have the schedule memorized, after a week of alternating between staring at the welcome email and obsessively rereading the two Orman books.

My mind wanders ahead to what his session will be like,

my head spinning with everything I know about Orman and Endsley.

While the first book—*The Forest Between the Sea and the Sky*—is about finding Orman and the power struggle set up between Ainsley and Emmeline, the second book—*The In-Between Queens*—is about Emmeline and Ainsley gathering their armies to fight each other for the throne. But because the Old Laws only let them stay in Orman for spurts of time, for parts of the book they are dealing with each other and their parents back in our world. They're rulers of their realms in Orman, but here in our world they still have to do homework and clean up Oreo crumbs they drop on the carpet. It's funny to watch them try to exist in such different environments.

Everyone thinks the third book is going to be set completely in Orman, but I hope not. I like to imagine the girls somewhere in this world with me—Emmeline running out of toilet paper after she pees and dealing with real stuff alongside me, but slipping back into Orman to take her place as the true queen of the kingdom.

They're the kind of stories that keep you up late at night, ones I sink into so fully I'm certain they are secret histories of a real world that I just haven't figured out how to get to. Reading them makes me feel as if I'm putting on a suit of armor over a beloved sweater, fierce and comfortable, nostalgic and adventurous.

And N. E. Endsley is some sort of absurdly young writing prodigy. He's only a year older than Jenna and me. Social media lit up a few weeks ago on his nineteenth birthday, and a few prominent sites ran articles recapping his improbably glorious success.

He started writing the stories when he was only thirteen

and published the first book when he was sixteen, the second book's publication following a year later. The third and final book of the trilogy was supposed to come out this year, but the release date was pushed back indefinitely.

No one knows why.

There are rumors, though. Some say that he has writer's block and can't figure out how to end such an epic story when it's become so popular. Some go further and accuse the fandom of being the root of the problem, using words like *vapid* and *invasive*. Expecting too much, putting too much pressure on Endsley's creative space.

Others still say he'll never finish, that he's become a social recluse before the age of twenty-five and that whatever has caused it, the story will end with the second book.

I hope it's not true, but I don't have much to hope on. Nobody does. Endsley rarely grants interviews. What the Orman fandom knows of him comes mostly in trickles and hearsay.

One night I couldn't sleep and I fell down an internet rabbit hole, reading comments from people who've run into Endsley in New York City, where he lives. One girl saw him at the public library and approached to ask for an autograph of the second book, which she happened to have with her. Endsley refused. But as he walked away, a different boy approached her. He apologized for Endsley's behavior and asked for the girl's address, promising to send her a signed copy, before apologizing again for Endsley's rudeness and disappearing into the crowd.

In an updated post, the girl claimed to have received the book.

Who knows if it's true. Maybe I'll be better able to judge for myself when I see him face-to-face.

"What about the 'Just Enough Cooks in the Kitchen' panel?" Jenna asks, interrupting my daydreaming. "June Turner and some of the authors from that anthology about feminism in high school are speaking. You know, the book I gave you to read last week that you never did?"

"How do you know I didn't read it?" I ask.

"Because you gave it back to me without a page out of place, that's how. There wasn't so much as a smudge on it."

"Are you suggesting I'm a book destroyer?"

Jenna gives me the same look I've seen Mrs. Williams level at Mr. Williams on weekly grocery runs, when he sneaks extra boxes of prepackaged muffins into the shopping cart, which he claims are "for his girls." It's a look of exasperation, but full of so much love it makes my insides burst.

I laugh. "Fine, I'm not a neat freak. Sue me. And you're right about me not reading it, but only because I was—"

"Rereading the Endsley books," Jenna interrupts. "I know."

I link my arm through hers, dragging her once more into the river of people.

"Feminism panel it is, JenJen. We better get moving if we want seats up front. I *know* that's where you'll want to sit."

Jenna is obviously resisting the urge to roll her eyes at me again as I stubbornly keep my arm linked through hers. It's difficult to walk side by side with so many people around us. She doesn't drop her arm, though. It's her job to make the big and not-so-big choices in this friendship. It's my job to make whatever she chooses fun, no matter how many faces she makes.

Both of us have an easy task today, because though she won't say it aloud, I know that Jenna's heart is beating just as eagerly as mine, marking time until we are closer to Orman and its creator than we've ever been before.

———

After the surprisingly hilarious talk on feminism, Jenna wants to squeeze in another panel before we get in line for the Endsley session, but I don't want to risk getting crappy seats. It doesn't take much whining to wear her down.

"Fine," she says, rolling her eyes. "But we're going to be in line for over an hour, and I'm not going to hear any of this *She's cutting* nonsense, so if you need to go to the restroom, go now."

"I don't have to go that bad."

"Bad-*ly*. You better start using proper grammar if you are going to be a professor of English someday."

It's my turn to roll my eyes. Jenna forced me to take an expensive career aptitude test last spring that made all sorts of promises about accuracy and reliability and blah, blah, blah. It spit out *Professor*. Jenna had said, "Perfect. You can teach English," and that was that. She had my ten-year plan sorted within the next two hours, my light red boxes lining up next to her purple ones on a spreadsheet.

The first entry of note—getting into the same college—has already been updated on our shared document, with lines drawn through it to signify its completion. The next, a university preparatory class at the local community college, is highlighted only in my red boxes, because I am to take notes—*careful notes, Amelia*—while Jenna is in Ireland. It's only a one-day seminar, but it's supposed to teach you all kinds of new study techniques and coping mechanisms for getting through college with your dignity and sanity intact. Jenna insists it's a necessity.

"Fine. I'll go," I tell her, answering for the bathroom run

but thinking of the stupid prep course. "Hold my book bag, will you?"

Jenna gives a long-suffering sigh. "Mine is already too heavy. I'll sit here and wait for you."

She points to a blessedly empty patch of carpet beside a roped-off hallway with a long line of windows overlooking the ocean. From the rope dangles a sign: NO CONFERENCE PARTICIPANTS. A soda and half-eaten pastry on the other side of the barrier suggest the presence of a volunteer who has abandoned their post.

"I'll be quick," I say. "I'll meet you right back here."

Jenna leans both our bags against the wall, rotating her shoulders and rubbing her neck as I scamper off, tripping over my feet in my rush.

The first bathroom I come across has a line that winds out the door and halfway up the wall that borders it. I consider using the men's restroom (Why is there *never* a line?) but decide to try my luck on the first floor, hoping the bathrooms there will be empty.

They're twice as busy. But it seems silly to go upstairs again so I spend twenty minutes in line, bouncing up and down on my toes, before washing my hands in record time and rushing back upstairs to Jenna and the line for *N. E. Endsley.*

My heart is already thumping in my throat, so it doesn't have a chance to react when I trip on the last step and fall head-first into the legs of a boy at the top.

He's all dark hair and white skin that looks sun-kissed, with warm eyes that are concerned when I meet them. This is what a human chocolate chip cookie must look like. A very *stressed* cookie. His forehead is furrowed so deeply, I have a headache just looking at him. I would probably care more—about how cute he is, about the lanyard that identifies him as being part of the festival, about whatever is provoking the forehead wrinkles—if I weren't so eager to get back to Jenna and to see N. E. Endsley.

"I am very sorry," the boy says. "I didn't see you there."

"No worries," I say, bracing myself against his elbow to straighten up. "My fault. I wasn't looking where I was going."

I'm already peering around him, my eyes searching for Jenna, as the boy slides past me and hurries down the stairs, his plastic lanyard blown to the side and bouncing against his shoulder like Clark Kent's tie.

At first I wonder if Jenna has left, but she's only moved to the other side of the hallway. She doesn't see me approach because her head is turned. Something about her posture reminds me of Gatsby looking forlornly toward the green light at the end of the dock, which makes me nervous.

"I'm back," I say, and her head jerks toward me, startled.

"What's going on?" I ask, frowning.

She blinks once, twice, and fidgets. "Nothing. Just lost in thought. Do you think one suitcase is enough for Ireland?"

I squint at her, trying to reconcile my in-charge friend with this skittish creature before me. She picks at an invisible piece of lint on her tights.

"Fess up, Williams. What is it?"

For a moment, she looks guilty, but when she speaks I realize I've misdiagnosed her foreboding.

It's not shame on her face; it's pity.

"Amelia . . . there's a rumor that's been floating around since you left. One woman walked by with a walkie-talkie and I overheard . . ." She tilts her head toward the hallway. "And another came out only a few minutes later with a team of volunteers. They're going to announce it shortly."

Something sick twists in my stomach.

"Announce. What?"

Jenna flinches at my hardened tone.

"Amelia, let's try to be as under—"

"Ladies and gentlemen." A voice booms from the overhead speakers and the din of the room hushes as much as is to be expected.

"This is Linda Lancaster, head of events here at CCBF. Due to unforeseen circumstances, N. E. Endsley is unable to attend today's festivities. We offer our sincerest apologies for this unexpected turn of events. Those who paid for the session will be refunded, or you may donate the difference to our charity partner. Representatives and volunteers will be stationed in the lobby should you have any questions or concerns. Thank you."

Rolling sounds of confusion and disappointment splash against the rocks of the blue polo–clad volunteers. I'm looking straight forward, my eyes resting on a booth that sells cloth book covers, but I don't really see it.

"Amelia." Jenna sounds like she's approaching a wounded animal. "Amelia, please talk to me."

I can't. I can't handle her trying to comfort me.

"This is a mistake," I say. "Right?"

"It's not a mistake, Amelia."

"Would you stop saying my name like that? I'm not going to"—I wave my arms above my head—"flip out or something."

"I know."

"I'm pissed."

"I know."

"Aren't *you*?"

Something in her face doesn't look quite right, but she doesn't answer. How can she be so cavalier about this? Endsley was supposed to be the main event of the festival—and *my* summer. The memory of breathing the same air as him was meant to keep me company during the long Jenna-less summer, while she was in Ireland.

Now I'll be alone to suffocate in my thoughts. I'll spend the next two months waiting for the people on the *Wheel of Fortune* reruns Mom watches over and over to guess the stupid puzzle, while Jenna enjoys her "Irish excursion," which most would treat as a vacation but she'll treat as a botanical expedition.

I would have done all of these things anyway, but the whole reason I told the Williamses I didn't want to go with Jenna to Ireland was because it was already too much—the last four years of them paying for dinners and weekend outings and this festival besides. A trip abroad felt like stepping over the invisible line I *know* I've been toeing since freshman year with them and their seemingly endless two-lawyer-parent income. I mentioned the line to Jenna once. She snorted and ignored my comment completely. But it's there, even if she can't see it.

It's as present as Jenna's not-so-subtle insistence that I do something sensible with my college degree instead of pursuing photography like I mentioned once. As present as the high-pitched sobs of a girl half my age who is clutching a worn copy of *The In-Between Queens* and pressing her face into her father's shirt.

It's all too much.

"There are a few more panels," Jenna begins, but she is un-characteristically cowed into silence when I whirl around to face her, tears that I didn't give permission to fall rolling down my cheeks.

She steps forward, and I wonder if this is the beginning of a rare Jenna-initiated hug, but she stops before we're touching.

"Maybe we should go back to the hotel and recharge," she says. "Eat some overpriced mini-fridge ice cream."

I'm relieved that it's her idea to go. I can't stand the thought of staying here and wandering from panel to panel while my heart does acrobatic maneuvers in my chest.

On the way out the sliding glass doors of the conference center, I drop my nicked wristband in the trash can.

chapter two

The long drive to the airport the next day is disastrously silent. I ask the Uber driver to roll the windows down because the air is cooler here than back home in Texas. I do my best to enjoy it, to find the magic in the dull heat of the sun dappling my cheeks, but I'm in no mood.

I'm thinking about the phrase "counting chickens before they hatch" and wondering how you're supposed to find magic in the world and all that crap if you can't have reasonable expectations of outcomes, when Jenna suddenly begins to roll up the window on her side of the car, forcing me to either close mine or have my eardrums burst from the pressure.

I'm about to protest, but she cuts me off with, "Don't be angry."

"A little late for that," I say.

"I met N. E. Endsley," she blurts.

In our four years of friendship, we've only had a handful of arguments—mostly about which inside joke originated where—but never a *fight*. The closest we've come was an intense row last year when Jenna insisted I attend the homecoming dance with the big group of single girls and I refused.

If this slow-boiling lava rising up my throat is any indication, our first fight will be the battle to end all wars.

"But the festival said he had to cancel," I say, trying and failing to keep my voice even and calm and adult. "They said he was unable to attend."

Jenna sighs. "I know. I saw him before he left."

"You saw him from a distance, you mean," I say. "You saw him getting into his private car or something is what you mean, right?"

Apparently, Jenna is incapable of starting a sentence without sighing, because she does it again before she says, "No. I met N. E. Endsley. I spoke with him while you were in the bathroom."

My mouth doesn't stop long enough for my brain to process this impossible information. "This is a joke, right? You've got to be joking." I can hear my voice rising.

"Please stay calm, Amelia. Please?" Jenna exhales. She is slipping into the tone her mother uses in court, the forced relaxation of someone who refuses to lose their cool in the face of hysterical clients, husbands, or—in this case—fangirls.

I try to make my voice more level. "*Where* did you see him?"

This is a betrayal of the highest degree, a purposeful withholding of my greatest desire—to meet the author of the Orman Chronicles—and I can barely hear her through the heat pulsing in my ears.

The Uber guy flicks his eyes to us in the rearview mirror, then away. I bet he'll tell his partner over dinner about the two insane teenagers whisper-arguing in the backseat.

"You know that rope I was standing next to?" Jenna is picking at the invisible lint again. "I guess it was blocking the way to the refreshment room they had for the authors. I heard a choking sound and thought someone was in trouble. I ignored the NO CONFERENCE PARTICIPANTS sign to check and . . . it was him."

"*Him*," I say bitterly. "Him. How can you say it like that? It wasn't just a him, it was N. E. Endsley, Jenna."

"I *know*, Amelia, but he's also just a guy, you know?"

Now she sounds sympathetic and motherly, and I know my reaction is unfair, but I can feel my temper rise even higher.

"No, I don't know that he's just a guy, because I wasn't there. *Remember?*"

Jenna is quiet. A bright yellow sports car comes roaring out of nowhere and jerks around us, the sound of the engine cutting through the silence.

"He was pacing and pulling at his hair," Jenna says. "And mumbling. A panic attack, I think. I don't know. I've never seen anything like it." Jenna's voice is almost a whisper, like she's afraid to speak too loudly.

When I say nothing, Jenna tries to fill the quiet, her voice pitching higher in exasperation. "He needed help, Amelia. All I could do was try and calm him down. Do you really think I could leave him there? *'Hey, one sec. Let me go find my friend. She loves your books. Hold that thought and that mental breakdown. Thanks.'*"

"You could've," I half shout, hating myself for the slight Texas accent that breaks through and how unreasonable I sound. "You could have come to find me. I could have helped!"

In the span of a second, I think of all the things that make up Jenna—her goodness, her quiet but fierce empathy, her infuriating need to be right—and wish I could shut up. That I could make the aching, disenchanted part of my chest stop hurting long enough to tell Jenna that I understand.

But when Jenna responds, "Oh, Amelia. You're being unreasonable," the angry swirling in my brain starts anew and I'm at the mercy of the storm.

"I'm not, though." I'm almost shouting. The Uber driver coughs, but we ignore him. "That was the whole reason we came to this festival, even though you *and* your mom said it was too close to your Ireland trip. Because we wanted to meet him and get our books signed, and I didn't even get to do *that* because whatever you told him to"—I pause to make air quotes—"*calm him down* actually made it worse, because he *left*."

"I refuse to talk to you when you're like this," Jenna says, her voice rising to be heard over my ranting.

"You know how much those books mean to me." I'm yelling, but I don't care. "You know what those books got me through!"

She flinches, thinking of abandoned-puppy Amelia that she found outside of Downtown Books. Of the countless times her parents had to claim two daughters instead of one because my parents never bothered to attend award nights or sit through cheesy high school Christmas programs.

"Yes, but nobody knows what those books got *him* through. It's not fair to ask too much of someone, Amelia, no matter how much we admire them *or* their work. He was desperate to get out of there. He looked trapped and lost and I . . . I told him that he had to take care of himself."

The smooth hum of the driver's BMW, the light, posh clicking noise of the turn signal, ticks into yet another pocket of silence. I wonder if it's true that there can be absolute quiet before a tornado.

"I told him about you," Jenna says after a while.

"I don't want to hear it," I interject. There is something else clanging around inside me that feels detached from our discussion of N. E. Endsley, and it's making my chest hurt. "I don't want to hear anything about it. You sent home the headliner of the festival because he was feeling stressed. I get it, but I'm disappointed, and I don't want to hear any more. Please."

The *Please* comes out on a hiccup. It's pathetic. I'm pathetic. And I can't bring myself to care.

We don't speak for the rest of the ride, or through security, wordlessly sitting next to each other as we wait for our boarding section to be called. We don't speak when the flight attendant brings sparkling water for Jenna, Coke for me.

When the plane begins its descent into the airport, I finally ask her why she didn't tell me sooner, why she waited until the car ride to bring it up.

"What difference would it have made if I told you sooner?" She says it like a fact, and I'm too emotionally exhausted to tell her that's not an answer.

I've cried in front of Jenna a thousand times, but I've only seen Jenna cry once.

We were barely fifteen, and our friendship was still new and unformed, but I knew her well enough to understand that her affection for the Williamses' ancient cat, Moot, ran deep, even if it was not readily apparent to observers. She would make a show of grumbling about how much he shed, how his sharp claws tore holes in her comforter, but if he wasn't at the foot of her bed when it came time to sleep, she would fetch him.

"He'll cry at the door," she reasoned. But she scratched behind Moot's ears affectionately when she thought I wasn't looking.

It was one of those days with a cold snap in the air when Moot slipped out past Mr. Williams's legs and scampered off into the wilds of the neighborhood. Nobody worried much until that evening, when it was time for me to go home and Moot still hadn't returned.

"He'll come back," Mr. Williams said. "He always does."

But Moot didn't. Not that night or the night after.

Jenna wouldn't admit that she was worried, but on the third night, instead of hyperfocusing on her *Romeo and Juliet* essay, she kept looking out the window, her brows furrowed.

"Jenna?"

"Yeah?" She didn't look away from the window. She probably didn't even realize she was doing it.

"Let's take a walk," I said. "It's nice out."

Snapping out of it, Jenna glanced at me. "It's fifty degrees," she said, but she was already pulling her sweatshirt on over her head.

After a few minutes of walking, Jenna and I gave up the pretense and used the flashlight on Jenna's phone to scan under trees and behind cars, hoping to capture in its beam a chubby, graying tabby with glowing green eyes.

An hour later, by some miracle—or curse—we found Moot's raggedy collar with the dented silver bell that no longer jingled, beside a bush in the neighborhood park. Even in the dim light I could see it was streaked with blood and a few too many strands of Moot's fur.

"Coyotes," Jenna said.

I fought back tears at the sight of the pathetic, hollowed-out collar.

"I'm so sorry," I whispered.

"He was old," Jenna said, her voice a dull monotone. And then, quoting the Frost poem we had read in English class that week, "'Nothing gold can stay.'"

That night I broke our rule and announced I was staying over on a school night. Jenna fought against it—*I'm fine, I'm fine*, she said—but I wore her down.

I woke in the dead of night to the sound of the window opening and the cold air chasing away the snug coziness of Jenna's room.

"What are you doing?" I asked, blearily pushing myself up from her bed.

She was silhouetted against the window, her long spine hunched into the warmth of her plush robe as she gazed out the window.

"I thought I heard him meow," she said.

I came to stand beside her. "I'm sorry."

She still didn't move. I glanced at her.

Tears, little diamonds shining in the faded light of the moon, cascaded down her face in steady streams.

Hesitantly, a little afraid she would shrug me off, I put an arm around her shoulders. I thought of a hundred things to say, but in the end I came back to Orman.

"You know the little river? The one across the street, that runs through the park?"

Jenna nodded.

"Maybe it runs to Orman," I said. "And maybe Emmeline

and Ainsley needed a tubby old cat to help them feel less homesick for this world."

Jenna was quiet. I was starting to feel really stupid when she said, "Moot will do well in Orman, don't you think? The cook at Siren's Point will probably feed him so much he won't be able to walk."

I laughed louder than necessary in my relief. "Yeah, or maybe Emmeline will love him best, but he'll choose to live with Ainsley, and it will make Em angry."

"Likely."

The corner of Jenna's mouth twitched, and she dropped her head onto my shoulder, wiping at the tears on her cheeks. The night air was freezing my face, but I didn't dare move, for fear of breaking the moment.

Jenna might never cry, but I do.

I force myself to dry my tears and bottle up my anger. We only have one day before Jenna leaves for Ireland.

One day to unpack—and in Jenna's case, repack—and to squelch out the bubbles of dead and empty space I have built up between us since she told me about N. E. Endsley.

We reach a strange equilibrium, placing Jenna's new books she got at the festival on shelves and trying again and again to fit her extensive botanist-in-training wardrobe into the two suitcases she is bringing. Jenna unrolls the reading poster we bought, making eye contact with me across her unmade bed full of sock balls, and smiles, holding it higher as if to say, *Look*.

I nod dully. *Yeah.*

She rolls it back up and puts it in the tube, setting it atop my tote bag to take home with me, and sighs.

I'm sorry, the sigh says, but I pretend not to hear it and continue to roll her tops into tiny little cylinders.

She asks me two different times if I'll remember to go to the college prep seminar. I still think it's going to be eight hours of people who like the sound of their voices talking into crappy microphones, but I tell her I will. She makes me pinky promise, a trick I started sophomore year to make sure Jenna was really, truly listening to me instead of concentrating on something else. I almost smile when she holds out her hand, and our fingers meet, but not quite.

"Take good notes," Jenna says. "You can tell me all the best bits when I get back."

I want to tell her the best bits will be the catered lunch and the closing statements, but I don't.

Things still feel off the next day when Jenna leaves. Neither of us wants to relive the book festival scenario and drag up the argument from where it lies dormant in its unsealed coffin, so we don't discuss it.

If the Williamses notice how quiet we are on the way to the airport the next morning, they don't mention it. Maybe they think we're exhausted from the California trip. Jenna didn't tell them about the Endsley drama.

When I give her a hug, I loosen my arms to leave space for our good-byes and for the stray specks of unease and mild indignation that I can still feel floating below the surface of my skin.

"You owe me," I say into her ear. "For Endsley, I mean. I want you to bring me a Highlander in a kilt to make up for it."

She huffs but doesn't break our hug. "It's Ireland, you idiot, not Scotland."

"I *know*, but it's only a couple hours by ferry, right? Surely you could spare one day."

Her grip on me tightens and I will my arms to move and follow suit, but they can't quite make it. My joke about Scottish travel time is as close to forgiveness as I'll get for the moment. It's only been two days since I was supposed to have been in the same room as N. E. Endsley.

"Fine," Jenna says, a smile tucked into the warm corners of her voice. "But if there are any magical standing stones that take me back in time, I'm not trying to come back."

"Fine," I agree. "Dibs on your library."

"Fine." She laughs. It's her sparkling laugh, which she doesn't use very often, with good reason. A man walking nearby almost stumbles over his suitcase when he hears it.

"Fine," I say. "Now go before I gag from your stupid perfume."

And just like that, Jenna is gone.

chapter three

I learn that books are liars when, less than a week after her departure, Jenna's mother calls to tell me that Jenna is dead.

"Car accident," she says. "The other driver sped through a red light."

"How?" I ask. Stupidly, brokenly.

"I don't know," she says.

"But she was in Ireland."

Was. I've only known for a minute and Jenna is already a *was* instead of an *is*.

Jenna's mother barely stops to breathe; she uses her attorney voice, her no-nonsense voice, the kind she uses for client calls or when Mr. Williams doesn't cut the Thanksgiving turkey into thin enough slices.

"Will you speak, Amelia? At her funeral, I mean?"

I say yes, but when the day comes and I'm standing in front of a congregation that moments before had been singing a hymn of celebration for Jenna and her "reunion with her creator," I lose it. I let myself bleed onto every surface—the podium, the hideous floral arrangements, her casket—as the stories and memories imprison my head and my voice.

If this were a photo I was trying to frame in my lens, I would stretch the shadows creeping from beneath her stupid casket as far as I could. I would stretch them until they smothered the somber faces in the pews and all that would be left unshadowed in the photo would be myself behind the podium and what's left of Jenna. I would call it *Survivor and a Half.*

But my imagination can only keep me occupied for so long. Countless pairs of eyes look at me with pity and heartbreak, and I feel the years of waiting in line for book signings, the late-night study sessions when one of us had procrastinated too long on research papers, the countless hours spent reading together. All that, and the stupid, stupid pictures tacked to her bedroom wall, work their way down from the lump in my throat to the choke hold squeezing my heart.

Eventually the pastor comes up to pat my back and lead me away from the microphone, my hiccupping sobs loud enough without the assistance of amplification.

It's wrong, I keep thinking. *Life isn't following its script and it's not fair . . . I'm not prepared.*

While some kids waited for their letter to be delivered by owl or for their closet to one day reveal a magical land with talking animals and stone tables, I'd waited for the other shoe to drop. Because if there's one thing I learned from books, it's that life is fair and unfair, just and unjust. When my father left us, I thought that was the end of it, but then Jenna found me and life was dreadfully out of balance again, too right and happy.

I waited for more hard parts, the ones books say begin when you're young but always, *always* end in the early teenage years to allow for happily-ever-after. The Final Big Bad Thing would happen before high school graduation. Everything bad happens to you in high school or after you've turned forty and have a spouse and six kids and a few decades of hard-earned disappointment under your belt.

Books lie. Life isn't finished with you when you are eighteen or when you think you've had enough.

It's never enough. You're never in the clear.

Jenna thought her books should be new and pure, untouched by anyone but herself. I prefer my books to have already been occupied, to have stories independent of the one carried on the page. I like to imagine my used books as little soldiers that have gone off to serve their duty elsewhere before coming into my hands. Books are something to be stepped inside of, to be occupied and lived in. Maybe that's why I tend to loan out my books while Jenna rarely parted with hers.

But Jenna is gone now. She's gone, and her parents have bequeathed me her library.

"She'd want you to have them," Mr. Williams says through tears, when he and Mrs. Williams come to check on me a few days after we watch Jenna's body get lowered into the ground.

This is only the second or third time they have been inside my mother's house, and they look out of place seated on the edge of my twin bed.

Mr. Williams is vying for me to spend the remainder of the summer with them, but something inside me balks.

"You wouldn't . . . you wouldn't have to sleep in Jenna's room," Mr. Williams says. "But we could get you all the help you need. Counselors and therapists and college coaches, whatever you need . . . whatever you want."

"I know," I say, rubbing my temples to try to stop the low throbbing. "I know."

"Mark," Jenna's mother says. Her tone is low, mildly chastising. "She doesn't want to be in our house."

She's right. I can't stand the thought of being smothered by the long hallways of their immaculate house, which hold almost as many pictures of me on the walls as of Jenna.

Pictures of us in mud masks and pajamas. Shots of us grinning in front of the ocean, with the tip of Mr. Williams's pinky in the corner of the frame. The one of Jenna looking back over her shoulder and smiling her devastating smile, the one she rarely let people see, the one that made her face glow and her eyes crinkle.

That's the photo Mrs. Williams had blown up and framed for the funeral service. During the reception at their house, Kailey Lancaster pointed to where the wrapped canvas picture sat on an easel and whispered to her boyfriend, "It doesn't even *look* like her."

It took everything in me not to "accidentally" knock her plate of cheese cubes and fruit out of her hand.

I shove the memory from my brain and half try to give Jenna's books back, to insist they return the six or so massive boxes to Jenna's shelves, but her parents refuse to hear of it.

When they finally leave, I spend what feels like hours going through Jenna's library and systematically destroying page 49 of each of her books, tearing the pages in half before sloppily taping them back together. The first roll of tape I grab from the kitchen junk drawer is double-sided. I numbly use it for about twelve books. I don't attempt to fix the others.

It was Jenna's rule of reading excerpts, the page 49 thing.

"Far enough to get a feel for what the author's writing is really like without going too far and risking a huge spoiler," she always said.

I don't know why I rip the pages. Maybe I'm hoping she will come back and chastise me for ruining her books. Maybe I'm trying to erase her, to make the books my own so I can forget perfect Jenna and her perfect books ever existed.

Or maybe I'm just stupid with grief and don't know what I'm doing.

Later that night, summer rain patters against the window and drowns out even my most melancholy thoughts, and I try to read the book I started before graduation. Over and over, I try. I switch to Orman, and I try again. But my eyes refuse to change the letters into sentences, the sentences into pages.

I reread the same sentence no less than five times before I give up. I close the book and lie on my back with my eyes closed.

My life has split in two. Before there was a *before* and a subsequent *after*, I imagined myself a talented reader. Reading, for me, has always been more like playing a video game than watching a movie, an active experience that used to leave me physically and emotionally wrought.

I could step into a page and roam the described landscape independently of the characters that inhabited it. I've plucked the ring from Frodo and felt its inscribed Elvish on my fingertips. I've sneaked gulps of milk from the Boxcar Children's hidden stash beneath the waterfall, borrowed Harry's broom while he studied with Hermione, and played with the Bennet cats while Elizabeth and her sisters were dancing at Netherfield. I've stepped in the forest-green prints of Orman, my footprints dwarfing Emmeline's and barely matching up to Ainsley's. I've rested my palm against the cool stone of the lighthouse fortress that first greeted them upon their arrival, and smelled the salt from the sea below.

I've lived in books. I've eaten and breathed books for so long that I took it for granted. I assumed that, if they saved me once, they would always be there to pick me up, even if Jenna wasn't.

But Jenna is gone, and the words stay on the page in their neat, orderly rows. The pages don't rise up to meet me like old friends, and the characters are marionettes pulled by visible strings.

If I were going to take a self-portrait, I wouldn't focus on my crumpled body curled on the bed with its mismatched sheets and pillowcases. I would take all of Jenna's books and wrap them so tightly with masking tape that the covers would wrinkle beneath the binding. I would take my books and rip out the last two pages of each, because this is what it feels like without Jenna here to see what comes after this—college, careers, boyfriends, whatever. None of it will matter, because in all of my imaginings, it was always the two of us, sisters by choice rather than blood.

I'd arrange the ripped pages falling on the taped books and I would call it *Time Heals No Wounds*. Or maybe I would focus on the crumpled edges of the removed pages and call it *Amelia Abridged*.

When I eventually fall asleep, tears still pooling in my ears, a shadow monster with teeth chases me through endless swampy marshes. In my hand is an instruction manual on how to defeat it, but since I can no longer read, I run and run and run.

chapter four

It has been ten days since the funeral, and Jenna is not here. It's like a mantra now, my personal maxim: I am wearing a sweater in June because even in the Texas heat I can't seem to stop shivering, and Jenna is not here. I count out change from my piggy bank and order pizza online so I don't have to speak to people with sunshiny voices unaffected by grief, and Jenna is not here. I walk to Downtown Books and stand at the window, telling myself I can stay there as long as I like, and Jenna is not here.

She's not here.

My phone buzzes in my pocket as I stare into the bookstore, and my heart leaps into my throat for one beautiful, terrible moment because I think Jenna's calling to tell me not to be a creeper.

But Jenna is not here. It's the next best/worst thing: her dad.

I think about hitting the Ignore button, even though that seems doubly terrible, since I'm in the family text group, which was mostly Jenna and me sending random photos of ducklings and Mrs. Williams reminding us when our college admission and scholarship applications were due.

My thumb is hovering between the Answer and Ignore options when the screen lights up anew, this time with the Downtown Books phone number. Why on earth are *they* calling? Do they know I'm standing outside of their storefront like a golden retriever waiting for its owner to return?

Even this makes me think of Jenna's funeral. Everyone was *so* intent on talking to me and offering their condolences, their voices jumbling over and around me in a cacophony I pretended to decipher. I glued myself to her casket, reluctant to leave her. I was a sentry, I told myself, and I would keep watch over her until I no longer could.

I shake the memory off. In a panic, I swipe to dismiss Mr. Williams and answer the bookstore's call, walking a short way down the sidewalk so the person calling can't see me through the window.

"Hello?" I clear my throat, which is scratchy from almost a full twenty-four hours of disuse.

"Amelia? Hi, it's Becky from Downtown Books. We got a package in for you today. I just wanted to let you know!"

"A package? I didn't order a book."

"It's not from our store, actually. It's the weirdest thing . . . It's some sort of transfer or something from a bookstore in Michigan, a place called Val's?"

I shake my head and then, realizing she can't see me, say, "What book is it?"

"Don't know," Becky says. "It came in an envelope and I didn't want to open it since it's not one of our usual packages. It has your name on it, though, and you're the only Amelia Griffin in our system."

"I wasn't expecting anything," I say again, but my mind is starting to piece together some insane hope that this is a gift from Jenna.

"Strange," Becky says. "What a mystery! Do you want me to open it for you and let you know what's inside?"

"No," I say quickly, looking back over my shoulder toward the store. "No, I'll come get it. I'm not far."

"Excellent! I'll keep it at the front register for you. See you soon."

I look at the time on my phone and make myself wait exactly ten minutes before I walk the twenty yards back.

In those ten minutes, I contemplate all sorts of wonderful mysteries, finally settling on the insane possibility that Jenna isn't *actually* dead and that she was kidnapped by pirates and made to fake her own death because of ransom demands the Williamses never met because Mr. Williams is just as likely to accidentally delete emails as read them. And instead of killing her, the pirates shipped her back to one of their boats in Michigan—because it's practically an island, surrounded by all that water, and there's probably a lot of pirate ships out on those lakes—and she is trying to communicate with me via this book she sent.

As a rebuttal, my brain keeps bringing up the image of her in the casket, her dark hair a sharp contrast to the white silk lining, her favorite silver tights tucked out of view. The reminder catches me off guard and I pretend to cough to hide the gasp of grief that claws its way up my throat.

I'm mostly under control when Becky comes to the counter and plops a square brown envelope in front of me.

"Open it," Becky begs, "I'm so curious!"

Blessedly, my phone buzzes, Mr. Williams's picture

lighting up the screen again, and I am saved from answering her.

"I have to take this," I say, which is true. I can't ignore him twice or he'll go into panic mode, thinking the worst. "I'm sure the package is nothing. Thanks, Becky."

I practically run out of the store, the package tucked under my arm, my phone against my ear.

"Hello, Mr. W—Mark," I say. He insisted I finally give up the *Mr.* and *Mrs.* bit once and for all at the funeral.

"Amelia," he says. His voice sounds sunshiny and round. "How are you?"

I'm thrown off by his tone but try not to let it show. "I'm okay, I guess."

"Just calling to make sure you're still okay with dinner this evening. We're picking up those chicken fingers you like."

"Yeah, looking forward to it," I say, wrestling the package from under my arm to hold it between both hands. The handwriting is sloppy, almost illegible, but it most definitely says "Care of Amelia Griffin" above the Downtown Books address.

"I'll pick you up around five then, okay?"

"Sounds great," I say, eager to get off the phone and further examine the package. "Thank you."

"And Amelia?" His voice loses a little of its sunshine. "Whatever you need, remember? Just let us know."

I stop thinking about the package, my brain flicking to last week's first biweekly Amelia-and-the-Williams "family dinner."

What I need—who I need—was devastatingly absent from the table.

"Thank you, Mark," I say again.

"Because it's . . . it's hard enough, hon. It's hard enough

going through what you're going through. Make sure you're eating, okay? Eat *well*, Amelia. Make sure you eat lunch, okay?"

"Sure thing," I say. "See you tonight."

I make myself obey, though this package is the first thing I've been remotely distracted by since Jenna's funeral. I promise myself I can examine its every corner if I stop by the grocery store and buy something to make Mom and me for lunch.

I make spaghetti and canned sauce—it's the only thing I know how to cook besides grilled cheese—and sprinkle enough salt in the water to fill the sea. I need it to boil faster, need to go to my room and shut the door and consider the hundreds of possibilities for this little book-shaped package.

I need to escape again.

Mom doesn't look up when I set a steaming bowl of spaghetti on the little table next to her recliner. I have to move an ashtray and an empty box of wine to make room. She's watching some talk show where the hosts pick live audience members to compete in stupid games to earn gift cards.

She's between jobs again. The gas station she worked at was bought out by a chain and they laid off most of the existing employees. She's been home since just before Jenna died, and I can't stand it. The TV is always, always on.

"I made spaghetti," I say.

She nods as the TV audience bursts into hysterical screams of laughter.

"I'll be in my room if you need me," I tell her.

I slurp spaghetti cross-legged on my bed, staring at the

package in front of me and telling myself that as soon as I'm done eating, I can tear into it. I am trying my best to make this moment last, to savor each second that goes by where something other than Jenna's death is competing for my attention.

But then I feel guilty for wishing Jenna away and open the package before I've eaten half the noodles.

I don't try and stifle my awed gasp.

It's a deluxe edition of *The Forest Between the Sea and the Sky*, bound in dark green leather, with the sigil of Orman stamped on the front. I scramble to flip the book open to inspect the inside of the front cover. "101 of 100" is stamped on the bottom. The internet buzzed about these limited edition copies for weeks before the release. They include four full-page illustrations by Endsley himself, plus a new color map of Orman. It's real leather, too. I don't remember exactly how much they cost, but it was hundreds of dollars.

And I have the 101st edition.

Jenna. It has to be Jenna. She must have ordered this as an apology for the Endsley fiasco, but I have to be sure.

A quick internet search pops up a number to a Val's in Lochbrook, Michigan. The pictures of the town that appear alongside the store's contact information are gorgeous— lakes and sailboats and sunsets and a lighthouse atop a hill that reminds me of Orman.

It's a sign.

I click the phone number on the page to dial, but immediately hang up. What am I going to say? "*Hey there, it's Amelia. Do you happen to know who sent me a one hundred and first edition of* The Forest Between the Sea and the Sky? *Because if it was my dead best friend I want to know, but also I haven't been able to read anything since she died. Do you have a cure for that kind of reading problem? Also, this edition technically shouldn't exist.*"

I put my phone down and flip through the book, the strong scent of leather tickling my nose. I'm looking for any kind of note or marking that will point to Jenna. When my search turns up fruitless after two slow perusals of each page, I flip to the illustrated map, my eyes drinking in every detail.

There is figure-eight-shaped Orman with its gloriously lush forests—the source of most of the island's magic—on the northern half, as well as on its southern half, the land there fraught from the encroaching and furious sea that is forever trying to swallow the island and its occupants whole. At the northernmost point is the reigning monarch of Orman's castle, Siren's Point. And even though they are smaller than my pinky nail, there are the sirens themselves, waiting to tempt sailors into the rocky depths of the ocean.

This time I do not hang up when I call. For every ring, my heart beats three times.

"This is Val's. Alex speaking."

He sounds nice, too nice, and this throws me off. I should have planned what to say, but I dig deep and borrow some of Jenna's authority and let it instill false confidence into my voice.

"Hi, Alex. I received a book today that was marked with your store's name as the return address. I would like to know who sent it, please."

I can hear this Alex person typing on the other side, the click of a mouse.

"Sure thing," he says. "What's the name?"

"Amelia Griffin."

The clicking stops. A full ten seconds pass before I say, "Hello? Alex?"

I can almost hear him jerk to attention over the phone. "Yes. Sorry. I'm afraid there has been a mistake." His voice sounds rushed. "There is no record of an Amelia Griffin in our system. Is there something else I can help you with?"

If I wanted to create a still life to represent this Alex person's voice, I would need barbed wire. A lot of it.

"That's weird," I say. "That's really weird. It came to me through my local bookstore. Like, it was sent there for me to pick up. Can you look it up by the bookstore?"

"We do not ship to other bookstores. Are you sure it was our address?"

"There's a round sticker on the back of the package that says Val's, Lochbrook, Michigan. Is that your bookstore?"

Another stretch of silence, then a low muttered word I can't quite make out.

"Hello?" I ask. Maybe our connection is bad, or maybe he doesn't understand the significance of the situation. "It's a limited edition of *The Forest Between the Sea and the Sky*," I tell him. "The first Orman book? It says it's the one hundred and first copy out of one hundred, but that makes no sense, right? Can you try looking for Jenna Williams? Maybe she's in your system?"

I can hear that he isn't typing. "There is no record of Jenna Williams or Amelia Griffin in our system, I'm sorry." And here, he *almost* sounds sorry. "Is there something else I can help you with?"

"No . . . I guess not."

"Sorry I couldn't be of service," Alex says, before I can add anything else. "Thanks for your call."

Click.

I have always loved stories that attribute the thrill of adventure to a physical force—a push of insistent wind or the tug of magic. I love the idea of adventure finding us in our day-to-day boredom and beckoning us to go on a quest for something better than we leave behind.

Jenna knew that.

And, as thunder rattles my bedroom window, I can't help but feel like this has something to do with her, that she is orchestrating it from wherever people go after they die.

It would be so like Jenna to send me a step-by-step manual for how to grieve the loss of her, and to use Orman to deliver her instructions.

For my birthday last year, she set up a meticulous scavenger hunt, using clues from my most beloved books—including Orman—that eventually led me to my favorite restaurant. When I opened the door, the Williamses were sitting at our usual table, Jenna's delighted grin sparkling in the light of the birthday candles on my bakery-bought cake. Her dad joked that if I had taken any longer to follow the clues, my cake would have been more wax than sugar.

"What did you wish for?" Jenna asked, later that night. We sat on the barstools in her kitchen, eating forkfuls of leftover buttercream cake while sharing a glass of milk.

"I can't tell you," I said. "It won't come true."

"Aren't we a little old for that?"

I shook my head as I downed the last of the milk.

"So tell me what you didn't wish for." She smiled.

I set the glass down. It clinked lightly against the marble countertop. "I didn't wish to never spend a birthday without you. That's for sure."

"Double negative." Jenna laughed, but I could tell she was pleased. "Amelia, you're going to have to be better at grammar if—"

"I'm going to be a professor," I finished. "I know."

I stared off into the distance over Jenna's shoulder, trying to look pensive and serious.

"What are you thinking about?" she asked.

"Oh, nothing." I sighed deeply. "Just . . . you know . . . Do you think it's too late to take back my birthday wish? Maybe I could trade you for someone less exasperating."

The memory makes me feel hollow, like my edges are blurred and I might not be entirely real anymore. So I try to flip through and read my favorite parts in this impossible 101st copy of one hundred, but my eyes refuse to string together meanings from the words. I turn to the internet, scrolling through forums and articles but never finding evidence of an extra printed copy. Is this edition even legit?

It doesn't matter that I can't read it. I just need to find out why this edition exists and how Jenna sent it to me from a store in Michigan that has no record of either of us. And why.

chapter five

When Mark texts to let me know he's outside, he punctuates it with a smiling emoji. I think about that stupid yellow happy face as I wrap the 101st copy in a clean hand towel I pulled from the dryer and carefully place it into the book tote I use as a purse.

A happy face. Even with the Orman book tucked against my side, whispering promises of mystery and distraction, I can't imagine using an emoji. There's not a face that can capture the expression of *My best friend is gone.*

I'm kind of mad about it—Mark and Trisha's attempts to make everything seem normal and happy—until I pass Mom in her chair, staring at the TV. There's just as many ways to handle grief as there are emojis, I guess.

They all suck.

Mark must have turned on the seat warmer for me when he left his office, because when I sit down, the cushiony leather beneath my butt and lower back feels warm through my shirt. I lean into the heat with a sigh.

"You do know that it is nearly eighty degrees outside?" He half smiles at me as he backs the car out, its tires jumping over my crumbling driveway.

I give one of my new false, dry chuckles, the humorless one that has replaced my too-exuberant laughs since the funeral.

"Yes, but like all Texans, you run the air-conditioning below freezing," I say. "Thanks for the seat heater."

"Don't mention it."

The windshield wiper blades squeak angrily against the rain as Mark drives us from my crappy neighborhood to downtown Dallas, to where huge homes sit in orderly rows behind wrought iron fences.

The first time I came to their house, it was obviously different from mine in every way. Most notably, it homed two parents who loved each other almost as much as they loved their daughter.

As it became my second home, I explored its nooks and crannies. It's a Croatian style, so it has almost as much stone inside as it does on the exterior, and Mrs. Williams—*Trisha. Call her Trisha*—has covered the walls with this great art.

My favorite is a piece by Vincent van Gogh. It's actually a print—the original is in a museum an hour away, in Fort Worth—and it shows brightly colored houses along a street in a small Mediterranean fishing village. Van Gogh went pretty heavy with the paint; the viewer can see clumps and heavy streaks on the vibrant rooftops, even in the print. It's like what he saw with his eyes was too much for his head to hold and he had to get it out in any way he could. It's a strange piece, melancholy and hopeful in the way the colors fight for attention, and it manages to suggest so much in just one frame. Even though it is an oil painting, it makes me feel as if I'll never be as good a photographer, never be able to capture anything in such a vibrant, genuine way.

I'm looking at the painting now, avoiding Trisha's and Mark's eyes as we eat chicken fingers on porcelain plates at the dining table. Trisha uses a fork and knife to cut hers, but Mark and I both use our fingers.

We studiously ignore Jenna's empty seat next to mine. Nobody comments on the empty place setting that Trisha must have put out by accident, but I can't stop myself from zeroing in on it and remembering, even if it makes my insides feel like an empty well and my skin itch.

Memory takes over. My plate morphs into a finer one with a tented cloth napkin placed perfectly at its center. The gleaming silverware twinkles against the polished wooden table. Mr. and Mrs. Williams will be meeting us any minute, but until then, Jenna and I are on our own in this very fancy restaurant.

I inhale, and the air has the clotted, close smell of spiced vegetables and butter and wine. There is a large elk's head mounted on the wall above the kitchen. He seems out of place, presiding over this fancy Latin fusion restaurant with his wide stare, but taxidermy is rarely considered unsuitable in Texas, no matter the theme.

I only break eye contact with him when Jenna puts down her phone and looks up at me, shaking her head.

"They're stuck in traffic on the other side of town. They said to go ahead and eat without them."

"*What?* But it was your mom's idea to try this place to begin with," I say. "Let's go, and come back when they're with us."

"We're already here, Amelia," she says. "Why not?"

This turns out to be a terrible idea.

The cheapest thing on the menu is something neither of us can pronounce, and it costs fifty dollars. Even Jenna, who wields her parents' credit card with a fair amount of confidence, balks at the prices.

"Maybe we should split something?" I suggest.

Jenna agrees, and neither of us thinks much of it when the waiter gives us a funny look, until he eventually returns with the world's smallest plate of thin, unidentified cooked meat and another, only slightly larger plate of . . . French fries.

"Thank God there are fries," I say, popping one in my mouth before it can burn my fingers. "Tastes kind of funny, but they're good!"

"Amelia," Jenna hisses, her eyes darting to a very well-to-do couple who are looking at us like we're a pair of mice that just scurried across their plates. "Those are plantains. Use a knife and fork."

I roll my eyes. "Jenna," I say, mimicking her tone, "these are called *fries*. You eat them with your *hands*."

I lean forward to grab another and demonstrate, but Jenna pokes at my knuckles with her fork. Her eyes get a fraction larger, the face she makes when she is trying very hard not to laugh at me.

"Look, Bambi," I say. "Why don't you take care of . . . well"—I reach with my fork to nudge at the thin meat— "whatever that is, and I'll take care of the fries?"

It took less than five minutes to eat the pathetic amount of food. When we finished, Jenna and I looked at each other for a long moment before Jenna's stomach audibly grumbled.

"Maybe this is just the appetizer?" I asked hopefully, but the waiter, eager to be rid of the plantain hand-eater and her friend, darted forward with the check.

"Answers that," I muttered.

We called Mrs. Williams from outside the restaurant, beside the valet booth, Jenna and I fighting over the phone in our eagerness to tell the story.

"We can never eat there again, Mom. Seriously." Jenna giggled into the phone. "Dad would have to order at least five main courses."

"Pick us up at the bookstore," I half yelled. Jenna tried to shove me away, but she was laughing too hard. "And bring cheeseburgers!" I added.

Her parents had a good long laugh at our expense as we reenacted the short meal over Whataburger that evening.

But here it's only me and Mark and Trisha, and as I exhale, the room goes back to smelling like chicken fingers and the plate goes back to being just an empty plate before an empty chair.

The show must go on, though, this charade that we're all okay. We chat about the rain, discuss what I'm reading—I lie and make something up—and when Mark brings up Missoula, I try my best not to wince.

"Soon you'll be at freshman orientation," he says proudly. And, with less enthusiasm, "I know it won't be exactly how you wanted, but I hope you're going to stay the course, hon. You . . . you have to live for you both . . . you and Jenna."

He is starting to sniffle, and Trisha puts down her fork and dabs at her mouth with a white napkin. When she takes it away, there is a bright smudge of reddish-purple lipstick imprinted on the cloth.

When Trisha speaks, my eyes stay focused on the smudge.

"Don't forget about that college preparatory course in a

couple of weeks. It can't hurt to be as prepared as possible for these upcoming changes, Amelia."

I can feel a manacle forming around my ankle, any hope I ever had of doing something other than what Jenna wanted fading away. I *cannot* disappoint her parents by not doing what Jenna had planned for us. I have to honor her memory, and the only way I can do that is by sticking to the plan . . . college prep course, Missoula, becoming a college professor . . . even if I was—*am*—totally unsure what I would do if nobody were watching.

I have no choice.

I pinky promised.

Smiling at Mark and Trisha, I rearrange the weight on my shoulders and make myself enthuse about Missoula and what lies ahead. I won't break their hearts or dishonor my friendship with Jenna. I *will* do the sensible thing and adhere to the route Jenna mapped out for us, for me.

My smile falters, my brain staging one last rebellion.

It's a stupid plan. I might not even be able to pull it off. But when Mark's homemade banana pudding is brought out, to be eaten straight from the serving dish, I clear my throat.

"So," I begin hesitantly, the plan seeming more ridiculous now that I'm voicing it aloud. "I'm thinking about driving to Michigan. I'll probably miss our dinners next week."

I say it to my spoon, but I don't miss the shared glance of worry. I eat a mouthful of pudding and try to summon strength from Jenna's empty chair.

"It's not a big deal or anything," I rush after swallowing. "I mean, I know it's a long drive to Michigan, but I got this book and—"

"Michigan?" Trisha interrupts. "What could possibly be in Michigan that warrants such a trip?"

"I got a book in the mail that I didn't order," I say, again wishing I had planned out a script. Suddenly telling the parents of my dead friend, *"Hey, I think your daughter is trying to communicate with me from the beyond using our favorite book, and/or she might be in a pirate's possession,"* sounds not only crazy but also insensitive. "I Googled the store it came from and it's in this really cool, tiny town in northern Michigan. There are sailboats and chocolate shops and—"

"And you just want to leave," Mark says. "You want to get away."

When he puts it like that, I feel guilty, because there's truth to his words. Part of me wants to run as far as I can go, to a place that has never borne the mark of Jenna and doesn't taste or smell or feel like her.

But I also want to see if she had anything to do with this mysterious 101st copy, if that knowledge will give me answers to questions I'm not even sure how to ask.

Is it possible to want to run both from and to someone's memory?

"How will you get there?" Mark asks.

"I was thinking about renting a car. It's the cheapest way."

Nobody is paying any attention to the pudding, and I can practically hear the bananas browning in the thick silence.

"You should go."

It's hard to tell who is more surprised at Trisha's sudden verdict—me or Mark.

"Trish, you can't expect her to go up there *alone*."

"She's eighteen. She'll be going to college in the fall and will have to navigate things on her own sooner or later, Mark. She is a very capable young woman. She will be more than fine. We *have* to let her go."

Trisha is giving him a look I don't quite understand, but Mark must understand it, because he sighs through his nose like Jenna used to and turns to me.

"Well, you can't drive that far alone. I won't allow it. I'll book you a flight. And for the love of God, Amelia, don't forget to text us."

My head is spinning, my half-formed revolt is turning into a full-fledged battle, and Jenna isn't here to be the general.

"You really don't have to," I say. "I can rent a car."

I don't tell them it would take every last penny of my birthday and babysitting money to afford the car rental and gas.

"*No.*" Mark's voice is the most forceful it has ever been with me. "No long-distance drives. No cars. Ever."

"Mark," Trisha whispers, a hand coming up to rub his arm. "It's okay."

We are all thinking about the photos of a smashed-up rental car. Jenna died instantly in the front passenger seat; the other three passengers were taken to the local hospital, where they made a full recovery.

I bet Mark is thinking the same will happen to me, that another freak episode will take me away and there will be nobody left for him to dote on or to call on long lunch breaks or to turn the seat warmer on for. I have no idea what Trisha is thinking.

"I'll fly," I say. "If that makes you feel better. I'll have to rent a car to get around town, I think, but I'll fly there if you want me to. I . . . I just have to see what's there. I have to go."

I have to go *away*.

Mark starts crying in earnest. "Jenna would want you to," he says. "She would want you to enjoy your summer the best . . . the best that you can."

Trisha rubs his back in soothing circles and says to me, "I see no problem with a trip, so long as you are back in time for the college prep course."

I don't tell her that I would rather have someone explain to me how I'm going to live the rest of my life without my best friend. That, I would take notes on.

Before Mark drives me home, I go to Jenna's room to tell her that I'm going to Michigan. It's strange, seeing her bookcases empty, half her clothes taken from their hangers and packed into boxes labeled "Donation" in her mom's handwriting. The other half—her formal dresses for school banquets and weddings and funerals—hang forlornly. I wonder if Trisha means to keep them or just couldn't bear to put any more bits of Jenna into boxes.

It feels too soon.

But there's the window where she cried over Moot, and there is the bed beside which I first stepped into Orman. There's the rug that covers a large Coke stain, from when we were too immersed in our books to hear the glass fall and the liquid soaked into the floor.

Maybe part of her lingers still. Maybe I am not entirely alone.

"I'm taking a trip," I whisper. My voice comes out reverent and hushed. "I'm going to Michigan. Mostly because of that book you sent. You probably think it's stupid, but . . . you're not here to tell me what a stupid idea this is, so I'm going to do it, okay? I swear on Orman, I'll come back and do everything you wanted. The prep course, Missoula . . . everything."

A light wind rattles against her bedroom window, the leaves on a tree branch casting fluttering shadows on the floor. I hope it's a magical, clever wind come to aid me in Jenna's absence.

I hope it stays.

When I stand between my mother and the television later that night to tell her I am going to Michigan for a week, that Mark took care of the flight, she tilts her head to look at me, cigarette held between her fingers.

"You know where the suitcase is?" she asks.

My father took the luggage when he left us, but I nod anyway.

"Great. Just leave me y'all's travel details. Now, can you move, Ames? This is the best part."

I don't correct her when she assumes Jenna's parents are going with me. Later, I hear her laughing in the living room as I pack my duffle bag with sweaters, T-shirts, and the 101st copy of *The Forest Between the Sea and the Sky*.

After hesitating, I pick up my camera case from where it rests on my dresser, a dust ring left in its wake. I haven't touched it since the festival, haven't wanted to, even if my head can't seem to stop trying to take mental photos.

I don't even think I'm that good at photography. My way of framing photos in my brain is too fantastical to be professional or skillful. I haven't won any contests. But I enjoy it. Since I started taking pictures last year, I made a rule that I could only take one photo of a subject at a time. A lot of YouTube videos I watched discourage this, telling new photographers to take as many shots as they can and to sift through and find the good ones later.

But I don't want every photo to be good; I want them to be *real*. I want to capture the exact moment where I stood and observed something about the world and thought it worth documenting in all of its crooked, imperfect glory. I want to catch myself by surprise, and the only way I know how to do that is to point the lens and snap what I see before me.

Once.

This trip is going to be a photograph. One snap, one chance, to figure out why and how Jenna sent that book, to put the loss of her far enough behind me that I can move on and do everything she wanted us to do, everything her parents expect me to do.

It's what Jenna would want.

chapter six

"Turn around. Turn around, when possible."

I'm trying not to take the squawking GPS that came with my airport rental car as a bad omen, but it's difficult when, no matter which way I turn, it tells me I'm going the wrong way.

Jenna is probably laughing at me, or watching me with her patented look of aggravation.

Somehow, I keep missing the elusive turn for Lochbrook from the main highway. It reminds me a little of Orman, actually, of how Emmeline and Ainsley have to walk past the entrance to the forest a certain number of times, the trees spreading apart to let them through only after the required number of passes have been made.

I must be right—or this navigation system is faulty—because as I take an exit I tried ten minutes ago, the voice happily chirps, "In twenty miles, your destination will be on your left."

Maybe this is all part of the balance thing, paying the piper for the ease with which I got through the airport and onto my plane. They make it remarkably easy to know where to go—

there are signs *everywhere*—though you wouldn't have known this from Mark's level of worrying.

When he and Trisha dropped me off, he told me at least five times to call if I had any trouble finding the gate, and Trisha said, "Amelia and Jenna went to California by themselves, Mark," and he said, "Yes, but Jenna isn't here," and then we all stood there looking at our shoes while Mark cried and Trisha pinched the bridge of her nose.

Trisha had kissed me on the cheek, holding me against her tall frame much longer than usual, when they finally left me at security.

"I hope you find what you're looking for," she said in my ear.

I would have asked what she thinks I'm looking for, but I bet she doesn't think it's a secret message left by her daughter.

Lost in thought, I don't notice when the road dwindles to a small, winding street, mingling in and out of clumps of cottage-like houses and quaint storefronts that are closing for the evening. It's a world dotted with the same trees that line the road. The sky is turning a brilliant pink, and though Lake Michigan has patiently been waiting for me to acknowledge her splendor, I am only now seeing her unobstructed.

It's achingly beautiful, a scene from a van Gogh.

I'm struck with wonder, drawn to the waves rolling onto the tiny shore just below the sloping road. How funny that it is only a lake and not the sea. There are no promises of dolphins or stingrays anywhere in its depths, but from here it looks the same.

I allow myself to imagine them, the sea creatures, and to dwell on the idea that no matter what happens to me, somewhere in the world there are whales swimming hundreds of miles a day. Whether I find the mysterious sender of the book or not, whether I read another book or not, the whales don't care; they swim on.

"You have arrived at your destination."

The parking lot for the bookstore is small and rectangular and I take the last available space. It takes me a moment to find the store itself in the grove of trees, because it looks more like a mansion than a storefront, a house made of gray stone with a dark red roof. All three stories have lines of windows lit up from within, some shrouded with gauzy curtains and others with chips of embedded stained glass.

Even the front door is idyllic, burgundy red and massive, with a bell that tinkles when I pull it open by the iron handle.

It's not what I was expecting.

Bathed in a yellow light I thought was only real in movies, I want to believe in stories again. I want to believe everything has a purpose, no matter how terrible. That the fairy tales were right, the stories are true, and at the end of all the muck and despair, light can be found.

It's the most enchanting bookstore I've ever laid eyes on. A chaotic, music-swirling, cinnamon roll–smelling, warm, inviting bookstore.

Somewhere the whales are singing a deafening chorus.

Every wall of the first floor is lined with bookcases stretching from the hardwood floor to the vaulted ceiling, and working ladders glide along the shelves.

My blood is humming with the familiarity and newness of this place, my throat closing with something caught between hunger and reverence. I haven't managed to read a single book since Jenna died, but my whole body leans in to this discovery as an insistent gust of wind blows from behind and disappears into the store, ruffling the pages of a book propped open on a small table display.

Jenna brought me here. *I can feel it.*

My eyes are eager, frantically dancing around the room. To my left, beyond a patchwork assortment of welcome mats, is what looks like a beloved family living room. There are mismatched couches and plush armchairs. A stone fireplace sits unassumingly in the middle of the room, with framed pictures on the mantel. A low chaotic din fills the air, a buzz from the patrons draped in various levels of comfort across the homey furniture. They're all holding the same book, some gesturing with wineglasses and others flipping idly through their copies. A book club. They are sirens lounging along the rocky seascapes of Orman. As I watch, an old man in a dubious plaid tank top says something that causes the entire group to break into laughter. The sight is storybook warm and makes my insides feel like Christmas and hot tea.

I can practically feel my camera back in the car, like a forgotten extension of my body, framing the photo in my mind as clearly as if it were already a print. *Home Sweet Bookstore.* It would be slightly cheesy and nostalgic and perfect.

The *ping* of a cash register draws my eyes to a woman behind the long wooden counter on my right. Her bright copper hair and white skin glow beneath the light of a rustic chandelier, giving her an ethereal look. She seems neither particularly young nor particularly old. She talks animatedly to a little boy who stands on tiptoe to pay for his small stack of books with a jar full of bills. Feeling my gaze, she stops midsentence and our eyes meet.

"Are you going to keep that door open all evening? We're

not here to cool all of Michigan, you know." Her voice is both regal and exasperated, one of those people who make complete strangers feel like they belong. Someone like Jenna.

Sheepishly, I turn to close the door behind me, but before I can, the sound of clicking toenails rushes up behind me and a solid furry mass runs full force into my knees, pushing me forward. I manage to catch myself in a less-than-graceful scramble before my face hits the ground, but my palms and dignity are scratched, and my knees will most definitely bruise from hitting the lip of the door frame.

"Wally!" a male voice booms. "That's a bad dog! For shame!"

A great, brutish dog towers over me, the wiry fur of his muzzle tickling the back of my neck as he sniffs and then licks my right ear.

I don't bother trying to imagine how I would frame this massive beast in a lens. He's much too big. Except . . . he looks almost exactly like one of those hounds of old that one would find reclining in front of a massive fireplace after a long day of hunting with his royal master.

I lie frozen as he licks my other ear and lets out a low *woof* of excitement.

"I am so very sorry." Hands carefully pull me by the elbows, up from where I'm sprawled on the floor. "He is insufferable and particularly rambunctious when he's hungry. But he's completely harmless, except for the small matter of believing he is less than half his size. Are you okay?"

The whirl of activity slows enough that I finally get a look at my rescuer's face, and I choke back a gasp. I recognize him instantly as the boy from the festival, the one I tumbled into at the top of the stairs. The last time I saw him, I had been running toward Jenna.

But evidently *he* doesn't recognize *me*, because he's looking at me with large eyes and a patient expression, so I mutter, "I'm okay. Thanks."

"You're sure? He's heavy," the boy says, his voice stern as he glares down at the dog, who looks up with a tongue-lolling, unabashed grin.

Something about his voice sounds familiar, too. When it clicks, I dig through my head in search of the name of the boy who helped me on the phone. "Are you Alex?" I ask.

His smile falls a little, bemused, and he tilts his head. "Yes. Have we met?"

I look past him, pulled from our conversation by the sound of claws scratching. The beast is jumping up to sprawl his front paws onto the counter next to the woman at the register, a long string of saliva dangling from his tongue and toward a stack of papers.

"Not now, Wally," she says. The woman doesn't even look at him as she roughly pulls him down by the collar, and his splayed front legs knock over a jar full of bookmarks. The dog busies himself with picking one of the laminated papers off the floor, biting at the flat surface.

This is the boy who said there was no record of Jenna here. It's like a daydream come to life.

"I'm Amelia," I say, sticking out my hand.

He reaches forward to shake it, but still looks confused. "Amelia?"

"Oh, right. Sorry. Amelia Griffin. I called about the limited edition of *The Forest Between the Sea and the Sky*?"

My voice sounds overly bright, desperate. We both know I'm hoping he will tell me something different than he did before. His grip tightens on my hand as he shakes it in earnest, and he smiles in a way that doesn't reach his eyes.

"Yes, I remember." He sounds careful, like a field mouse trying not to draw a hawk's attention. "Sorry I couldn't help you. Did you come all the way from . . . wherever you came from . . . to check out the store?"

"Dallas," I say. "Yeah, something like that. I don't suppose you know anything else about the edition, do you?"

He shrugs. "Sorry. Wish I could help."

I sigh. "Me, too."

We stand awkwardly—him probably thinking I'm some kind of stalker, me wondering if I came all this way for nothing. Maybe the clever wind is the court jester of magical weather individuals. My certainty that coming to this bookstore is an act of Jenna's delayed will is slipping the longer our silence stretches on.

"Well, since you're here to look, you might as well enjoy yourself." Alex brightens somewhat and points to the woman behind the register. "That's Valerie, my mother and the owner of this fine dog-riddled establishment. She'll help you if you have any questions."

"We should have invested in a cat, like all of those sane bookstores," Valerie calls to me. She still hasn't come out from behind the counter, so our conversation has turned into some sort of odd oblong triangle. "Though I don't suppose we had much choice in the matter."

Alex shoots her a look I can't quite read as Wally trots to my side, two slobbery plastic bookmarks held between gleaming teeth. When I don't take them, he drops them on my foot and plops dramatically to the ground, sighing at my lack of interest.

"Well, I've got to get back to working the café." Alex sounds relieved to be done with me. "It was nice to meet you. Enjoy your stay in Lochbrook."

Part of me thinks I should be more forceful, demanding answers, but a quieter part—a Jenna part?—warns me to wait.

A dormant piece of my soul is stirring at the thought of exploring this bookstore, though, so I make my own magical wind and let it propel me forward to investigate.

The store is not only a bookstore; it's a community hub. The first floor has a corner devoted exclusively to studying students and writers, though I can't imagine how anyone could get anything done in the constant wild rumpus that serves as the store's soundtrack. There are some low shelves by a piano tucked beneath the staircase, populated by customer favorites taken from the rest of the store. Bits of colored index cards and spare paper jut out from the shelf, informing passersby "READ THIS BOOK OR ELSE" or "I skipped gym class to finish this. (Sorry, Coach G.)" or "Valerie made me read this and I'm so glad she did."

To get to the stairs and the floor above, I have to walk around the piano, where a teary student is being taught by a stern Valerie, who has left her post to loom over the keyboard.

The café is on the second floor, adjacent to a separate kitchen space that is used for weekly cooking classes. According to Alex, Valerie pays cookbook authors to come and be the "cook in residence" sometimes. Alex, who is behind the counter wearing a dark green apron, tells me the chefs teach classes or make tons of food they can sell in the café along with their books. He tells me all of this when I come to the café to get a sandwich.

He seems happy enough to talk about anything other than the mysterious 101st edition, but I feel like he's watching me closely, and I'm not sure why.

The second floor is filled with books, loosely organized into seven distinct rooms off of a long hallway. Each room is decorated to reflect the genre it holds. A mystery room with curious elongated shadows painted on the walls. A Victorian room filled to the brim with romances, historical fiction, and a potbelly stove. A children's room with a ceiling completely covered in papier-mâché balloons. An adventure and science fiction room that looks like it might double as Indiana Jones's study if his office were in space. A travel room full of guidebooks, but with some beloved classics shelved next to their respective countries. A nonfiction room with walls as diversely decorated as the books themselves—everything from printed articles on deep-sea fishing techniques to signed photos of comedic actresses tacked to any space not occupied by shelves. The last room, at the end of the hall, is so clogged with people that I don't bother fighting the throng to enter.

Even with the crazy-tall shelves downstairs, the bulk of the books are in these rooms, loosely organized by the whims of Valerie and her employees.

I overhear one girl telling a friend, "They battle it out all the time, whether *The Princess Bride* belongs in the romance-y Victorian room or the adventure room."

"How does anyone find anything in a place like this?" her friend asks, skeptical.

"You don't come to Val's to find something specific. You come to Val's because you hope something finds *you*."

Her words make my heart pound a little harder in my chest, but then the girl's friend makes an exaggerated gagging sound and they both burst into laughter. It reminds me of Jenna, and my heart constricts painfully, so I hurry on.

It's almost too easy to let myself lapse into what I once was: an avid reader with little care beyond what I might read next. Once or twice I pick up a book and fight the impulse to carry it to the register. Reading is no longer an option, and there is no point in buying something I won't use. Old habits die hard, though. I find myself running my hands along the spines before I remind myself to turn away, remembering the piles of shredded books back home.

Jenna and I used to guess at the personalities of people by watching how they browsed bookstores. Endlessly practical Jenna argued that there were only two types: the Amblers and the Directs. And I could *almost* side with her, if not for the hybrids, the people that are neither purposeful nor wanderers, the ones who stray from shelf to shelf, half checking their lists of books to read but allowing themselves room to be taken in by a beautiful cover or title.

"Three, then," Jenna said, when we first argued about the categorization.

I agreed for the sake of simplicity, but really I think there are too many types to count.

There must be, because I need there to be a category for an ex-reader with a hole the size of Texas in her chest wandering around a bookstore that seems determined to turn everyone into Amblers. Surrounded by the smell of coffee and books, I'm suddenly grossly aware of Jenna's absence beside me, a black hole sucking all the air from the room and my lungs.

I'm in the travel room, about to panic from lack of oxygen, when the lights dim briefly before returning to full brightness, like a theater indicating the end of an intermission.

I breathe in harshly, taking stock of who and what and where I am. I am Amelia Griffin. I am in Michigan on a mission to uncover my dead best friend's reason for sending me an impossible book. And I will find out why she sent it—with or without air.

Filled with a sense of purpose and the strange relief that comes from having ridden out a particularly large wave of grief, an emotion I'm already uncomfortably familiar with, I promise to return tomorrow to more thoroughly investigate. Starting with Alex.

"All right, you lot, glasses and mugs back to the café please, and it's the last call for books if you insist on purchasing them tonight." Valerie is shouting from the first floor. Wally joins in with a chorus of barking. "Round up the upstairs stragglers, won't you, Alexander? And for the love of all, Walter, you are in *enough* trouble today without causing that racket!"

I make my way downstairs, letting one or two patrons on my heels step around me. When I reach the first floor, Valerie is arguing with the remaining book club members.

"Aww, come on, Val," the plaid man is saying. "We've only just started our *discussion*." He says "discussion" like *dees-cussion*, with phony importance that I think is meant to mock Valerie's imperial air.

"John, this group has been reading the same book for two months because you can't get past the wine to talk about the plot. *Out!*"

As the group moves toward the back of the store with much good-natured grumbling, Valerie turns to me and opens her mouth to speak, but Alex interrupts her as he steps off the stairs.

"You're still here?" He's a breath shy of polite, and there's something buried in his tone that I can't decipher.

"Alexander! Where are your manners?"

Without the counter or piano blocking her, I can see Valerie is dressed in a long skirt and a frilly shirt that glimmers with layers of draped necklaces. Her ears glitter with two very large diamonds that match the sizable wedding ring on her left hand. She looks like she might be off to a gala or a movie premiere. She reeks of sophistication and grace, and I immediately feel underdressed and overwhelmed in my shirt and jeans.

"Mom, she—"

"I don't care if she's the White Witch or Moriarty. You do not speak to guests that way, Alexander, do you hear me?"

"But—"

"Butts are for sitting and cigarettes," Valerie cuts him off. "Apologize."

Alex rolls his eyes before turning to me. "Look, I'm sorry. But if you're still here about the book thing, I've already told you: it didn't come from here."

"And which 'book thing' would this be, Alexander?" She rolls out his name like a song: *Al-ex-an-der*.

This conversation is a spinning top that is going to topple over at any moment, but my sluggish brain is slowly putting context clues together. Alex definitely knows something about the 101st copy that he's not telling me, and he doesn't want his mom to know about it.

"It's nothing," he tells Valerie, and then turns to me. "I'm really sorry about Wally earlier . . . and that we didn't send the book."

Exhausted from traveling and afraid to ask him more in front of Valerie, I shake my head to stop the brain fog from settling in.

"Okay, I get it. You don't know where the book came from. Sorry I asked." I say this with a pointed tone I hope Alex interprets as *You're hiding something, but I'll play nice and not bring it up in front of your mom.* "But can you point me in the direction of a hotel? I'll be here for a few days."

Alex says, "The ones in town will be booked up with summer travelers," right as Valerie says, "Nonsense. You can stay here. My personal apartments are on the third floor. It's the least I can do, after your trouble with Wally and"—she shoots a look at Alex that could melt flesh from bone—"my son."

"But *Mom*—"

"No more *but*s, Alexander, I mean it. And where is *that boy*? I know he didn't feed Walter, but did he ever go retrieve that package I sent him to the post office for?"

Alex grows very still. I watch, feeling out of place and forgotten in this conversational detour, as he slowly shuts his eyes and lets out a lot of air from his pursed lips before answering, "No. I did."

Alex shoots me a look of dread as Valerie's perfect posture grows rigid.

"So, he refused to go to the post office, did he?" Valerie's voice has gone from benevolent queen to warlord in an instant. "And you just closed up the café to run and do his part for him?"

"I was only gone a minute. Nobody noticed—" Alex starts, but he is quickly cut off.

"It isn't about the package, Alex. That boy needs to learn he can hide from the world and his books and his problems but he can't hide from Valerie Stroudsburg."

She already has one hand resting on the bannister to the stairs when Alex, exasperated, moans, "Your *knees*, Mom. Remember what Dr. Krown said about taking the elevator."

She turns around and glares in such a way that even I want to cower, but Alex only throws up his hands in a surprisingly dramatic gesture and says, "Fine. But remember that I'm the one who has to live with him, not you."

When she's halfway up the stairs, Alex turns to me and sighs, a look of resignation on his face.

"It's my roommate. He and I share a house down the street. He's not very good with people. My mom is . . . well, she's trying to change that."

"Does he work in the bookstore, too?"

Alex looks at me hard, like he would shove me out of the store if he could, but since he can't, he's going to level with me against his will. "No. He's a writer."

"Why are you saying it like that? Does he write embarrassing advice columns for the paper or something?"

"No," Alex says carefully. "You'll know him on sight. And, no offense, but I don't know you, so I'm going to have to *beg* that you don't write about him on social media or Twit or whatever it is everyone is using. He's—"

Stomping feet and shouting voices come from above us, and Alex and I both look toward the second floor.

"Endsley," Alex says to me under his breath, as the voices

draw nearer. "N. E. Endsley. Nolan. Don't ask him about that limited copy, either. Please. He's got enough going on."

I don't need the magical wind to blow or Wally to knock me over to feel like I'm being shoved to my knees.

Of course.

"N. E. Endsley," I say, disbelieving. "Upstairs? Here? I thought he lived in New York!"

"He did," Alex says, but that's all he can tell me before our subject comes clomping down the stairs. *Where was he? How did I not see him in my second-floor wanderings?* Valerie and Wally are close on his heels.

"And another thing," Valerie is saying. "Your imbecile of a dog managed to wreak havoc on a poor girl visiting the store."

Endsley seems to be ignoring her, to the point that I wonder if he is deaf. I'm not even the one being yelled at and I am fighting the impulse to duck behind Alex, who is looking agitatedly from me to Endsley, gauging my reaction.

Valerie is significantly shorter than Endsley, but when they reach the bottom of the stairs and she comes to stand toe to toe with him, she somehow looms larger. Endsley's head is bent, his hands stuffed into the pockets of his sweatshirt, and the only word for his attitude is *pouty*.

Somewhere the clever wind is chortling—no—*screaming* with laughter. The pages of Jenna's manual have dumped me right where I wanted to be only a few chapters ago, standing feet away from the creator of the Orman Chronicles. Here is *the N. E. Endsley*, not in New York but in a tiny Michigan town off the beaten path to nowhere, which I wouldn't have known existed except for the package that I *know* is from my dead best friend.

"No appreciation for responsibility," Valerie is saying, when

I tune back in. "No consideration for others. I've had it up to here with you, Nolan Endsley. Up. To. Here."

With each word, she raises her hand higher until it is level with Endsley's head, taking his worn red baseball cap from his midnight hair and hitting him across the shoulder with it. Wally is barking and running circles around them, and it seems more chaotic now with only the five of us than it did when the store was crawling with people. Alex sighs beside me and moves to step into the fray while I try to blend in with the counter.

"As much as I am enjoying this," Alex says, "I have a hundred things to do in the morning to get ready for the bazaar. Can I take him home, Mom?"

Valerie and Alex share a meaningful look, and he darts his eyes toward me. *Not in front of her*, the look says.

She considers, after directing another glare at Endsley, who is looking at his feet, and gives a nod of acquiescence.

"Fine. But first, any progress today, Nolan?"

N. E. Endsley is braver than I. He pulls a few folded pieces of paper from his pocket, shoving them into Valerie's outstretched palm without looking at her. She chooses to ignore the attitude.

"I expect more from you tomorrow" is all she says.

It's a dismissal. Endsley turns sharply on his heel and stalks past me and Alex, toward the large wooden door, unlocking it and wrenching it open so hard I'm worried it will come unhinged. Without turning he says, "Alex. Walter."

The New York Times described him as "enigmatic." *The Washington Post* called him "complex." And this was *before* he stopped giving interviews and making public appearances, which happened fairly soon after the publication of his first book.

If my mind were focused only on the wonder of meeting the famously reclusive N. E. Endsley, I might describe him as petulant at best and standoffish at worst. I probably would have spoken up, explained that Jenna was my friend and that we had bonded over his books, his words.

Except, no matter how far I drive, or whom I meet, everything will always come back to Jenna.

Jenna is not here.

Wally is the only one who has moved to carry out the command, happily sitting on his haunches and panting beside Endsley's clearly expensive jeans in the doorway. Alex looks split between following Endsley and staying to reason with the incensed Valerie.

"Come *on*, Alex." Endsley's tone is expectant. He finally turns, frustrated. His eyes meet mine, noticing me for the first time. I force myself to hold his gaze, blue on blue, and his eyes widen slightly.

He's not pretty like Alex; nobody would mistake them for brothers, though their hair is almost identical in color. Endsley's is a bit curlier, twisting around his ears and toward the collar of his T-shirt, but everything else about him is fair—his skin, his eyes, his lips. I've seen this face in so many stylized portraits, namely the small author photo on the back flap of his books, but the reality is sobering.

His nose is slightly crooked; it leans a little to the right side of his face. His cheekbones—sharp and shadowy in his professional photos—don't look like they might cut through glass without the aid of professional lighting. His shoulders are not at all proud and stalwart, as they appear at the end of the Orman Chronicles. Instead, they are slightly hunched and deign to make the great N. E. Endsley a mere mortal.

He is staring, and it's the most eye contact I've managed in weeks. My cheeks warm as something inside me both fortifies and breaks. The anger I felt after the festival floods away and leaves me with one simple need: to know if he remembers Jenna, too.

"She met you," I blurt out, taking a shaky step forward. When I realize this won't make sense to anybody but me, I add, "Jenna. My friend. She met you at CCBF. She said you were . . ." I pause, looking for a tactful word. "Troubled."

N. E. Endsley still doesn't break our weirdly charged stand-off. It feels like mutual recognition, which is impossible, since he's never laid eyes on me.

He opens his mouth and takes a minuscule half step forward and I think he's going to say something. Instead, he stares for another stretch of uncomfortable time, his mouth partially open, before turning to Alex and saying, "I'll wait by the car." And he disappears into the inky darkness.

When I meet people, I always imagine what world hides inside them. Most people are the same: rows and rows of busy cubicles with pictures of their kids tacked to the walls and piles of paperwork waiting to go *somewhere*. I prefer the different ones. Those are the people I love to photograph, the reason I try so hard to shrink entire worlds down into a single shot.

Behind Jenna's eyes was a shopping mall that ran like a well-oiled machine. There was never trash on the food court floor, no crying toddlers wailing from strollers. People walked with purpose from store to store, with a task to be accomplished, but sometimes one of those mall playgrounds would suddenly form and everyone, no matter their age, would scramble to play.

Adults would abandon bags of protein bars and vitamins and compete on the swings. Little kids would throw down their new school clothes and clamor onto monkey bars and scooch down slides. Old women would chuck aside their canes and take turns spinning each other on the merry-go-rounds. And just as quickly as the playground appeared, it would disappear, and the shoppers would return to their tasks.

That was Jenna.

Endsley is different, too. I had caught a glimpse, like a flickering photo that won't come into focus, but it's enough. I see dark forests that neither threaten nor welcome. Hot, humid nights trapped among trees and branches, wolves that may or may not be friendly, and streams of black water promising nothing. It looks like the perfect, most frightening hiding place one could create.

This is how I finally meet N. E. Endsley—the best seller, the recluse, the enigma. Not at the festival, but here. Wherever *here* is.

Clever wind.

chapter seven

After Alex apologizes to his mom at least three times for Endsley's behavior—"I'll talk to him. I'll talk to him," he tells Valerie—and an imploring glance at me, he and Wally follow Endsley down the gravel path into darkness.

Valerie again insists that I stay the night in her guest room. I am too terrified of displeasing her and too tired to argue, even though I've only just met her and she could be the bookshop equivalent of the old witch in the candy house, luring innocent bookworms in with her promise of endless stories and tea before cooking them in her oven.

I comfort myself with the knowledge that I will most definitely not fit in a standard-size oven.

She relocks the large wooden door at the front of the store, mumbles about Alex not shutting down the computer system—"I'm not a technical wizard, for heaven's sake"—and presses a few buttons on the wall, which dim all of the visible lights in the store to a dull glow.

What would Jenna do? I wonder. I dig through my memories for an answer, which, after the lack of air in the travel room, feels like running barefoot on gravel. When I find nothing remotely similar to spending the night in a stranger's bookstore to guide me, I turn to my imagination, trying with all my might to turn the black hole beside me into a Jenna-shaped thing. That doesn't work, either, so I let my mind slacken and instead count whales floating in and around the kelp of the darkened bookshelves while Valerie closes the store.

"Well," she says, coming from behind the counter, sending the whales swimming from view. "I suppose this is as good a time as any for a proper introduction. I am Valerie Stroudsburg. I run the store, I teach piano, and I do not suffer idiocy, my dear, so try to keep that to a minimum. You aren't predisposed to idiocy, are you?"

Here, a wry smile and an arched eyebrow from Valerie. From me, a thin upward turn of the lips and a shake of my head as I fight every impulse to ask a string of questions about N. E. Endsley, the book, and Alex.

"Good," Valerie says. "This is the part where you offer a name and intention, dear."

One of the things I love—loved—about books is that no matter how dreadful the characters' plights or how insurmountable the conflicts, everything turns out for the best in the end. Not necessarily happily ever after, and maybe not happy at all, but necessary and true. If there was pain, it was to be for personal growth. If there was loss, it was so something better or more essential could be introduced.

Standing here on the ground floor of a bookstore that is drifting into sleep for the night, with a woman who looks like she fell out of a picture book with her gauzy dress and bejeweled everything—not to mention the proximity of the creator of the Orman Chronicles—I can feel the hint of a story peeping its way from the ashes of the last couple of weeks and I wonder if maybe there really is such a thing as a benevolent wind. But when I wonder why the wind wasn't there to save Jenna, I feel the magic ebb.

"Amelia," I say. "My name is Amelia Griffin."

"Pretty name, that," Valerie says. "And what brings you to Lochbrook, Amelia?"

This is all said with her same regality, which coming from anyone else would seem fake but from Valerie seems natural and appropriate.

"A quick getaway," I finally say. "To clear my thoughts."

"You must have a great deal of thoughts if they brought you all this way from . . . Texas, was it? Well, no matter. You will find Lochbrook a charming town, though I will be the first to admit, your welcome committee was found lacking this evening. Do you want to take something up to read?"

My eyes have wandered to the second floor and the distant room I did not get to explore. When my gaze darts back to her face, Valerie is smiling.

"You've got that hungry look about you," she says.

"I used to," I say. "Read, I mean. I . . . I don't do it much anymore."

It's not a lie, but it's not the whole truth.

Valerie gives me a long, slow look that is not altogether different from the one my mother used to give me, back when there was little wrong in our world, well before the divorce. Mom used to be able to look into my eyes and know what was wrong in a matter of seconds.

Now there's nothing behind my mother's eyes except TV static.

I fear Valerie has the same power, that she's going to lay my confusion about Jenna, the mystery book, and my future bare at my feet and I'm going to have to examine it too closely, but instead she says, "Suit yourself. It's bedtime, I think."

A little piece of me decides to love Valerie for the rest of my days for this one small mercy.

Valerie asks if I need to grab my bags, but I tell her I'm too tired to go to my car tonight. I'm exhausted enough to dread walking up the grand staircase, but Valerie walks past it to the far left corner of the store. There's an elevator I only half noticed earlier. It doesn't smell like elevators usually smell. This one smells like flowers and has piano music pouring from nonscratchy hidden speakers. There is a label next to the third-floor button that says, "Private Residence," and a handwritten sticky note next to it that says, "Enter at your own risk. Dementors on duty."

The ride to the third floor is short, but I have time to examine the numerous flyers stuck to the walls. Author events, cookbook signings, a dueling piano competition, and a summer bazaar benefiting the library of an elementary school. All are advertised on various colors of luminescent copy paper, all claiming to be held at a place called A Measure of Prose, with the exception of the bazaar, which simply states "Valerie's."

"A Measure of Prose?" I ask.

Valerie, who is cleaning her glasses on a lacy handkerchief I didn't see her extract, nods absently.

"The official name of the shop, dear. Though everyone calls it Val's for short."

Another bit of gravel sticks in the sole of my foot. Jenna

loved places with quirky monikers or multiple names. It was one of the few times our roles were reversed; I found it inefficient, but she found it charming. Is this yet another reason she sent me here, to a bookstore that uses its unofficial name for its official postage stickers?

The elevator dings a greeting and opens to a small entryway that holds a fake spiral-shaped plant in a blue pot, a welcome mat with chickens pecking on the words "Home Sweet Home," and a tiny framed picture of a wheelbarrow on the wall. Valerie pulls a long chain from inside her shirt and uses the key at its end to unlock the door.

We are deposited directly into a small sitting area with matching furniture and a coffee table, which looks far less cozy than the inviting living room of the store. It looks more like hotel decor, except the ceiling is slanted to a point, and I've never seen a hotel room with a private elevator.

Valerie removes the rings from each of her fingers and lifts the necklaces from around her head with no less grace than a prima ballerina, setting them in a series of colored trays on a tall table before showing me to my room. There is a queen-size four-poster bed with thick midnight-blue curtains, an armoire, and a small sink in the corner, with no attached bathroom. The sink is rather an eyesore, jutting out near the bedside table.

"Inexplicable, that," Valerie says, following my gaze. "I find it rather charming in its oddness. You may brush your teeth without leaving the room, but little else, I'm afraid. There's no television, and the top floor has just the one bathroom, but I promise I don't spend above an hour or three getting ready in the morning."

An hour or *three*? I hope I can hold my pee that long.

"It's a joke, dear," she says, laughing at my expression. "It's the door exactly opposite your quarters, so you won't become lost. I tend to wake early most days, so I'll likely be out of your hair before you rise."

She reiterates that the café is downstairs, should I need a midnight snack or drink, and that the shop opens whenever she feels like it—and she almost always feels like it around eight. I thank her, which she waves off with a hand that holds one remaining ring—the wedding band—as she closes the door behind her.

After I send a quick text letting the Williamses know I've checked into a hotel, a white lie I don't bother feeling guilty about, I drift into a restless sleep under a deluge of thoughts about Jenna, N. E. Endsley, and 101st copies of books.

I manage a few hours of sleep before despair and fear reach their dark, oily fingers from beneath the floorboards to play with the tendrils of my hair. I've heard grief compared to a tide, but tides are predictable. These feelings are not. I try to think of whales swimming, to imagine myself in a small boat, watching them glide around me, but I can feel my heart constricting, tight pain booming through my chest, so I extricate myself from the sheets wound around my legs and let myself into the dark hallway of Valerie's apartments. I'm in the elevator with the glowing second-floor button pressed before I fully realize what I'm doing.

If Valerie wakes and asks, I'll say I was thirsty. She'll pretend to believe me, but we would both know my bluff. Even then, she wouldn't ask what's wrong or ask me to tell my story, and I thank the god of the whales for adults that do not pry or presume.

The flyers on the elevator walls blur as I realize I'm technically supposed to be one. An adult. I'm supposed to be able to make my own life choices, be self-sufficient, and generally be more *something*. Mature, maybe, but I know plenty of immature adults.

I feel old, a tattered sail on a boat that has barely weathered the storm. Losing Jenna, or maybe understanding how the people I love will all die someday, makes me feel apart. Funerals are supposed to be for really old relatives, not for friends that were in the isle of green. Not for friends whose lives had only begun.

Yet somehow I also feel far too young to be a high school graduate, too unprepared for what lies ahead. Is the fear I feel about school because Jenna is no longer beside me or because I never wanted to major in English in the first place?

A memory: Jenna muttering to herself as she compiled notes on one of her many spreadsheets. *This* school didn't have a program that emphasized pharmacognosy, Jenna's chosen narrow field of study about turning plants into medicine. *This* school had poor placement for PhD students who wanted to pursue teaching at a college level.

"No, no, no, *no*."

I didn't look up from my math homework to acknowledge Jenna's increasingly distressed protests.

"What is it?" I asked, my voice flat. Geometric proofs were kicking my butt, and her racket wasn't helping.

"Don't use that tone," Jenna said. "This is for you as much as it's for me."

"And what *this* is this?" I asked.

"Our *futures*, Amelia. Our futures. Or do you not want to go to the same school?"

I set down my pencil and uncurled my legs, scooching to sit shoulder to shoulder with Jenna. She turned the laptop toward me and dramatically threw her arm over her eyes while I scanned the screen.

"A&M, University of Washington, University of Alaska . . . What is this?"

"Candidates," Jenna said, her eyes still covered by her arm. "For schools. For us." *Duh*, her tone said.

I ran my finger along the trackpad. Beside each school was a list of criteria, all rated on a one-to-ten scale: pharmacognosy program strength, English program strength, diversity, on-campus life, off-campus entertainment, proximity to major airport, professor-to-student ratios, number of AP course credits accepted.

The list went on. She had already entered data for at least twelve schools, and their "grades" were typed in bold at the top of each column.

"Jenna, this is ridiculous. You can't decide where we're going to college this way."

She moved her arm, her eyes narrowed. "Why ever not?"

"Why *ever* not? Because, Miss Prim-and-Proper, you can't possibly know"—I glanced at the screen—"the overall quality of the locally sourced coffee down to a numerical rating without having tried it."

"Yes I can," Jenna argued. "They're called online reviews. They're very popular."

"Okay, but why should that factor in to where we're going to school?"

Her arm went back over her eyes and she growled in the

back of her throat. "We're going to be there for *four years*, at least, Amelia. Don't you want to make sure we'll be happy there?"

I laughed. "You can't be serious. You don't honestly think this spreadsheet is going to guarantee us happiness, do you?"

But she did. A week later—after a lot more frustrated grumblings on her part—Jenna ordered informational pamphlets from the top three contenders on what I had come to call her College Deathmatch Spreadsheet. When they came in, we pored over them at her dining room table. Glossy photos of campuses in ideal lighting, bookmarks with the numbers of admissions advisors, and detachable sheets of majors littered the table.

"I don't even know," Jenna said, what felt like hours later. "What do you think?"

"There's something about the campus of this one," I said, pushing the University of Montana packet in front of her. "The snow and the hill behind the admin building, and did you see the photo of this professor? Her professional head shot is a photo of her dogsledding."

Jenna stared at the flyer, her lip curling upward. "You like it because the trees remind you of Orman, don't you?"

This hadn't even popped into my mind, but when I looked back to the photo, I nodded.

"Me, too," she whispered.

"So let's *go*." I smiled. "Where did this one rank in the deathmatch?"

"Second," she said. "But only by three-tenths of a point."

"Let's apply," I said. "No harm in trying. And maybe this will be the only place we both get into our programs."

It was. I called it a sign, and Jenna called it a statistical

probability, based on her research, but I took it to mean that we were on the right track. Jenna and I were supposed to be with each other, always.

But she's not here. What am I supposed to do with a sign meant for two?

My thoughts are swarming like flies, and I wave them away when the elevator door slides open. I'm drawn past the café, through the maze of eerily empty tables and couches that echo the sitting area downstairs, to the far hallway that contains the book rooms. Three hushed electric candelabras dimly light my way through the darkness, though the book rooms appear completely unlit. The large window at the end of the hall looks out over the grove of trees and I let myself imagine I am a high lady walking through silent castle corridors. A feeling of reverence steps on despair's grimy fingers long enough for me to half lunge myself at the window to look upon a unicorn as it steps gently from the shelter of the trees into the moonlight. Or a night rider, cloaked and mysterious, riding a noble steed across the clearing before retreating into the darkness of the forest. I have the fleeting thought that maybe, in the absence of reading, my mind will make its own stories.

I wonder if the college prep course will advise against day-dreaming. I can't bring myself to read a single page of a new book, but the idea of being a droid focused on academia almost physically pains me. I untangle myself from the thought. It's not like I can back out. I pinky promised, and I won't break that, even if Jenna's not here to give me a pep talk.

My imaginings must block everything out, because at first I don't see the muted light coming from my right, the book room I didn't get to explore. My feet slow, my body bracing itself like it knows something I don't.

Glowing electric lanterns with flickering bulbs are mounted on top of every curved bookshelf and sporadically along the walls. It's the largest book room I've seen here, almost perfectly circular, with a large area rug designed like a compass just beyond the door. In the pale light of the lanterns, I can make out a mural on the wall, so realistic and unexpected that I immediately sober, despair and mystery alike falling off me so quickly I'm half convinced they make an audible clang against the floor.

It's a depiction of the first big scene from the Orman Chronicles, when Emmeline and Ainsley row their canoe into another realm by accident. They don't realize they've left their world until they see the looming cliff, a lighthouse castle perched atop its crest, and the gentle ripples of the river beneath their stolen canoe suddenly become the large waves of a great sea.

This room has fallen out of my imagination, like someone shadowed me as I explored the corners of every page of those books and jotted down notes about my favorite details. My entire body is drawn to the mural, and I'm having a hard time convincing myself it is only a painting and not a secret portal to a world I ache to find.

Used to ache to find.

I wonder if Endsley had a hand in its creation. Maybe he knows about the room but disapproves. He's obviously not a fan of attention.

I walk toward the lighthouse but am unable to reach it, even on tiptoe. I feel this impulsive need to try, though. Jenna was much taller than me. If she were here, I would tell her to touch the lighthouse for both of us and she would tell me that's stupid or ask why, but I would break her down. She would roll her eyes and reach a palm up to the wall, but her hand would linger for a second longer than necessary because she had wanted to touch it all along.

I'm stretched against the wall, my palm flattened against the painted rock face, when he coughs.

N. E. Endsley is sitting in an armchair tucked between two bookcases. I jolt as he rises to his feet, and the lanterns on the cases gently sway as if in a breeze.

When I was little, my father used to read me the same book every night before I fell asleep. It was called *The Forest Girl*. It didn't have many words, but the illustrations were in lovely shades of blue and gray and green all muddled together to make looming castles and tall haunting trees that soared high above the little golden-haired princess. I loved that book, but it was lost in one of the moves we made, when my father's job took us from Washington to Kansas to Texas.

Years later, while wandering a used bookstore with Jenna—she knew I loved them—I went to the picture book section on a whim. Old friends fluttered their pages and stretched their bindings toward me and I fondly stroked their spines. My eyes came to settle on a picture book crammed between some illustrated children's Bibles, forgotten and worn, and my entire body came alive in recognition of the narrative that used to sing me to sleep. *The Forest Girl* sat unassumingly on a shelf, waiting for me to recover it, nostalgia and love and regret for our time apart wrapped into a few colored illustrations.

This is as close as I can come to describing what it is like to find myself far away from well-laid plans, from Jenna and common sense, and instead standing, quite alone, before N. E. Endsley.

What comes out of my mouth first is unplanned and rawer than I would like.

"Jenna loved your books," I say, tilting my head back to meet his eyes. "Did she tell you that when you spoke?"

He stares at me so long I wonder if he'll turn around and disappear without a word, a phantom prince returning to his silent castle.

Or maybe I'm a fool and he doesn't remember meeting Jenna at all and has nothing to say.

"I don't know what you're talking about," he says.

His tone is haughty and imperious, like he's all-knowing. It's not at all similar to the warm cadence of Valerie's voice, though she could get more accomplished with a single word than most monarchs could with a sentence.

No, N. E. Endsley is using his voice to belittle, and the part of me still surviving with my head above water refuses to be made small.

"You know exactly what I'm talking about," I say. "She met you at the festival that you ditched. She *helped* you."

Even in the low light, I see him flinch.

"See!" I point, my finger nearly grazing his chest. "See? You remember."

"I don't," he insists, a frantic undercurrent in his voice. "I don't know what you're talking about or *who you are*."

While his voice rises, mine recedes, not in fright but in desperation. My whole body suddenly needs N. E. Endsley to acknowledge the existence of Jenna Williams more than I've ever needed anything in my life.

"Why won't you tell me?" My voice is quiet, splintered. I hate myself for losing my cool, but there is nothing I can do to stop the oncoming runaway train of grief.

He takes an agitated step closer, like if he physically lunges at this conversation he can make it go away. "Why do you need to know?"

"Because she's dead," I say. I sob a little on the last word, tears spilling over my cheeks. "She's dead, and I'd like to know what she said, and what you said to her, because she died a week after the festival, and we both loved your books, and I—I just want to know."

I don't have the energy to care how hopeless I sound, how broken. I don't have the energy to compare my daydreams of meeting N. E. Endsley to the reality, alone in a bookstore, Jennaless.

I'm not surprised when he abruptly leaves the room. This is too much to handle, I know. Numb, I stand in the middle of the compass rug, with Orman at my back, and think of whales swimming. I imagine their sleek bodies peeking in and out of waves, their songs calling to one another in the twilight, the infant whales playful and happy to be alive.

I *am* surprised when Endsley abruptly returns, tissue box in hand.

"Here." He holds the tissues at arm's length like he's afraid to get near me in my state, but even with both our arms outstretched, I can't reach. He gently tosses the box to me and it falls to the ground between us, loud in the silence.

I scoot it closer with my foot and bend to extract a tissue before raising my eyes to meet his. In this light, they are a thunderstorm, the kind no photographer could ever truly capture.

"You can leave," I say thickly. I can feel the fight seeping out of me with each traitorous tear. I want to be mad, vengeful, but all I am is crushed. "I know you hate people. I've read your interviews."

Maybe I'm so pathetic that even this reclusive author who hates the world has taken pity on me, or I'm hallucinating, but I swear something in Endsley's expression changes. His eyes briefly leave me, staring over my head to the lighthouse, his jaw tight and his eyes slightly narrowed, and when they return he seems resigned. After a sigh, he takes two long steps to my side and not-so-gently tugs on my arm.

"Sit," he says. Another command from a king used to getting his way.

"What?" I ask, startled. "Why?"

"Because not so long ago somebody did the same thing I'm about to do for you. Sit."

Curious and disoriented, I fold myself down beside him so we are both cross-legged on the compass rug. He turns ever so slightly to face me, sticking his hand out.

"I'm Endsley," he says.

It's like having Taylor Swift introducing herself at a concert. It's preposterous, giggle-worthy, but I don't laugh.

"I know," I say, shaking his hand, only realizing after we touch that I'm using the hand I wiped away snot with. "Amelia."

"Right," he says. "Right." He digs around in his pocket and extracts a flip phone, a chunky thing that looks grossly out of place in a world of slim, keyboardless touch screens.

"I don't really like smartphones," he says.

I nod, imagining whales free to roam hundreds of miles in a day, sunset after sunset.

He types in a four-digit passcode and uses the archaic arrow pad to navigate to a large icon labeled "Digital Photos." A grainy photo of an emaciated gray dog appears on the tiny screen.

"Wally," Endsley says simply, extending the phone so it's in front of me. "He was something of a legend for a few weeks in New York. He was living in Central Park but would periodically run into the street to try and cross to the food vendors on the other side. He kept evading animal control. The car I was riding in was the one that finally hit him. I took him to the vet—don't ask me why—and he's been with me ever since. Valerie figures that's why he throws himself at things when he's hungry. His pea-sized brain probably affiliates physical distress with positive outcomes."

This is beyond bizarre. The mighty N. E. Endsley is showing me phone pictures? A fever dream, that's what this is. I'm dying, and this is apparently all my brain can manage to give me in my final moments.

Jenna, I think. *Give me Jenna instead.* But Endsley takes the phone and clicks a few more times. He shows me another image, this one of a gnarled tree.

"This is a tree from the backyard where I grew up. I used to climb up to the little V, see? I would sit there with a legal pad and write story after story. Repetitive, formulaic things, but I liked them. I hated being inside. Sometimes my father would bring me a sandwich so I could picnic in the tree, but that wasn't often."

Click, click.

"This one doesn't really have a story behind it, but I liked this footstool. It was in an antique store and I wondered who carved it and painted the design on top and how it ended up in that forgotten shop. It's stupid," he says.

The whales are dissipating, replaced by the oddest turn of events. The photos are taking over my thought process, and the great N. E. Endsley has shrunk down to the size of a normal human boy, only a year older than me, a couple of inches taller, sitting on the floor of a room designed for his own fiction. The questioning in my brain is numbing to a quiet roar and I'm just trying to take in every moment of this encounter. I'm sure it will be the last, on account of my immediate, hallucinatory death.

I scoot the slightest bit closer to him, not brave enough to let my arm touch his, even though I suspect one or both of us is incorporeal.

He glances at me but says nothing, until another image pops up on the screen.

"This is Alex in Times Square. He came to visit me . . . when I lived there, in New York."

Alex beams at us, bundled in a scarf and beanie, with comically large hipster glasses that look out of place on his round face. I almost comment on the glasses—he wasn't wearing any tonight—but I haven't found my voice yet. Endsley glances at my face and almost smiles.

"He bought those on the street," he says. "To annoy me, mostly. He didn't take them off the whole time he was there."

He takes the phone back and begins to click buttons, presumably looking for another picture to show me. I've stopped crying.

I want to thank him, but instead I'm hastily putting together clues about his strange, authorial existence: the flip phone, the well-made jeans faintly stained with mud around the knees and hems, the litany of photos he deems worth keeping.

Part of me wonders if he is just distracting me from Jenna. Why doesn't he want to talk about her?

I can feel myself spiraling, so I quickly say, "Thank you for showing me the pictures."

He doesn't look up from his phone. "It's fine."

An unspoken *You're welcome* hangs in the air, but he doesn't grab it and pull it down, so we sit in silence.

I let my head fall back as I try to take in the whole mural, but I only manage to see the tip of the lighthouse, a smudge of a lantern hanging from a bookcase.

If Jenna were here, she probably would have already put herself and Endsley at ease.

"Can I see you tomorrow?" I ask the lighthouse, too cowardly to watch his face as he rejects me. "When we're both more awake?"

My eyes focus on the painted waves that crash fretfully at the bottom of the jagged hill the lighthouse sits upon. Somewhere, an entirely new pod of whales is born and dies before N. E. Endsley—author of beloved books and potential co-Jenna acknowledger—sighs again, and says, "Maybe."

I straighten, surprised, and we look at each other for a long time, his eyes narrow and circumspect. If this looking could be personified, his blue would be the rough gray-blue of a terrible storm and mine would be the lighter blue of the ocean rising up to meet it.

I want to make concrete plans, pick a time and place and reality when we will meet tomorrow, but trying to pin N. E. Endsley to a plan would be fatal. Storms have no masters.

His stare is unrelenting. I wonder what worlds he sees behind my eyes.

I wonder if he knows that sometimes, in the quiet of my

head, I imagine myself in the Orman forests. That I walk in the crushed-grass footprints of the girls, my own tread covering theirs completely, until their stories become my own. If he knows that, even though the books have stopped speaking to me, the world behind my eyes still looks very much like a living, breathing library.

Without a word he rises, his elbow accidentally bumping my knee. He is halfway down the hall, his muffled steps barely registering in the silence, when I find my voice.

"So, you'll talk?" I ask as I find my own feet. "About Jenna? And," I can't resist asking, "maybe Orman?"

I haven't left the room, but I hear him pause at the top of the stairs.

No answer. I can sense the storm gathering strength, so I amend.

"Okay," I say. "No Orman. But . . . you'll tell me what Jenna said?"

I'm in the hallway now and can just barely make out his silhouette on the stairs—his back straight, head bent as if scanning the floor for something he's dropped, his left hand sprawled on the railing, fingers tapping a beat. He is a human computer calculating risk and reward. He hasn't said anything, but he also hasn't said no.

"So, I'll see you tomorrow?" I prod.

I've pushed too far. He doesn't answer, doesn't look my way as he glides down the staircase with familiar ease, even though I'm almost to the stairs myself.

I watch as he opens the front door to leave, can't help but torture myself with what I suspect is the last time I will see N. E. Endsley in the flesh. I let my mind run circles around his meeting with Jenna, his books, the pictures on his phone. I'm so lost in my own head that I almost don't hear his voice intermingled with the jingling bells of the front door.

"Maybe."

chapter eight

The morning greets me with the scent of coffee seeping through the guest room floor from the café below. Yesterday's sandwich forgotten, my stomach forces me from my nest of pillows and tangled sheets to hunt down food. I've slept in my clothes, the sweatpants and bookish shirt, so I'm even more wrinkly and unkempt than usual, but somebody has brought my duffle bag in from my car, the keys set neatly on top. I rush over and check that my precious 101st copy is still inside, wrapped in a dish towel and zipped into a huge protective baggie. I let out a sigh of relief when I see it, and I continue to stare at it while I change into jeans and a clean T-shirt.

When I reach the café, there is a small group of women sitting around one of the tables, strollers nestled at their sides, and a lone man reading a paper in the corner, but no sign of a familiar face. I had half hoped Endsley would be waiting for me, coffee and breakfast burrito in hand, ready to talk about Jenna.

"Amelia?"

A head appears above the marble counter, next to a glass

case stuffed to the brim with breakfast pastries. It's an older man, gruff and unshaven, crinkles upon crinkles on his sun-weathered face. He cocks his head to the side.

"Val said you'd be down," he says when I near. His voice sounds like an old car on a gravel road, rough and meandering. "She also said to tell you that she came into your bedroom while you were sleeping to take your car keys and fetch your overnight bag. Well, she may have told me to omit the bit about coming into your bedroom while you were sleeping, but I figured you would ask."

"That's fine," I say, too hungry to think of anything but the pastry case. "How much are the Danishes?"

"I'm Larson," he continues as if I haven't spoken. "Most young folk call me Mr. Larson, but you can call me whatever you want so long as you don't complain about the coffee being too strong. Your generation doesn't know what coffee is supposed to taste like, with all the sugar and creamers and that artificial sweetener you dump in by the handful."

I am definitely not awake enough to follow this conversation. If Jenna were here, she would already be poking her credit card across the counter in a borderline unfriendly fashion, asking to be served now and chitchatted at later.

"Mr. Larson, may I just have a Danish and some water?" I ask.

"Since when is coffee supposed to taste like ice cream? And who on God's green earth decided that *pumpkin*, a gourd of all things, ought to be a coffee flavor?" There is no end to his chatter in sight, but he blessedly moves toward the pastry case with tongs and wrestles with a Danish, unable to open the tongs wide enough to grasp it.

"It's cereal, you know," he continues. "All that sugar and

those marshmallows. It's ruined you. Your whole generation thinks breakfast food and coffee—and life, for that matter—is supposed to be sweet enough to crack a tooth. But sometimes life is bitter, and you might as well get used to it."

He gives up on the tongs with a *bahhh* and roughly manhandles the offending Danish onto a white ceramic plate.

"It's the government that's doing it. All that sugar. If they can keep you fat and lazy and dependent on the health care system, it keeps you pliant. Like religion. Or Netflix."

Now he's pouring me a mug of coffee, and it'd be useless to even try and tell him I didn't ask for it.

He plunks the mug next to the Danish and gives me a hard look over the case.

"You're awfully short," he says decidedly. "It's the sugar. No charge, missy. Val's orders. She said your tab for the remainder of your stay is to be on the house."

"Thanks," I say, reaching into the pocket of my jeans for cash. "But I can pay."

"Did you hear what I said, missy? These are Valerie's orders, not mine. Have you met Val?"

"Yes, sir," I say. "We met last night."

I mean, obviously. I slept in her guest room.

"Well, if you think it would be productive to argue with her, the sugar epidemic is worse than I thought." With that, he grumbles away to the small back room attached to the café.

I take a seat far from the strollers and eye the coffee. One sip raises the hair on my arms and makes my eyes water, and I stuff a piece of Danish into my mouth, hoping to quell the sudden urge to leap out of my skin. I let out a short, desperate cough, trying to rid myself of the acidic landslide in my throat, and am answered by a low *woof* from the mouth of the stairs.

"No," I say. "Absolutely not." Wally's tail is already wagging, and he's prancing in place with excitement. "No," I repeat firmly. "Wally, don't you dare."

His long legs tear across the carpet to my corner table, immediately launch up to my shoulders, damp paws eagerly scraping at my clean shirt, tongue joyously reshaping my eyebrows.

"Wally, stop it. *Stop it!* Get *down*."

The stroller brigade has stopped talking, its members holding their coffee mugs prettily with both hands and staring at Wally and me with slightly open mouths.

After I finally manage to bribe Wally with a piece of Danish to sit at my feet, his tail still thumping happily against the leg of my chair, Mr. Larson comes to my table with another cup of coffee.

"Thanks, Mr. Larson, but I have plenty of coffee." *And I don't want to smell like burnt tar.*

"It's not for you. This is Wally's daily brew. Here you go, boy." He sets the mug down in front of Wally, who stops licking my pant leg long enough to let his huge tongue plop into the cup.

"I thought caffeine was bad for dogs," I say.

"My coffee is good for anyone and everyone," Mr. Larson says, and I can't tell whether his tone is proud or defensive. "Walter here has been drinking this coffee every morning and he's had no side effects, except for maybe a little extra pep in his step."

As if to prove a point, Wally's ears perk upward, the tips of his scraggly ear hairs rising from the nearly empty mug of coffee in answer to some unseen call. He stays completely still for about a second before bolting to the stairs, a streak of murky gray lightning that no photographer in the world has a prayer of capturing.

A moment later, there's an awful lot of barking and shouting downstairs. I recognize Valerie's voice straightaway, rising above the hubbub in swooping tones of disapproval, and Alex's, exasperated but laughing. I hurriedly stuff the rest of the pastry in my mouth and make my way downstairs, eager to see Endsley.

"Amelia, dear, you're awake. I hope you slept well."

"Thank you," I say. I let my eyes run across the store, but he's not here.

Alex's forced smile slips down his face when he sees my search.

"He's usually pretty busy during the week," he says. Nobody needs clarification on who *he* is. "He doesn't like much company, to be honest. I *am* sorry about his behavior last night, though."

So. Endsley didn't bother to talk to Alex about our Orman room discussion.

"But when I talked to him again last night, he said we—"

"*Again?*" Valerie interrupts. "You mean you spoke last night? Beyond your introduction, in which he was abominably rude?"

"Yeah," I say. "I went to get some water and I may have wandered. He said we could meet today . . ."

Maybe, my brain interrupts. *He said* maybe.

Valerie turns toward Alex in astonishment. "Alexander, did you know about this?"

Alex looks between us doubtfully as he rearranges a weighty messenger bag on his shoulder.

"I didn't know they spoke last night, if that's what you mean."

"Well, of course that's what I mean. Where is he today?"

Alex runs a hand through his curls, eyes closed. "I don't know." It's almost a whine. "There's not enough time left for me to get everything ready for the summer bazaar as it—"

"Alexander, it is important for that boy to be encouraged in the social arena at every opportunity. Now, where is he?"

Another odd look is exchanged and I'm once again a living set piece, something that will participate when needed but is otherwise ignored.

I watch the silent conversation unfold. Valerie tilts her head the slightest bit and turns her palm upward by her side. *This is unusual.* Alex shrugs with an almost imperceptible lift of his shoulders and blinks twice. *Yes, but you're the one who says he should be encouraged.* A not-so-subtle head swing in my direction. *But do we trust her?*

"It's Wednesday. Fort day, isn't that right?" Valerie says, to me, I think, though she is still looking at Alex. "Alexander will take you."

"*Bazaar business,*" Alex argues. His tone suggests that he has his own answer to the question of my integrity, and that it isn't good.

"You're confirming the booth rentals today with Mr. Sampson, correct?" Valerie asks.

"Mom, no. I'm supposed to—" Alex begins, but he is quickly cut off. I'm beginning to wonder if anyone ever finishes a complete sentence around here.

"I will call Mr. Sampson and check on the rentals," Valerie says. "And I will hear nothing more on the subject. Don't make me put you on my bad list alongside Mr. Endsley."

"But I've just been taken *off* the bad list," Alex mutters, and I watch as his face transforms from handsome college student to chagrined five-year-old.

Against my will, I am dreadfully amused.

"Come on," Alex says. "I'll take you to Nolan. Wally! Come!"

Wally is busy surreptitiously licking a wooden box of matches that sits on the fireplace seat.

"Walter," Alex shouts. "Come on!"

And this is the story of how I ended up in a rusted brown pickup truck with the best friend of N. E. Endsley and N. E. Endsley's stupid, no good, very bad dog.

We don't talk much during the drive. The diesel engine is so loud that even the shortest of conversations would strain the vocal cords. Wally is supposed to be sitting in the truck bed, but after he pushes his huge head through the open rear window to lick my hair once or twice, he decides he might as well come all the way in and make himself comfortable. He sits between Alex and me on the bench, panting with delight, his front paws atop my left knee.

"Nolan's fault," Alex yells over the engine. "He never bothered to train him."

He sounds at once chastening and indulgent of Endsley, reminding me with a sharp pang of Jenna.

She's not here. It's like a sneaking fog, the sudden jolting realization that, a few days ago, would have greeted me right when I woke. But today is different. Today I woke up in a bookstore after meeting N. E. Endsley and ate breakfast in the same bookstore and am being shuttled to his presence by none other than his best friend and keeper, and I have only just now remembered why I ran away from home in the first place.

Have I really forgotten her this easily? I spend the rest of the ride staring out the window, trying to make sense of all the green. I imagine whales swimming in the air between the trees, the forests of Orman rising up with their dark branches to mingle into the Michigan landscape. I pretend I am not real; Wally and Alex are not real. The world is one giant story and I'm only a figment of some author's imagination, a discarded character that never made it onto a page. Strangely, it makes me feel a bit better.

Alex maneuvers the truck through an iron gate that's been propped open on each side with stones. There's a sign saying the beach is private, but the rocks are deeply embedded in the soil and I get the feeling that the gate never closes.

Lake Michigan is back in full glory, stretching out toward the horizon in leisurely strokes of blue. Alex stops the truck near a narrow dirt path that leads to the water's lapping edges. When he shuts off the engine, Wally squeezes himself back through the window and out of the truck bed, his sprint only slightly slower than his coffee-fueled efforts as he rounds a clump of trees and disappears from view.

My ears are still adjusting to the relative quiet when Alex sighs. I think he's about to tell me where to find Endsley, but instead he closes his eyes, leans his head back, and breathes, "He's my best friend."

I don't know what to say, so I say nothing.

"He's my best friend and I don't want anything to hurt him."

I watch as the world of Alex comes into focus. Alex is everything kind and good and naive without being stupid. His insides are a carnival full of possibility and wonder and intelligent machines that do not detract from the quaintness of his old-fashioned bizarre. Everyone is welcome here, everyone given first and second and third chances to enjoy the bounty of cotton candy. Nobody is too poor or too odd or too anything to be excluded. Alex is whimsy and hope, but he is not ignorant. Encircling the carnival are tall walls decorated with murals of smiling children and hot air balloons—bright and joyous, but walls nonetheless. They are meant to keep the bad things out.

He is wondering if *I* am one of those bad things.

I don't blame him.

I want to tell him that the bad things will find a way in, no matter what he does. I want to say that I, too, thought I was safe because I loved friends and stories and life more than I liked material possessions, but it turns out that even the safest things can be ripped from you between one heartbeat and the next.

"I don't want to hurt anyone," I say instead, and Alex stares at me for a long moment.

"I almost believe you," he says, and he sounds surprised. "I don't know what happened last night, but it says something that he talked to you at all." He pauses. "You should know he never talks. To anyone."

"I figured," I say.

"No, but really." His voice is stern, almost admonishing. "No one. I can count them all on one hand for you."

"I get it, Alex. I don't want to hurt anyone."

Alex's eyes bore into mine. "He needs *friends*. Not fans."

And there it is, the underlying concern, the fear I'm a

mindless fan drone that, given the chance, will rip off N. E. Endsley's sweater and sell it on eBay. Or maybe he and Valerie are worried I'm an undercover journalist gearing up to write a big tell-all. I look down at my decidedly unprofessional rumpled shirt and decide it is probably the former.

"I won't hurt him," I say. "I swear."

Alex makes no move to get out of the truck, so I don't either. I hear a sharp bark from Wally in the distance.

"You remind me of my friend Jenna," I say. I stare straight at the windshield, afraid if I look at Alex when I say her name, the air will leave me. "She was . . . protective. She had to be, because when she found me, I didn't have anyone to do that for me. Jenna was . . ." I pause and take a deep breath before continuing, "Jenna was my sister and my dearest, dearest friend. I swear on her grave, I am not trying to hurt him."

I'm proud of myself for not crying when I meet Alex's circumspect eyes.

"I'm sorry about your friend," he says. After a pause, "You'll have to walk a ways down the beach. I would drive you, but walking is quicker. The back roads here are weird. It's about a ten-minute walk to the fort. He'll probably find you before then. I texted him to make sure he wanted you to come."

I'm glad to not be unannounced. It settles some of the jitters I tried to blame on Mr. Larson's coffee but know are from the prospect of seeing Endsley again.

"Thanks, Alex," I say.

"No, thank *you*, Amelia. It's unusual for him to have any kind of company. Just . . ." He looks more than a little lost as he tries to articulate what he's thinking. "Just remember that you are visiting my unvisitable friend and I would very much like for him to still be intact when you leave. Okay?"

Today is a day of forgetting. I have also forgotten that I am only in this place temporarily, borrowing six days from Texas, and my future, and all the responsibilities that roll out before me in a blanket meant to comfort but that feels more like prolonged smothering.

I look out the window of the truck and try to ignore Wally's distant excited barks. It's a demanding sound, an insistent come-and-play, but I feel like my conversation with Alex isn't finished.

I'm about to get out of the truck and let the moment pass when Alex says, "Amelia?"

"Yeah?"

He's staring at me again, like I'm a puzzle and if he can just flip the correct switch I'll be complete and whole.

"What?" I ask, when he doesn't say more.

"Nothing," Alex says, and he leans back in the seat and starts the engine. "Nothing. I've got to get back to working on the bazaar. We'll see each other later."

There's a smile hiding in his eyes as I slip from the cab. I give a halfhearted wave to Alex and walk down the rocky slope to the sand. The truck roars into motion as soon as I'm out of sight.

Wally's barks float from the trees and my eyes trail upward to where the wind is pushing the branches sharply away from the water. The distant dark clouds promise buckets of water, should they make it across the lake to Lochbrook. How strange that one day I am in Dallas, tucked neatly into my untidy world, and the next I am transported to an entirely different place. There are no tall buildings here, no police sirens, no smell of asphalt melting in the Texas sun, and no lingering suggestions of Jenna's presence, like her house or Downtown Books.

The whales drift, their underbellies skirting the tops of the trees, before swimming off toward the storms with a confidence that comes from being too immovable for weather or time or a girl's problems.

"Amelia?"

I jump, a hand flying dramatically to my heart like a goofy southern belle from a movie.

"Nolan." His first name is startled out of me at his sudden appearance. It's what Alex and Valerie call him, when Valerie isn't calling him "that boy," and I find it's what feels most right.

He doesn't correct me.

He's managed to sneak up on me by emerging from the foliage that lines the beach, appearing like one of the tree knights from the Orman Chronicles, from one of his *own books*. He stands beside me, following my gaze to the trees, a look of confusion on his face.

"Bird-watching?"

It will do me no good to pretend I am the bubbly book-loving person I once was. In a matter of days, I will wake up in my mom's tiny house, as alone as a person can be without actually being by oneself. I will look at the pizza in the fridge and decide it is probably too old even for me and will order a new box. I will put away Jenna's books I ruined, empty my mother's ashtrays, and prepare to start the rest of my life.

I will go to Jenna's college prep course. I will tread faithfully down the path put before me and I will be grateful for the privilege of it and I won't care so much about *what* I study. I will listen to the battle cry of my heartbeat: *I am I am I am.*

But for now I will be my truest, most unadulterated new self. I am Jennaless and I am broken, but I still have my wits and a healthy dose of curiosity about Nolan Endsley, and I will guilelessly use both to see what he remembers about Jenna, or if he knows anything about the 101st edition I left tucked under my pillow in Valerie's guest room. I will use every bit of charm in my arsenal to collect this piece of Jenna to store in the mausoleum of my heart.

What do I have to lose?

So, in lieu of coming up with a socially acceptable answer like *I was watching the trees*, or *I was lost in thought*, I tell him the truth.

"More like whale watching."

Nolan Endsley doesn't miss a beat, squinting hard at me and back up to the sky. "In the trees? Are they flying whales?"

"Sometimes," I say. I am surprised but glad that he is joining in my game. "Most of the time I think of them swimming way out in the middle of the ocean."

The wind rattles out another symphony of rustling leaves, accented with the staccato huffs of Wally's heavy breathing. He's skirted the trees to stand between Nolan and me.

Nolan and me.

"I come down here once a week and never have I imagined whales flying through the trees," he says. His eyes are trained upward. "What kind of whales?"

I frown. "Usually they're orcas, but today they are most definitely blue whales."

"Did you know that orcas aren't technically whales? They're part of the dolphin family." He's still peering up, like he can really see what I see. He's not smiling, not totally taken by my whimsy, but he's not dismissing me, either.

"I did know," I say. "You, on the other hand, have never seen the flying whales before."

"And now I have," Nolan says simply.

"And now you have," I echo.

I peek at him, not wanting to stare outright. He's calmer outside the bookstore, less calculating and hard. He's still a storm, but it's a muted one that promises only heavy rain instead of torrents of wind and destruction. It's as if last night and the photos of Wally, Alex, and trees have floated away with the whales and we have been left new and unsure in their wake.

But this is all I am guaranteed. Who knows if he will even want to see me after today. So I force myself to break the silence. "Alex said you have a fort?"

Nolan snorts. "*Fort.*"

"Is it not a fort?"

Nolan Endsley doesn't deign to reply. He begins to walk up the beach, hands shoved in the pockets of his jeans, his brown sweater making his frame look bulkier than he is. Wally trots obediently behind him and then sprints ahead, his impressive leg span reaching full gallop.

I half expect to walk behind Nolan the entire way, but he suddenly pauses to let me catch up. After, we walk side by side, our feet crunching in a sloppy tune.

I miss walking with Jenna this way, to classes or through rows of books at festivals and libraries and bookstores. She always said she preferred to browse alone, but she never argued when I insisted on linking arms with her. She would act annoyed, but she became very efficient at browsing and opening books one-handed. I did, too.

For a moment, I forget that I am walking beside N. E. Endsley, and he morphs back into the boy on the rug with the crappy cell phone. For a moment, I push away the voice insisting that I am too devastated, too pathetic, to be anyone's friend, and I boldly push my hand into the crook of his elbow.

He stops and my heart catches. I've ruined it all before it had a chance to begin. This is too forward, and he doesn't want to be touched, certainly not by me.

But he only says, "Amelia," and it sounds less like a warning and more like a simple acknowledgment.

"Nolan?"

He looks down at our linked arms. "You're short," he says.

"That's relative," I say. We haven't resumed walking, but he hasn't dropped my arm yet, either, so I pretend I am brave enough to look him in the eye without blushing. My cheeks do not obey—I can feel my face flushing an unflattering red—but my eyes are steadfast. I can see the dark forest behind his eyes again, but there is a spark, a borrowed bit of magic from Orman glittering from the depths. It gives me hope.

"She warned me that you are persistent," he says.

He says it offhandedly, a slip of the tongue, but I recognize it for what it is. He *does* remember talking to Jenna, and what's more, they talked about *me*.

A thrill goes through me, that they spoke long enough for her to tell him I'm stubborn. I feel buoyed, like Jenna is reaching forward from the past to hold my arm in the crook of Nolan's elbow, insisting I stay by his side long enough to find out what was said, to figure out how she sent the book to me undetected. The whales in the lake sing their songs as they joyfully breach.

"I am," I finally say. "Persistent, I mean."

Nolan Endsley nods like he believes me, or maybe like he's made a decision. I hope the decision is to not hate me.

"Okay," he says.

"Okay," I say.

I don't even mind that there are pebbles in my shoes as we begin to walk.

chapter nine

The "fort" ends up being a renovated boathouse that sits down-hill from a rather large blue-brick house toward which Nolan nods. "Home sweet home."

"That is your *house*?"

He drops my arm, like my wonder has offended him some-how, and sighs. He sighs a lot.

"It's my *family's* house."

"But you live here?"

"Yes."

"With Alex?"

"Yes."

"Does your family live here, too?"

"No," he says. It's a hard, sharp word that fills me to the brim with curiosity and chagrin, but I have no time to ques-tion him because Wally is barking and running between us and the boathouse like it's Christmas morning and he's waiting to open gifts of squeaker toys and rawhides.

We work our way up the stairs from the pebbles and sand to the fort, which is about the size of my living room. I worry it's going to smell grimy and damp, like old seawater—*Not the sea; not the sea*, I remind myself—but when Nolan unlocks the door, it creaks open to reveal a cozy room humming with the modern luxuries of electricity and central air.

Despite the bland exterior, the inside of the fort looks like it belongs in one of those high-end children's room decor magazines. A children's tent sits in the far corner with folds of blankets and throw pillows spilling through the opening, an oversize stuffed bear guarding the entrance with a dopey smile. One of his ears looks damp and matted and I suspect Wally is to blame. The other corner is stacked high with bean-bag chairs, the large kind that you can buy at shopping malls for the price of actual furniture. I used to lust after them. I even tried to convince Jenna to buy one for our dorm room, but she said they were "unsanitary and ridiculous." She did, however, buy me a much smaller, less expensive version from Target not two hours later.

Jenna is still not here, but my curiosity about Nolan and my reluctance to think about the world that awaits my return is something of an anchor, and for once I feel truly present.

I can smell the lake and the trees and the dampness of Wally's huge paws. I can feel the pebble in my shoe rubbing against the side of my foot. I can hear the waves lapping against the long stilts of the renovated boathouse. I'm here, in this space, with *the* N. E. Endsley, and I sense that he's at least not *not* trying, and I can work with that.

The aforementioned world-famous author drags two beanbags from their stack and into the center of the floor, which is covered by a large area rug made to look and feel like the world's softest grass. I can't help but watch him, curious how he moves and breathes and exists. He's taken off the bulky sweater and his muscles move beneath the sleeves of his shirt. I look away, embarrassed for noticing. Authors are supposed to be wan and tormented, not flushed and leanly muscular.

Nolan gestures for me to sit, an invitation. Still feeling like I might as well push my luck—*Six days; only six days* echoing in my mind—I drag my beanbag a smidgen closer to his before sitting.

"So. This is your fort?"

"This is the fort," Nolan says. He's looking around the room, too, like maybe he's trying to see it through a newcomer's eyes. I can almost see the inability, his eyes blandly running over the familiar kid's tent, the rug, Wally already snoring in a dog bed that sits beside the writing desk, the bulletin board full of thumbtacked sheets of stationery and greeting cards.

"Fan letters?" I ask.

A grim shake of the head. "Of a sort, I guess. They're thank-you letters. From my publisher."

"Really? So many?" There are at least a dozen.

"The sales of my second book warranted a Christmas bonus for some of the employees directly involved in the business stuff. Many thought it was thank-you-note worthy."

"That's amazing," I say, shifting forward. I move to stand and examine some of these letters, but before I can rise, before the thought is even fully formed, Nolan juts his arm out and pulls me back down.

"No," he says. "Don't."

I hear what he doesn't say: he doesn't want to talk about his books.

"Okay," I say, holding my hands up in mock surrender. I give a pointed look at where his hand still grasps my arm.

"Sorry," he says, quickly dropping his arm back to his side. "Sorry. I'm not used to being around . . ."

"Girls?" I finish for him.

"People."

This I should have known, but there is plenty I *don't* know. And as Alex reminded me in the truck, there's not much time to find out. I try to warm up with an easy question.

"You lived in New York, right?"

"I did," he says.

"And now you live here?"

He looks at me impassively, his eyes having lost all traces of the spark I saw on the beach. Maybe he's like Alex, worried I am some crazed fangirl on a quest to steal snippets of the final Orman book.

Maybe this will never work.

"I live here now, yes," he says, but he's waited too long. My mood starts to sink.

"Okay, different question," I try. "Is the pen collection real? Everyone says you have a pen and journal collection, but you've never talked about it in any of the interviews I've read."

God, that *does* sound too fangirl. But I feel a need to fill the silence, so I recalibrate quickly.

"Sorry, that was creepy," I admit. "I can get that way sometimes. You're not good with people and I'm not good at holding conversations, I guess." I laugh awkwardly and trudge on through this marsh of one-sided dialogue. "Do you miss New York?"

Again, blank staring from him, a slow burning crossness from me. Where is his playfulness from earlier with the whales? Did I already manage to say something wrong or offensive? And even if I did, am I only given the one chance and then he shuts up like a clam holding on to the world's most exquisite pearl?

Orman is wonderful and successful and all those things, but he doesn't get to be a jerk or withhold information about *my* best friend.

One last chance.

"Nolan, are you going talk to me? About Jenna?"

Whales become extinct in the time it takes Nolan to fiddle with the rug and finally look up and say, "I thought we *were* talking."

I stand up, restless.

"Is this how the day is going to go?" My voice is rising, as last night's desperation comes creeping back and Nolan's mask breaks enough to show a small amount of alarm. "Because this is useless," I continue. "This isn't helping you or me or anybody."

"Helping?"

"Yes, helping," I say. "I came because of Jenna . . . because of you, really. I mean . . ." I scoff in disbelief, gesturing between the two of us. "You *met* her and now *I'm* here and you won't even talk to me. What did she say to you? What did you say to her? I know you talked, because who else would have told you I was persistent? Did she mention anything about sending me a copy of your book? Just say *something*."

I'm standing over Nolan Endsley with my hair falling everywhere and my shirt sticking out at odd angles because of the beanbag. I look unkempt and probably irrational in front of the person I once had the most ambition to meet, but I don't care. I'm suddenly and inexplicably furious at everything. At the world, for taking Jenna away and leaving me with such a strange, unlikely, and poor substitute as this, the author of my favorite books. I'm angry at myself, for not having cultivated backup friends, ones waiting in the wings to take Jenna's place should she—most probably—grow tired of my antics or—least probably—die in Ireland.

I'm both irritated and relieved that N. E. Endsley is actually just Nolan Endsley and that he doesn't open portals to Orman, but I'm let down by how he seems incapable of carrying on even the smallest of conversations. He is entitled and grouchy and I'm desperately sad that all my imaginings of him don't hold water, but even more sad that he will not play along with me like he did with the whale watching. And I am *livid* that he won't share what he remembers of Jenna.

I'm mad at Jenna, at Nolan, at the lying books, and even the stupid whales.

"Look, I'm going to be honest," I tell him. I feel myself gearing up to shout him into the ground. Wally snorts himself awake at my tone and shuffles over to sit by Nolan. "I'm pissed. You're rude and unsociable and moody. Just because you wrote some of the greatest books the world has ever known doesn't make you special or particularly tortured."

Here, Nolan raises an eyebrow.

"Well, it doesn't," I say. "Make you special, that is. I mean, everyone is special, but you're not special-er. And don't you *dare* raise your eyebrow at me, because I know that's not a word. And when I asked to see you today, I thought it would be a chance to get to know you better and to hear about Jenna—my best friend, who is *dead*, but what the hell do you care? Your best friend is alive and well and your biggest worry is that your precious third book isn't finished because of your stupid writer's block."

Nolan is calmly petting Wally. They have their heads cocked to the side like they are examining me, an erratic migratory specimen of a girl, driven out of her mind by grief and confusion, who has come to rest in their private sanctuary.

"Anything else?" Nolan asks archly.

"I'm pissed," I say.

"That has been well established," Nolan says.

I stare at him for another beat, disbelieving the words even as they come out of my mouth.

"You know what? I don't have time for this. I'm leaving."

He shrugs. "Somehow I doubt that."

Even though he is echoing my thoughts, I'm incensed enough to stop, hand on the surprisingly flimsy doorknob. If Nolan Endsley's personality is any indication, I would have thought he would have nothing short of a fortress guarding his precious lakeside hideaway.

"And why is that?" I ask.

"Because of *Orman*." He says it like it's a curse, and I want to roll my eyes, so I do. "Because you're just like everyone else."

I wish *I was like everyone else*, I think. *Everyone else our age is smuggling microwaves into dorm rooms while I'm here arguing with an antisocial writer and his batty dog.*

"Think what you want," I say. "I'm still leaving."

I half expect him to come after me, to act like a human and show regret, and that I will hear the door open behind me by the time I've reached the sand. When it doesn't, I redirect to the tree a few yards ahead.

Nolan doesn't come.

When I am almost to the gate where Alex first dropped me off, I realize Nolan really isn't coming after me, that he failed this small test, and I'm mad again.

I shouldn't be. It's not like we're friends. It probably didn't mean anything to him, the pictures last night or the whales this morning. But he did promise to tell me about Jenna. *Maybe.*

I stomp back down the beach toward his fort, because where else *can* I go? The dark storm clouds gathering over the lake personify my mood. How lovely to see the weather finally co-operating with the events of the day.

As I keep checking my footing in the rocks and sand, I imagine myself a powerful sorceress with the ability to bend the weather to her whims. I look down to my feet and let my clothes flutter and change until I am dressed in an emerald green cloak with golden trim. *Too cheerful*, I think. It changes to black, and with narrowed eyes I direct a lightning bolt to strike the little fort and command the storm to kick up a cresting wave that bashes the stairs.

I'm considering a tornado to get Nolan and his little dog, too, as I approach the door, but I stop when I hear the low murmuring of Nolan talking on the phone.

"I know," he says, muffled. "Alex, I know."

Not giving myself time to decide if it's right or wrong, I creep beside the wooden stairs and press my ear as near to the insubstantial door as I dare.

He must be getting an earful from Alex, because it's almost a full minute before Nolan says, "But I blew it. She asked *so* many questions and I didn't know what to do, because I can't tell her about what happened at the festival without telling her about . . . I know." Another long pause and a sigh. "I know. I'll try. . . . Alex, I said I'll try. What more do you want? She's leaving soon, right? She's not my problem."

I don't want to hear any more. Serves me right for eaves-dropping. I shouldn't have gone back to the fort in the first place.

On the long, unavoidable walk back to the bookshop, I conjure snow, the desolate soaking kind that doesn't make for good snowmen or snowballs and only messes up transportation and happy plans. It takes all my powers of fancy and I have no energy left for the whales. They fade away, one by one.

A memory: a visit from my father a year after he left.

I sit beside him in his new used car. (I know it's new because he won't shut up about it, but the odometer reads 63,075 and the seats are worn.)

He's either oblivious to my silence or doesn't care enough to stop yammering on and on about how *great* his life is now and how *great* his girlfriend, Bianca, is and how much I'll like her when I meet her at Christmas.

When my phone rings, I gratefully dig it from my purse and it's Jenna. We planned this yesterday, when my father randomly dropped by my house to tell me he was in town and he wanted to take me to lunch the next day.

It's a quick call. Jenna talks loudly enough that he can hear her without being on speakerphone. She says we need to rework a part of our science project and she needs my help to do it.

"It's our last day before it's due," she says. "You need to get over here, stat, got it?"

"But I have plans," I protest, hoping my disappointment sounds genuine.

"This is about your future, Amelia," Jenna stresses, and I almost laugh at how much she sounds like her mom.

"Fine." I sigh. "I'll be there as soon as I can."

When I end the call, my father seems less concerned with

me not going to lunch with him than he is intrigued with my cell phone cover.

Jenna had it made for me just a month prior, when she declared my old case "decrepit." It's a collage of pictures from our first year of friendship: us on jet skis at the lake, eating beignets in New Orleans, Moot curled atop my head as I sleep, the Williamses and me in a poorly angled selfie in front of the local mall's huge Christmas tree.

"That your friend?"

I nod. "Yep."

He looks over at me, gross, stale flecks of at-home self-tanner getting lost in the folds of his neck. We're at a red light, so he leans forward to closely examine the phone case.

"Jet skis? Trips?"

I know what he's asking, and my heart and head are quickly trying to erect a wall to keep him out, to keep his oily presence away from the Williamses.

"Was a gift." I lob the words over the wall like grenades, half hoping they'll hit him square on the head.

They don't. He huffs and polishes the steering wheel with the bottom of his polo, oblivious to my clipped tone.

"Some friend," he says. "Take what you can from them while you're on their good side, you hear? Nobody who's not kin will treat you like that forever. You're not their problem."

After everything he's done, it's silly that this angers me as much as it does. I want to yell at him and jerk his key ring with the terrible rectangular keychain that reads, "You're my favorite Asshole <3 B," from the ignition to scratch the paint on the side of his stupid car.

Whose problem am I, then? I want to scream. *Where am I supposed to go?*

He drops me off at home because I don't want him to see where Jenna lives, don't want his gaze to defile my safe haven. Jenna and Mrs. Williams are there not five minutes later to pick me up and actually take me to lunch, where—halfway through the salad—I excuse myself to go to the bathroom because I can't stop the flood of tears.

I refuse to open the stall for Jenna when she comes into the bathroom. I tell her that I'm feeling a little sick and I'll be right out, but Jenna ignores me. She lies flat on the floor and scoots under the stall door. Her light blue dress is covered in God knows what now, but I don't think about it as she wraps my head in a bear hug and my nose is filled with the smell of her perfume.

I tell her everything Dad said, about how terrible it was to hear that Bianca is already pregnant, about how I *must* have known things weren't going to work out between him and Mom.

Jenna lets me dampen the front of her dress for a long while before pulling back and saying, "That's not all."

I shake my head, and more tears fall as I tell her what my father said about exploiting Jenna and her parents before they get rid of me. An ugly sob escapes my throat, and it clashes strangely with Jenna's exasperated sigh in the echo chamber of the stall.

"Oh, for God's sakes, Amelia. Is that what this is about? *This* is why I slid around on a dirty bathroom floor?"

She tears some toilet paper from the dispenser and roughly wipes it across my eyes and nose. As she mops my face, she mutters words like *ridiculous* and *absurd* and *melodramatic*.

When she's finished, Jenna looks me in the eyes and enunciates, "Amelia Griffin: I hereby declare that you will be *my*

worst and most persistent problem forever and ever. Now, can
we go back to eating lunch? Please?"

"But how? How could you know?" I ask, and my words drip
out watery and blue over my thick tongue.

Jenna rolls her eyes and juts out her hand, pinky extended.
"I *pinky promise*, okay? Good? Good. Now stop crying. Of all
the things to cry over. I thought maybe he told you that you
were going to have to come live with him and his terrible hair
in Florida. Now *that* would be something to cry about."

I laughed easier for the rest of the day, easy in the knowledge that if I had to be a problem, at least I had somewhere to
belong.

Valerie is teaching an adult student at the piano when I come
into the shop. I hurry to run upstairs and hide in my borrowed
bed, unseen, but she steps out from behind the piano and mo-
tions me over.

"Amelia, back so soon? Where's that boy?"

"Still at the fort," I say, trying to keep my voice neutral.

She stares at me over the rim of her glasses, her mouth
quirked in thought.

"Was he rude to you?"

"No," I lie. I'm not about to rat him out to Valerie. "No, he
had some work to do, so I walked back."

Valerie's eyes narrow. "I am certain *that* is a fabrication. No
matter, I will deal with him after I finish up this lesson. In the
meantime, make yourself at home. I'd keep to the shop for
the rest of the afternoon if I were you, dear. There's a mighty
storm coming this way and I'd hate for you to find yourself
caught in it."

I'm too emotionally wrought to try to deflect the oncoming rain with my imagined powers, too tired wondering where I belong now, so I head up the stairs and wrangle a lunch of tomato soup and grilled cheese from Mr. Larson. I sit on a worn couch and watch the sky darken alarmingly over the grove of trees surrounding the store, feeling—stupidly—a little guilty for causing the thunderstorm.

With my first mouthful of hot soup, a crash of thunder shakes the walls. By the last bite of my sandwich, the electricity has gone out, rendering the store eerily quiet as most of the customers flee to the safety of their homes.

I'm about to go upstairs and nap to the sound of rain pounding on the roof when, I swear on Jenna's grave, I hear a distant shout.

Help!

"Valerie?" I call uncertainly. "Mr. Larson? Did you hear that?"

There's some general clanging from the café and a muffled "Hear what, now?" from Mr. Larson. Valerie startles me with her close-in-proximity sigh as she makes her way up the stairs to the second floor.

"I didn't hear anything," she says.

"I thought I heard somebody calling for help."

"Only the storm, girl. The wind plays tricks up here. Help me collect the emergency flashlights, won't you?"

"Sure," I say, but I'm conflicted.

I know I heard something, a cry for help carried on the back of a clever wind. I stand suspended between Valerie's retreating form and the stairs, between reality and another realm, where imagination and actuality are nearly indistinguishable.

Anybody?

The voice is louder. Like it's right by my ear.

I didn't know when Jenna died. I didn't feel a disturbance in the Force or have any kind of premonition, and I hate myself for it.

Help!

"Are you coming, Amelia?" Valerie calls.

I don't answer; I just run.

It makes *no sense*, but I sprint down the staircase and out the front door, losing my worn-out flats in the squelching mud and not caring. What if I'm right? What if somebody needs my help?

I've never been athletic, but my legs are sure and strong as I race across the flooding two lanes of deserted road, down the hill to the beach that earlier today was filled with kids wading in the shallows. There is a pull inside me, a stirring that feels like intuition mixed with knowing how a story is supposed to end, chapters before the conclusion. The pull is telling me where to go. In the distance, a lighthouse lamp winks in and out of the torrents of rain and the high, high splashing waves.

I'm coming! I don't say it aloud, but somehow the wind will carry it where it needs to go. *Hang on. I'm coming.*

The rain is falling in sheets and I'm soaked through when I reach the edge of the lake. The waves are diligent in their insistence that they could hold their own in the roughest of oceans. I can feel their spray through the rain. They crash against the base of the lighthouse with such ferocity that I'm sure it will go tumbling into the water. Even I, a keen whale watcher, cannot conjure any dorsal fins poking up from the choppy surf.

But I do see Nolan, a few yards away, standing in front of the narrow, rocky peninsula that juts out to the lighthouse.

He's hunched forward like he's screaming or vomiting, the waves almost licking the toes of his shoes. He covers his ears with clenched fists, and in the eerie light of the storm he looks like he's drowning on land.

"Nolan!" I yell. "Nolan, what are you doing?"

He jerks his head toward me, his eyes wild.

"Wally." He points to the lighthouse. I don't hear the words so much as see them. "I . . . I can't. I can't do it."

I squint, and in a flash of lightning between one wave and the next, I make out Wally, huddled against the lighthouse, his tall body pressed flush against the bolted door.

"Can't, can't, can't." It's a litany from Nolan's lips, and I wonder if he even knows he is saying it.

My brain flashes to Jenna, to her explanations I refused to hear about her accidental meeting with Endsley at the festival. A panic attack, she called it, and I had doubted her; I wanted her to come and get me.

But, looking at Nolan, at the whites of his eyes, his distress, I know I couldn't leave him here, even if it meant seeing Jenna again. It's a startling thought, but the same wind that brought me the sound of Nolan's terror through the storm lets me hear Jenna's snort, and for one shining moment, her assured voice.

Don't be stupid, Amelia. He's your problem now.

"Wally!" I call. "Wally, come!"

It becomes very evident that Wally would rather die and haunt the lighthouse than let us miss the opportunity of retrieving his sorry tail ourselves. I groan.

"We can reach him!" I shout to Nolan, grabbing one of his hands and pulling him toward the lighthouse. "Don't let go."

Nolan jerks away when I begin to tug us down the rough path, literally digging his heels into the beach.

"I can't," he repeats. "I can't."

I point to my feet. "I lost my shoes. It's too slick for me to go it alone. I can guide us out there, but I need you to work as an anchor. I'll go first and grab him by the collar, but I need you to not let go."

Nolan's eyes dart from me to the lighthouse, like an animal trapped in a corner with no means of escape.

"I . . . I can't." His voice sounds far away. "I'm sorry. I'm sorry. God, I'm so sorry. I'm so *sorry*."

His voice fractures into a million sharp pieces, and he looks out at the waves like they will drag him under and kill him . . . like they already have once before and now he's going to be made to drown again. His eyes are wet with tears and rain, but there's something else there, too. Anger. The defeated kind. The kind that only comes after long nights of despair and bewilderment and wondering what you could have done differently, if you could have saved them.

It hits me all at once: Nolan Endsley has lost someone, too. And I'd wager it had something to do with water.

I squeeze his hand once, trying to catch his eye, but he's unmoving, staring at the lake, and we're running out of time. I'm worried Wally will try to move on his own and get swept out beyond reach.

I have to do it alone.

In all the stories I've read of kick-ass women who save the day, none of them have ever been short, muscularly puny, *and* devoid of magical abilities. Come to think of it, none of them risked life and limb to save a mongrel from a watery grave, either. They were all too smart for that.

But I'm not doing it for Wally. I'm not doing it for N. E. Endsley, either.

I'm doing it for the boy who's hunched over at the waist again, the boy who—when I thought my grief would tear me in two—showed me photo after photo until the pain shrank back down to something manageable.

I'm doing it for Jenna. Because she saved Nolan first, and I must finish what she started.

The wind whistles as another crash of thunder courses through my body. I don't say anything to Nolan as I begin to inch my way toward the lighthouse, but I can't stop the low, guttural noise I make when a wave sweeps up to hit me, either. I have nothing to hold on to, nothing with which to brace myself, so I think heavy thoughts and wait for the lashing to pass.

Wally is barking, evidently happy that someone is coming to his rescue. I grip the rocky pathway with my toes when another wave comes, frozen just a few feet up the walkway.

Something hits my shoulder, and fear of being knocked downward races through me, but then it's grabbing at my hand.

Nolan's eyes are narrowed to slits, like maybe if he can't fully see the storm, it can't see him.

"Don't talk about what we're about to do," he says through gritted teeth. "Just don't."

The path is barely wide enough for one person, so, in the interest of being as rooted as we can, we walk sideways. Every time a wave splashes against us, Nolan shudders, but he does not let go of my hand. It is already much easier, having his solid body as a counterweight to my swaying.

It's not a terribly long peninsula, but it feels like an eternity passes as we creep our way along the path. Sharp rocks cut through my callused soles, but I continue to lead us in our slow crab walk.

"Almost there," I shout to Nolan. I dare a glance back at him and the drowning look has only worsened. His eyes are almost completely shut.

We finally reach the cowering Wally, who, for the first time since I've met him, appears unenthusiastic about his circumstances. He barks, his tail low but wagging.

"Come on, you stupid boy." I spit out lake water as it splashes into my mouth and grab Wally's collar. "It's going to be okay. We've made it one way, we can make it back." I say this last bit loudly to both dog and master, but Nolan is looking back toward the shore.

"We can make it," I say again, squeezing his hand. "But you're going to have to lead us back."

His breath comes too fast, his nostrils flaring in steady pulses and his chest rising up and down. He did not think this through.

"There's this picture," I say, and I pray to God this works, that he can hear me, "of Jenna and me at the aquarium when we were sixteen. We're smiling in front of a tank. They had just fed the sharks and one is directly behind her head with a dead fish hanging out of its mouth. Over her shoulder, there is a little girl looking at the camera and pointing at the shark and bawling, but it looks like she's pointing at Jenna. It's one of my favorites."

His breathing hasn't slowed, but he seems to be focusing on me rather than the waves.

"You had to pick a photo with *more* water in it?" he asks.

If he were anyone else, if we were talking anywhere else, I would laugh.

"You can hate me for it after we get back to the shop," I say. He nods, squaring his shoulders and gripping my hand tighter in resolution. I resituate my hold on Wally's collar, and Nolan begins to slowly, *slowly*, lead us back to the beach.

When a rogue wave crashes against us, halfway down the walk, and Nolan loses and immediately reclaims his footing, I panic. If he freezes up, there's no way I can work around him to pull us to shore. We could be stuck out here. Quickly, I yell another photo description over the wind and rain, the first that comes to mind.

"The city cut down a tree in our park to make room for a playground. One of the trees had a family of squirrels in it that got crushed in the process, and a little boy found their bodies. He rallied five of his friends and they picketed the building of the new playground. Nobody cared or paid them any attention, except for this one guy who made a little squirrel headstone, so the kids could feel like they were heard. I walked by it one day and somebody had sprinkled the area with peanuts. There were about ten squirrels congregating around the headstone. The photo looks like I stumbled across a squirrel wake."

Nolan yells something over the wind, without taking his eyes off the shore.

"What? I can't hear you," I say.

He turns his head toward me. "Another."

When I hesitate, in search of another description worth mentioning, he adds, "Please."

It feels as if I'm bartering tiny pieces of myself in order to reach safety. And because the situation isn't a calm one, it feels like the descriptions have to be particularly poignant to do the job right. I don't have time to choose carefully.

"My dad gave me my camera for my birthday. I was surprised because sometimes he forgets my birthday entirely, but it's a really nice camera and I wanted to use it right away. I took a picture of my mom. She didn't notice me, so in the photo she's looking down into the sink with a blank stare. But there's something about the curve of her back that matches the line of a hanging plant in the kitchen. It looks like she grew there. Like she will always live in the kitchen."

I'm not sure how much he heard over the storm, and I don't get a chance to ask. We're only feet away from solid ground when I take my turn at losing my footing, but unlike Nolan I don't catch myself. My legs stumble into the water, my ankle knocking against the side of the ledge with a painful thump. I let go of Wally's collar and Nolan's hand before I can drag them down with me, confident I can make it the last few yards to shore on my own.

Though my feet can reach the lake floor, waves bash over me, blurring my vision and rendering me immobile. I reach out to grasp the rocks of the peninsula as a guide, but my fingers curl over air. I choke as sprays of water trickle into my lungs.

When my eyes clear between waves, I look up, expecting to see Nolan frozen on the walkway, but he's gone. He's fallen, I know it. I kick against the floor of the lake, my foot connecting with something large and moving.

Nolan grabs my forearms, pulling me through the angry waves to his chest, a look of pure resolution plastered over the terror on his face.

"Nolan! I'm fine," I yell, unsure if I'm lying. Everything beneath my waist aches.

Nolan doesn't answer, and he doesn't let go, which turns out to be necessary. My ankle begs for me to stop, with each flog of the waves. When we're a few feet from shore, a displaced rock smashes into my injured foot and I can feel a scream vibrating up my throat, though I don't hear it. Nolan stoops, tries to grab me behind the knees and hoist me, but another wave knocks us both into the shallow water.

Maybe Jenna and the clever wind want me to die out here, to give my last breath to Nolan and Wally and let my body float out past the chorus of whales to wherever Jenna is. Maybe this is why I'm so conflicted about my future . . . I'm not supposed to have one. I close my eyes and imagine never opening them, to see how it feels.

But I remember Nolan and jerk my eyes open, scrambling to find my footing in the water. He's still half holding me, dazed.

"Are you okay?" I ask, pulling on his shirt when he doesn't move. "Nolan, answer me!"

He remains still, one hand cradling my head and the other awkwardly cupping my elbow. Then he is looking down at me, and in a rush he says, "If they had lived, if I saved them, there would be—" He's cut off by a wave, and once we rid our mouths of water, he finishes. "There would be no Orman."

It's dark, we're both in over our heads—literally and metaphorically—and we need to dredge ourselves from the lake, but I find his eyes in the storm. I don't know who *they* are or if Nolan could have truly saved them, but I know Orman has rescued countless people, in the way only powerful stories can, and that can never be a bad thing.

"Just because it came from something terrible doesn't make Orman less beautiful," I say. "You weren't wrong to write it, Nolan, no matter where it came from."

This is not the time or place for a meeting of souls. More waves knock against us, their frequency and magnitude breaking our eye contact, but I must have said something right because Nolan finds it within himself to drag us to the shore, our bodies impossibly heavy as we emerge from the water.

We crawl when we reach solid ground, elbows bumping, as Wally barks and runs in mad circles around us. Nolan looks over his shoulder at the waves and shudders. His face pales and I wonder if he'll faint. Instead, he fumbles in the back pocket of his jeans before extricating his cell phone and flipping it open.

"It must be ruined," I say, but the screen shines through the darkness like a tiny beacon, illuminating his face as he dials Alex's number. God bless brick phones.

Nolan tells Alex to bring his truck and then hangs up and leans forward to where I lie flat on my stomach.

"You're okay?" he asks. His hands are shaking. I reach up and hold the one on his knee. It's cold from the water, but I don't think that's why he's shivering.

"I'm okay," I say. "Are *you* okay?"

He looks out over the water before he answers, but he doesn't move his hand from beneath mine.

"You didn't have to do that," he says.

"I know," I say.

"But you did."

"I know."

He hesitates. "How . . ."

When he looks down at me, I can tell he's not a supernova like Jenna, an old star burning its way out of this galaxy and into the next. He's brand new, a soul still learning how to navigate this odd world of whales and clever winds. Like me.

So I tell him the truth, even though it sounds crazy.

"I heard you."

When Alex's headlights flash through the sheets of rain, they highlight Nolan's silhouette and nearly blind me, but neither of us is willing to move our eyes away, still taking each other's measure.

Alex's car door slams. "What are you guys doing? Get out of the rain! Let's go!"

Nolan and I don't move.

"That's impossible," Nolan tells me. "There's no way."

I chuckle dryly, looking away as Alex nears us. "I know. If you had put a scene like this into Orman, everyone would chalk it up to magic."

His reply is too quick. "Magic isn't real."

I look hard at the boy who stood by the lake and saw flying whales, the same one who took an unspeakable horror that has left him terrified of water and made Orman. He fashioned his despair into something the world could hold and admire and feel comforted by, and he doesn't believe in magic.

It's absurd.

"If you think of another explanation, let me know," I say, and then Alex is hoisting me up on one side and taking me to the car.

"Come *on*, guys. What are you doing out here?"

Nolan fills Alex in on the way back to Val's, the three of us, and Wally, bouncing around uncomfortably in the small cab. Nolan and I don't say another word to each other about magic or anything else.

We don't need to speak to feel something has changed. We can't go back to being the same two people we were in the boathouse a few hours ago, before I answered his unspoken cry for help, before he conquered whatever fear forbade him from entering the water in order to help me. Before he confessed that he, too, has a *before* and an *after* and that it has something to do with Orman and someone he couldn't save.

It feels rather like we just took out a giant troll in the bathroom, or fought our way to Mordor, shoulder to shoulder. It's true: there are some things you can't go through together without ending up friends.

chapter ten

Nolan wants Alex to drive his truck around the trees and through the sodden miniature meadow that encircles the bookstore. He wants us to bypass the parking lot entirely and pull straight up to the door.

"She can't walk that far, Alex," he says across me. "Her ankle is probably twisted or broken or—"

"I am *not* messing up the ground when the festival is only three days away," Alex says as he puts the truck into park. His voice is quieter than Nolan's, nearly drowned out by the rain that coats the windows.

Nolan has no such problem. He's practically yelling. His eyes are not as wild as they were beside the lake, but they are still a tinge feral.

"Ask me how much I care about your festival right now. She's hurt. It's my fault. We're pulling up to the door."

Alex opens his mouth to respond, but my movement stops him.

I turn my body toward Nolan and—as slowly as we crept to the lighthouse—raise my hand to his cheek. I blush a little, knowing Alex is watching our every move, not knowing why this feels so inexplicably natural.

Even though it is still damp from the rain, Nolan's cheek is warm in my hand. I watch his face closely as my fingertips, my palm, my wrist, rest against his head. His eyes soften, the untamed energy sapping from his body as he slackens his face into my hand.

"I'm okay to walk," I tell him, my voice steady. "Really."

There is a time to talk about what happened at the lighthouse, but it is not now.

"I don't want . . . I don't want you to be hurt anymore," Nolan says, and—not to be outdone—he brings both of his hands up to cradle my face. "You've been hurt enough."

Alex makes a funny coughing sound in the back of his throat. I can feel him trying to make the fact that he is looking out the window as obvious as possible, but it also helps when he loudly says, "I'm looking out the window."

Nolan's half-smile presses his cheek more firmly against my hand, and I smile in return.

"I'll get the golf cart for you," Nolan tells me. "I don't want you walking on that ankle."

"Try to keep it on the path. Alex will kill us both if you mess up his grass."

"Thank you," Alex mumbles. "*Still* looking out the window here."

"I'm going, I'm going," Nolan says, but he waits another six heartbeats before he drops his hands from my face.

I try to watch him race across the muddy grass, but the rain is too heavy to see much past the hood of the truck. Wally goes berserk when Nolan leaves, and Alex quickly opens his door to let him out.

"I suppose it's safe to stop looking out the window?"

"Yes," I say. And we turn toward each other, his eyes as startled as I feel.

Alex folds his arms. "Are you going to tell me what really happened, or am I going to have to pry it out of Nolan?"

I drop my gaze to my feet, pretending to look at my ankle. "What are you talking about? Nolan told you what happened. Wally ran out to the lighthouse and we had to bring him back."

I glance over. He's tightened his arms.

"Nolan doesn't cavort around water willy-nilly. Spill."

I make myself look directly at Alex when I tell him about Nolan and me holding hands as we worked our way to the lighthouse. His face is carefully composed as I speak, but he unfolds his arms when I say we almost got stuck when Nolan had to lead us back to shore.

"How?" Alex asks. "How did you get him to cross back?"

I shrug and look back out the window, unable to meet his gaze. "I . . . I distracted him."

"*How?*"

A number of lies spring to mind, but none sound plausible enough to have worked. Alex would know how frantic Nolan was. He must also know *why*, but I don't ask.

Maybe it's that I'm soaked through and the truck's heater isn't doing much to warm me up, or maybe it's because Alex's silence has lapsed into the comforting kind instead of the judgmental kind, but I tell him the truth.

Eye contact is too much, so I tell it to the window. I tell the raindrops about the pictures of Jenna, my mom, and the squirrels. I tell about leaving little bread crumbs of myself up and down the walkway to the lighthouse to lead Nolan, Wally, and me to safety.

"That's how," I finish.

My voice sounds small, and I guess Alex can hear it, because when I turn toward him, he finds a way to inelegantly wrap his arms around me in the small space of the cab.

"Oh," I say, my head turned awkwardly against his shoulder. "Oh, we're hugging now?"

"Yes." Alex's voice is definitive, no room for argument. "We're hugging now."

"Um, why?"

I'm certain this will make him pull back, but he doesn't.

"You know why," he says.

"Because I saved your grass from being turned into soup by a golf cart?"

He pulls back and looks toward the roof of the car like maybe the god of the whales can somehow help deal with me.

"Because you saved *him*."

My heart hammers faster in my chest, and it makes me agitated.

"No, I didn't," I answer too quickly. "I saved *Wally*."

"Don't be stupid when you're not," Alex says. "Nolan could never like somebody stupid."

This conversation is not helping my heart rate, but blessedly I can hear Nolan returning in the golf cart.

"What makes you think he likes me?"

Alex levels a look at me that reminds me so strongly of Jenna it hurts. But instead of wanting to sob, I find myself laughing and shoving him in the arm.

"Don't give me that look!" I say.

"Then don't be stupid," he says, shoving me back. He's laughing, too.

Nolan opens the door on my side while Alex and I are

midshove. He stands and watches us in bemusement, which should sober the moment, but instead we laugh harder, until Nolan groans.

"It's cool. Just have fun while I stand here in the rain."

His hands are everywhere when he helps me slide from the tall cab of the truck, to the ground, to the cart. He brushes my waist, my arm, my back, and even though he's just trying to keep from hurting me, I blush.

After Valerie inspects my ankle—badly bruised but not twisted or broken—and fills the three of us with enough hot cocoa to drown a greedy kid in a chocolate factory, I'm sent to nap and to "not catch my death." Valerie won't listen to my arguments that I am fine and don't want to go to sleep at three in the afternoon. She directs Alex to help me to the third floor, and when Nolan makes to follow us, she calls him back with a sharp "Not you, boy. Let the girl get some rest."

Nolan and I lock eyes as the electricity-restored elevator doors snap our gaze in two, but our new, tenuous bond is still intact, an unbroken twine that extends from his body to mine.

Despite my protests, I fall asleep as soon as my head hits the pillow, the station empty of thought trains and the whales barely on the periphery. I wake hours later to Valerie at my bedside, a bowl of pasta in her hands.

"Hungry?"

I'm famished. My head is pounding from sleeping too long and from the exhaustion of the stormy afternoon. The sliver of sky I can see around the curtains is gray streaked through with pink. The storm has passed and the sun is setting.

"Starving." I scrunch up into a sitting position against the pillows and shovel the noodles into my mouth, only noticing three bites in that it is filled with mushrooms. I hate mushrooms. But I eat them anyway.

Valerie stands by the bed, her look expectant.

"I've closed the shop early," she says. "Because of the storm."

"That's too bad," I say, not sure why she's telling me.

She tilts her head. "I don't think so. How's your ankle?"

I turn it in a slow circle beneath the quilt. "It's fine."

"Hmm," she murmurs. If I weren't so busy shoving food in my mouth, I'd wonder why she's acting strangely.

The bowl is almost empty, and I wonder briefly if my future ought to include competitive eating. I'm scraping the sauce off the side of the bowl with my fork when Valerie says, "You should walk on it a bit so it doesn't stiffen up overnight."

"You're probably right," I say, swinging my legs from the bed, my ankle protesting with the dullest of cries. "I need to use the restroom anyway."

"You'll be wanting these."

The empty bowl in my hand is suddenly replaced with an ankle brace atop a folded blue dress.

"What's this for?" I ask suspiciously.

"Oh, I had the brace. It was one of Alex's from an old sports injury."

She's definitely up to something. "Valerie, not the *brace*. What do I need a dress for if the store is closed? Or if it's open, for that matter?"

"You ought to shower, get all that lake off your skin and hair. It will make you feel better. And give my old dress a spin. It hasn't seen anything other than the back corner of my closet for years."

I wonder if this is what having a mother is like when you're old enough to care about clothes.

I don't want my morose thoughts dragging me back to losing Jenna, to my mother, so I say, "Fine. But it's silly, because I'll just be taking it right back off to go to sleep."

"Everything is silly, dear. Life is too brief to be anything else."

The hot water feels supernaturally good. I massage shampoo into my scalp until my hair is so sleek my fingers can make squeaky noises against it. There are about ten different jewel-tone bottles of body wash on a copper-colored rack in the corner and I settle on one that smells like vanilla and sugar. It smells a bit like Jenna's perfume, but I don't mind.

Jenna was always trying to get me to dress up more. She took me on back-to-school shopping trips at the mall under the guise of going to the big chain bookstore, only to steer me to clothing boutiques.

"Try *this one thing*," she would say, before shoving me into a dressing room. "Just the one, I promise."

She never offered to pinky promise. It would have been a lie. Once she had me trapped in the fitting room, hanger after hanger of gauzy blouses, linen pants, and rompers with lace trim would form a chic barricade on the door, keeping me locked inside. Most of the time, this ended in me throwing a fit until she relented.

"Why do you hate it so much?" she asked once. "The clothes thing?"

She was appeasing me, post-tantrum, by letting me roam

the electronics store with the fun gadgets everyone wanted to try but never bought. I slowly put the Bluetooth-compatible race car back on the display shelf to buy myself some time to answer.

It was a multifaceted creature, my hatred of clothes. It had been around since elementary school, when the other girls would have new pink jackets at the beginning of every school year while I was stuck with whatever Mom found in the clearance section. We'd always been lower income. I hated that you could tell by looking at my clothes.

How could I explain to my beautiful, fearless fashionista Jenna that her elegance and grace intimidated the hell out of me? You could put us in the exact same outfit, down to the socks, and she would look like she belonged while I would look like a kid trying on her wealthy cousin's clothes. The Williamses *always* looked like a family in a catalog, even on the rare occasion you glimpsed them in their pajamas, all silken pants and button-up tops. They were willing to include me in their catalog spread, they wanted to, but it felt like another line that shouldn't be crossed.

And when I looked at Jenna's chosen outfit of the day—a ruffled red miniskirt and off-the-shoulder blue-and-white-striped top paired with strappy sandals—I wanted to cry.

"It's not who I get to be," I finally told her. "Maybe later it will, but right now it just feels . . . fake."

Jenna didn't miss a beat. "So? Fake it until you make it, right?"

"No," I say. "No, it . . . it feels dishonest. Like I'm tricking people into thinking I'm something I'm not."

But when I emerge from the shower and slip Valerie's blue dress over my head, my hair wet and slicked back behind my ears, I feel more like myself than I have in weeks. I don't feel fake when I tie the gossamer ribbon around my waist into a bow, even though the torso sags slightly and the dress hits oddly between ankle brace and knee.

I feel clean and whole, despite the stress of the day still pinging inside of me like a smoke detector whose batteries are running low. But with so much new information to process, the ache of Jenna is lessening, and with each retreat of misery's hold on my heart, my head, I can breathe a little easier.

I can breathe easier, until I remember Nolan's hands on my face.

A deep breath shakes away his imprint on my skin as I reenter the guest room, ignoring my ankle's whining, to do a tiny twirl of gratitude for Valerie . . .

Who isn't there.

I thought she would be waiting for me, to inspect me in my dress and fawn over my health. *Some fairy godmother.* Though she did straighten the bedsheets and take away the pasta bowl. Maybe she went down to the store.

But she's not in the café, at least not the part I can see from the elevator. I walk behind the counter and look into the attached kitchen. Nothing.

I lean over the bannister and look to the floor below. The store is deserted, the bell above the door unmoving and the fireplace cold and barren. No sign of her.

My ankle throbs dully after my short journey, but, as if summoned, I move to the end of the hallway. The lights are on in the last room and I understand instantly why I've been put in this dress and the store closed early.

The bond, as thick as rope now and loosened with sleep, pulls tighter as I near Nolan and the Orman room.

When I step into the dim lantern light, I pretend I'm stepping into the real Orman. I am Emmeline. My hands morph into hers, smaller and chubbier, the right thumb bearing a ring made entirely of sap from the sacred ash tree of Orman. But instead of reaching for an enchanted snow globe or a bejeweled sword, as Emmeline would, I reach to wake the sleeping prince from his slumber.

I look down at N. E. Endsley and Nolan Endsley, both sleeping within the same body. He is half curled on the center of the embroidered compass, using his sweatshirt as a pillow, his hat dislodged to reveal hair still wet from showering. A tiny bit of drool is pooling at the corner of his mouth. I wonder who will present himself upon such an abrupt awakening—N. E. or Nolan—as I lean forward and gently shove his shoulder.

At first, he is no one, like everyone is no one when they first wake. There is a moment between sleep and waking where anything can happen and it feels like a person might be wiped clean, their entire life rewritten almost by accident. The boy blinks once, twice, and immediately he is N. E. Endsley, as his eyes settle on my person but not my face. His arms tense into action as he jerks himself up to sitting, legs outstretched. But when he sees it's me, Nolan peeps out from behind the vulnerable author wrapped in the aggressive shell, and the writer who created worlds between his hands blurs into the boy who is scared of water.

"Hi," I say softly.

"Hello, Amelia."

My name on his lips yanks the thread between us, and rather than resist, I lower myself to the ground beside him.

"How is . . ." He trails off, waving his hand at my ankle.

"It's not too bad," I say. "I'll have to cancel the rock climbing plans I have for this weekend, but that's fine. Those can be rescheduled."

"Did you *have* rock climbing plans?"

"No." I laugh. He doesn't smile, but his lips twitch like he considered it.

"Well . . ." He rakes a hand through his hair and, realizing it's still wet, runs his hand over the rug to dry it.

"Is Wally here?" I ask, throwing him a line. "He seemed no worse for wear earlier."

"He's at home with Alex, the cretin. He's fine."

"Good," I say. "That he's okay, I mean."

"Yeah."

We both look anywhere but at each other, a clock downstairs ticking away our silence.

If I was framing us in a camera lens, I would cut one of us out completely to spare the viewer secondhand embarrassment.

"Was there something else?" I finally ask. "Why are you sleeping *here*?"

We both watch his palm trail over the rug.

"In Orman," he says without looking up, "the Old Laws dictate that when someone saves you, you owe them your life until the debt is repaid."

I blink. "I know. I've read them."

He waits half a beat. "So?"

"So?"

His hand stops moving, and we look at each other, searching.

"How would you have me pay my debt?"

My first thought is of Jenna—of asking what was said in

their short encounter, the 101st edition, how she comforted him, all of it.

But asking him would be a betrayal, a queen decapitating her knight as he bows to do her bidding. To ask Nolan Endsley to articulate a traitorously human moment so soon after the lake would be taking advantage. And I want him to *want* to tell me.

Asking about Jenna could sever the new tie between us, which makes my heart ache to even consider.

I laugh off his offer, give him an out. "I didn't save your life; I saved Wally's."

Nolan does not want an out.

"He isn't equipped to pay back a life debt, so, as his keeper, I'll act on his behalf."

I look away first, dropping Nolan's intense stare to reach down and pluck at the rug fringe dangerously close to where his hand rests. His pinky stretches the slightest bit toward my fingers, like he's fighting the draw of a magnet and losing.

"I thought you didn't believe in magic," I say.

"I don't."

"Then what's with the adherence to the Old Laws?"

"The Old Laws are more of an honor code than a magic system. All worlds—fictional or otherwise—must have morals."

"How noble," I mutter.

If he doesn't want to drop the subject, he must have something in mind . . . something he's willing to offer.

"What do you suggest?" I ask outright.

I'm caught in his stare again when he says, "Val said you haven't picked up a single book since you got here. Why?"

I am startled—that she noticed, that she mentioned it to Nolan, that he cares—but I try to hide it. "I've barely been here a full day. Besides, you can't answer a question with a question."

"I just did." His lips quirk but quickly flatten into a somber line. He manipulates the thread between us, pulling to test its strength. "I can answer for you, if you'd like."

I snort. "Good luck with that. May the odds be ever in your favor."

"It's Jenna," he says. "Her death. You feel guilty, like you shouldn't enjoy anything you both shared, because it's dishonoring her memory."

"How do *you* know what we shared?"

"You were at the festival, weren't you?" Nolan is expressionless as he lays me bare for our mutual examination.

All I wanted, less than a month ago, was to be in the same crowded room as N. E. Endsley. In an alternate universe, that's what I'd get. He'd show up at the festival but never meet Jenna. He would sign my book (maybe), nod politely (doubtful) as I tried to express my every thought about Orman in the span of one minute (definitely), and it would be over.

I'm having a hard time reconciling myself to this universe without Jenna, and an even harder time acknowledging that this is probably the only universe where Nolan's hand reaches forward and holds mine. In all the universes where I meet Nolan Endsley, Jenna is not there, and I don't know how to feel about it.

"I've had something similar happen," Nolan says carefully, oblivious to my musings. "But it was with music, not books."

I swallow. "Did it ever go away?"

"Eventually," Nolan says. "Or rather, I got through it. One day I decided I was going to listen to music even if it killed me, and it didn't. I managed."

The air kicks on overhead, the sound of it whooshing through the vents filling the room with an almost round noise, another layer of the cocoon we're weaving between us.

"It *is* different, though," Nolan says. "The music isn't the same as it was before."

"How is it different?"

Nolan turns my hand over, tracing the lines of my palm like he's deciphering my future.

"The melancholy is harder to ignore." He's nearly whispering. "And the happy parts, the full orchestral crescendos I used to love, sometimes make me feel more sad than happy. I think it has to do with the spectrum of emotion. Everyone tells you that you will feel more as you get older and experience life or whatever, but I think it's actually *less*, you know? Like, we start out here"—he drops my hand and spaces his own a shoulder width apart—"but the more that happens to us, the more we realize all of our emotions are connected. They feed off each other." He brings his palms closer together. "Even the good things, the big things that make you feel alive, only make you feel that way *because* you've experienced the bad things. Because you know that you won't always be on this planet. It's not a completely sad thought, because there's nothing else you would rather be doing, but it's not happy, because you wish you could go on feeling this way forever."

His palms touch as he looks at me expectantly.

I bite back a smile. "All that to say there are more sad parts in the music now? You really are a writer if it took you that long to explain something so simple."

Nolan laughs for the first time since I've met him, a surprised bark that jumps from shelf to shelf in this circular room.

The heaviness of the moment broken, I shift my legs to adjust my ankle. We sit in comfortable silence. Nolan is the one to break it.

"Amelia?"

"Yeah?"

"Can I read to you?"

A month ago, this would have been a dream come true. A month ago, I would have sold a kidney to fund such a venture, to sit alongside N. E. Endsley and have him read to me in a magical bookstore that feels like every reader's dream come true.

But maybe he's right about emotions getting squished together, because I'm thinking that Jenna is still dead. And I have nothing left of her except her oddly specific ten-year plan that does not include Nolan Endsley sitting beside me, smelling of soap and pine trees and making me wonder if maybe there isn't more to life than anyone could possibly plan for. Even Jenna.

"I can read on my own, thanks," I say, the words scratchy in my throat. I do my best to play it off as a joke. "I've been doing it since I was five."

He leans forward, inching his legs closer until we are almost touching.

"Please?" His breath stirs a few wispy hairs into my eye and I blink them away.

"Why?"

"To repay my debt."

Does he mean for our lips to be this close?

"You don't owe me anything," I whisper. "Really."

"Call it a gift, then."

Nolan doesn't wait for my answer. He stands up and shakes out his legs as he turns toward the shelves. With the darkness enfolding us like a warm blanket, and the waking world as far away as the line where the waters of Lake Michigan meet the sky, I feel infinite and safe and reckless all at once, and so I don't flinch when Nolan asks, "Any requests?"

Alex's warning of *friends not fans* hisses through my head, and I swallow down my answer, but what I want must be written across my face, because Nolan turns to pull one of his books from its snug place on the shelf.

"This one?" he asks, watching me carefully. And before I have a chance to respond, he adds, "It's okay if this is what you want."

"It is," I say.

He licks his fingers—a habit I abhor but find fitting for him—and flips through as he folds back onto the floor.

He inhales to begin reading, but instead says, "At the risk of sounding cheesy, I think it's appropriate to start in the middle, if that's fine with you. Since that's what *we're* doing."

"I'm okay with that," I say. My voice is small and scared in my ears. I wonder if Nolan can hear the nerves I won't admit to. What if the world doesn't spread and rise around me? What if reading is dead to me forever?

The whales come, and I let them. If this doesn't work, they can take me out to sea, where nothing—not even the lack of books—can touch me.

I can hear Nolan's purposeful turning, the sound of a reader—a writer—delving into a mountain range of words in search of one stray sheep. He has something specific in mind, and my curiosity is burning away the anxiety.

"This is my favorite part," he whispers, so quietly that I wonder if he meant to say it aloud. He begins to read.

They were, in fact, lost. Emmeline found this terrifying. Ainsley had never been more excited about anything in her life.

"Come on," Ainsley groaned. "It's an adventure."

"It's suicide is what it is," Emmeline said, extracting her foot from a particularly goopy swamp of mud.

"And so what if it is? We don't even know if we can be hurt here. We're probably sleeping, have you thought of that?"

Emmeline reached across and pinched her sister's arm, hard.

"Ouch! What is wrong with you?!" Ainsley, always melodramatic, rubbed her arm ferociously, as if she could rub the pain right out.

"Not a dream," Emmeline said, and in a movement that would confound her sister until her dying day, Emmeline—the girl who refused to watch princess movies because princesses were always saved from dragons and dragons often meant blood—grabbed a sharp rock and slit her palm in a slow, deliberate motion, three perfect drops of blood falling wetly to the ground. "And not safe. We could die, Ainsley."

Nolan's voice has dropped to a rough whisper. My eyes have fluttered closed, the story playing out against my eyelids, my heart quickening, every bone in my body wanting to drop to the forest floor of Orman and have a look at the blood that started it all.

Slowly, I open my eyes to steal a glance. He reads on, and if I let my eyes blur out of focus and watch the corner of his lips—the only part of him I can see around the cover of the book—I can believe he is weaving an incantation around us.

Nolan notices my distraction and says, "Do you want me to stop?"

"No, I don't."

The words come swirling back to me in a flood more powerful than any vortex. The characters I've missed running forth, arms outstretched, as I drift on a lazy river of words and stories and feelings, propelled along by Nolan's gentle and deep voice. I'm stuck between life and dream. I could be anyone.

The girls were much too preoccupied to see the knights, though if they had taken notice, they would have been hard-pressed to find words to describe them.

Nolan's voice flickers in and out of my consciousness as I lie sprawled on the floor, the world breaking and re-forming itself around me.

Tree knights, they were called, mostly human, but with an ounce of tree magic in their veins. They had the ability to become nearly indistinguishable from foliage to human eyes. They were known to be tall, stoic women—they were, almost without exception, all women—with very little in the way of humor or wit. They were the guardians of the forest, the keepers of the outside realms, and they were, in a word, terrible.

Ainsley was the first to spot one, gasping and whirling her sister around excitedly to point with a shaking finger.

"Look, Em! Do you see? Do you?"

The strange moment when she cut her palm forgotten,

Emmeline found herself shaking for a reason entirely differ-ent from excitement.

"Wh-what are th-they?"

When she spoke, it was as if the forest came alive. Doz-ens of women pulled themselves from the trees to stand tall and proud, encircling Ainsley and Emmeline. The tallest of the knights leaned forward, bowing before Emmeline.

"Your Highness." Her voice was the sound of a thousand tempests ransacking a thousand forests, hard and enchanting. "We have been waiting for you."

Ainsley loosened her arms from around Emmeline and stepped forward, her chest puffed out toward the sky. "My sister and I are honored to make your acquaintance."

There was a pause before the knight said, "It is your sis-ter, lady, of whom we speak. Your presence was not foretold here."

And, like that, the stories have come back to me. They are sitting in my throat, working their way into my bones, my blood, the tips of my hair. They are altered, like me. Parts I skimmed before now seem desperately important, and parts I thought were vital, less so.

I am different, but like the stories, I will hold up to more readings, even if those readings are drastically changed in my *after*.

I reach over to touch Nolan's arm.

"Thank you," I whisper.

He pauses. I watch as indecision flickers across his features before he drops a hand to my hair, gently smoothing it away from my face in a touch so tender I feel like everything inside me might break. His hand shakes as he pushes hair behind my ear, and I reach up to hold it against my face and still his tremors.

Being here with Nolan is like listening to every good and bad part of music at once, ingesting all the happiest of endings with the most grueling of in-betweens.

He returns to his reading, and I lose myself in his voice.

chapter eleven

When I wake, before I remember who I am and what pinky promises I have made, I am a photographer. I can feel the weight of the camera between my hands, see the frame my lens makes, without looking through the viewer. It doesn't matter what I am photographing. It just matters that I *am*.

But I come back to myself. My heart slowly pumping into wakefulness, ticking down the minutes until I'm back on the plane headed to Texas, to the Williamses' open arms and their plans.

I wake with my head in Nolan's lap and his hand resting uncomfortably atop my eye. The first Orman book is wedged between us, poking at my neck, and Valerie's borrowed dress has bunched into a gauzy blue lump under my knees. Nolan groans and cracks his neck, equally unhappy about our sleeping arrangements.

"We fell asleep?" I ask, a stupid question.

"I guess," Nolan says, a stupid answer. He has spent the night slumped against the side of a bookcase.

"Geniuses, the both of you," a deep voice adds. I startle,

jerking from the floor and crushing Nolan's nose in the process. The room has suddenly shrunk to the size of my rental car and we are all crammed into too few seats.

"Walter, heel. Wally, stop. *Wally!* That's enough!" Nolan helplessly tries to bat the overeager mutt away while I pull on his collar, with no luck.

Mr. Larson, seemingly unperturbed by the commotion that is partly his responsibility, steps around the mass of fur and tangled body parts and sets a tray of steaming coffee mugs on the low reading table.

"Val said to send this up. Make yourselves presentable and then she wants to see you both in her office. One of those mugs is for Walter, so don't go gettin' greedy, understand?"

Nolan half glares at Mr. Larson over his cupped hands, trying to contain the trickle of blood coming from his nose. I grab a napkin from the tray and shove it at him, panicked.

"Are we in trouble?" I ask.

"I sure hope so," Alex says, appearing behind Mr. Larson's shoulder with a wicked grin. The room shrinks another two sizes as his smile fills the space. "I mean, seeing as how you spent the night together under Mom's roof and all."

"Good morning, Alexander," Nolan says drily. "You appear to have slept well."

Alex's grin widens. "I did indeed. But clearly not as well as you."

"Don't you have to attend to the bazaar or something?" Nolan asks, swapping out the bloodied napkin for a tissue that Alex pulls from his messenger bag. Is it possible to die of blood loss through the nose?

"Only the one meeting. Christ, that's a lot of blood. Amelia, if you wanted to kill him you could have just asked for my help. We could have spiked his cereal or something."

"I'll keep that in mind," I say. "Do you know where Valerie is?"

And because I'm pretty sure this bookstore is enchanted, my question is a summons. Valerie stands at the door, hands on hips.

"Mr. Larson. Alexander. Would you give us a moment?"

They scatter, Mr. Larson grabbing his tray, Alex hurriedly rambling about final bazaar preparations and being back later while still managing to get in a suggestive eyebrow wiggle at Nolan and me, with drank-all-three-cups-of-coffee Wally jittering his way out of the room as if possessed by an evil caffeinated spirit.

Once it's only the three of us, Nolan glances at me over the wad of tissues and shrugs, but I'm much too nervous to be so cavalier.

"It was an accident," I tell Valerie's stern face. "Sleeping together, I mean." I feel myself redden and quickly amend, "Sleeping in the same room together, not *together*, together. We didn't, um . . ."

"Nolan Endsley." Valerie spares me. "What *have* you been up to?"

Nolan takes the tissue from his nose long enough to say, "I expect you know exactly what we've been up to, seeing as how you're the one that sent her down in her Sunday best to disturb my work."

"Work?" I gape at him, turning to Valerie. "He was sleeping when I came down here!"

"Traitor," Nolan says under his breath.

"I know very well what you were doing," Valerie says.

"And you have spent entirely too much time alone together in this store, and I won't have any more of it."

An irrational part of me wonders if she knows Mark's and Trisha's numbers and is going to call them so they can ground me.

"Go spend time alone together out there." She points a long finger at the window. "Preferably not by the lighthouse, though the lake is significantly calmer today. Go. Have fun. Maybe catch the remote control boat races down by the pier."

Nolan surprises us both when he says, "I'm showing her Orman today."

Valerie looks at Nolan like he just revealed he has seven extra toes and they're all behind his right ear.

The thread between Nolan and me pulses, glows.

He shrugs at Valerie's gaping and doesn't look at me when he says, "She has to know."

Eight toes. Twenty toes. An entire extra head. Valerie looks caught between astonishment and uncertainty.

"You're sure?" Valerie says.

Nolan gives one deep nod and looks at me, a half-smile playing on his lips.

"If she says anything to anybody, I'll sic Wally on her."

"A fate worse than death," I deadpan.

I feel a bubble of satisfaction trail along the invisible thread between us. It's more like a thick yarn than twine today. Malleable but strong. I brush my fingertips against Nolan's knee, my whole body warming at the shy touch.

Valerie is looking between us, her expression easing into motherly affection.

"Well, off you go," she says. "And for God's sake, comb your hair, the both of you. You look like you slept on the floor of a bookstore."

We're going to the fort first. Nolan has to tell me three times that Orman isn't in the boathouse before I believe him. With Wally following dutifully at our heels, we make our way through a rain-soaked Lochbrook to the gate held open by rocks.

Nolan keeps his head down, his hands tucked into the pockets of his sweatshirt like he is trying to make himself smaller and smaller until he becomes invisible.

Lochbrookians and tourists wander in and around the tiny shops, brightly colored shopping bags and beach totes tucked under their arms. Kids in bathing suits and flip-flops sit on the curb outside an old-fashioned ice cream parlor, licking hot-pink ice cream droplets that slide down their cones. From the crest of the hill, I can see a group of boys shoving and wrestling like puppies on the peninsula that leads to the light-house. Adventurous adults bob in and out of the rough waves left over from yesterday's storm.

"You okay?" I ask Nolan when he jerks his head to face me. A group of girls our age passes us on the narrow sidewalk.

"Fine," he mumbles.

I don't press him.

When we reach the private beach on which the fort sits, Nolan lets out a half groan, half yell and drags his hand down his face.

"I hate it," he admits.

"Hate what?"

"Walking through town. I'm always worried a tourist will

recognize me and send out their internet Bat-Signal and that will be the end of my privacy."

"Wasn't it worse in New York?" I ask.

"Much. That's why I decided to come back here." He gestures at the fort.

His keys jingle as he unlocks the door and stomps his feet to clear them of sand.

Our beanbags are exactly as we left them.

I take a seat, expecting Nolan to follow, but he goes to his writing desk. Wally happily bounds over to me and sits on my lap, his gargantuan furry body blocking my view of anything else. I can hear Nolan opening a drawer, the rustle of paper, the clattering of pens.

Wally is more than happy to leave my lap when Nolan sits back in his beanbag. Nolan is so fully concentrating on the spiral notebooks he's brought over that he doesn't even notice when Wally knocks the hat from his head. He flips through the pages of one and hands me a standard college-ruled red number and some plain black pens. I guess this answers the question of the expensive journal and pen collection.

"Can you draw?" Nolan asks.

"No," I say. "I mean, stick figures and stuff."

"Good enough," he replies, businesslike. He pokes a finger at my spiral. "Draw stick figures of thirteen-year-old you and thirteen-year-old me."

"What? But you're a year older than me."

Nolan rolls his eyes. "Fine. Draw twelve-year-old you and thirteen-year-old me."

"But why?"

"It's for a project. Friends work on projects together, right?"

Still too confused to process his use of the word *friend*, I ask, "And what are *you* going to be drawing?"

"I . . ." Nolan pauses for dramatic effect. "I will be writing."

"Writing what?"

Nolan picks his cap off the ground and puts it back on his head, a bit smug.

"We will be creating the fictionalized shared history of Nolan and Amelia. We started in the middle, remember? We have to fill in the beginning."

And like that, the absurd boy from the Orman room, the one with the flip phone, the one who reads to distressed girls until they fall asleep, has returned and stuffed the angsty famous author who is afraid of being seen into a car trunk. In the gleam of his eyes, I can almost see the boy that imagined Orman into being peeking out from the darkness of too-sad and too-happy music.

While I doodle pictures of stick figures frolicking through meadows of poorly drawn flowers and swimming in a sloppy square marked "public pool," Nolan asks me questions and writes the answers down in his spiral.

"Favorite movie we saw together?" he asks.

"I don't know. What movies did you like when you were a kid?"

"It has to be a made-up movie, Amelia. This is all made up. The movie has to be one we create." He says this like it's the most obvious thing in the world, fake fiction to accompany our fake history.

"*Unicorns Rule and Werewolves Drool*?" I suggest, and feel silly.

Nolan pauses. "Good. But what's the plot?"

"Unicorns rule the world, and werewolves—with their poisonous drool—try to destroy it." I try to make this sound as natural as his reasoning, and I must succeed, because he writes it down.

"Animated?" he asks.

I stare at him over the top of my spiral and desperately wish I could raise one eyebrow like he can. "No, Nolan. It's live action, with real unicorns and werewolves," I say, deadpan.

He throws a pen at me, which bounces ineffectively off my shoulder. "It could have been one of those cheesy B movies with live actors and CGI animals," he protests. "Do you buy candy at the theater?"

"I sneak candy in my purse," I say. "You?"

"Popcorn with enough butter to make it soggy."

"That's gross," I say. I throw a colored pencil back at him for good measure.

Nolan looks at me sadly and writes something, shaking his head.

"What are you writing?"

"That you clearly have no taste for culinary delights and are showing signs of violence. Unfortunate."

"If by 'violence' you mean *retaliation*, I'm okay with that." I laugh.

We spend the afternoon this way, creating a golden childhood for two fictional creatures that happen to share our names. Nolan manages to extricate real facts to apply to my fictionalized persona—the names of my parents, the kind of house I grew up in, favorite and not-so-favorite childhood memories—but I only learn the barest facts about him. He likes popcorn at the theater, enjoys listening to classical music when he writes, and his favorite thing to do is walk.

"Do you listen to music when you walk?" I ask.

"Nope. I just walk. It helps me think when I want to think and helps me not think when I don't."

"That's nice," I say dreamily. I've given up drawing caricatures of our invented friendship and am lounged sideways in the beanbag, oddly comfortable sitting in such an unflattering position. Nolan scribbles away.

"Tell me something else," I say to the ceiling. "Something about you."

The scratching stops, and I crane my neck to watch him as he thinks.

I tug on the line between us.

"Come on," I tease. "It doesn't have to be anything major."

He's quiet for a long moment.

"How does this story end?" Nolan asks.

"What?"

"This." He raises his notes and gestures to my drawings. "How do we end?"

The line between us is so taut it could be plucked like a guitar string. I don't know if it's going to hold or break.

"How do you *want* this to end?" I ask, an evasion.

A slow smile. "You can't answer a question with a question."

And even though the room is filled with wisps of tension, uncertainty floating between dust particles, I smile back.

"Well, I just did."

I think of all the things he could say. He could (improbably) confess his undying love for me, or he could (most likely) tell me he's not interested in more than a five-day fictionalized friendship that ends as soon as I step foot on the plane out of here.

He doesn't do any of that.

"After she left, I wanted Jenna to stay," he says slowly. "She didn't care who I was but *how* I was, and that mattered. She mattered. She was only there for a few minutes, and she mattered to me. So what's going to happen when you leave, after you've mattered to me for days?"

Dear. Lord.

It seems unfair that the world is often critical of finding meaning in another person. We're allowed to find ourselves in places, books, music, nature, but not in another human. We aren't allowed to mourn losing a piece of ourselves for *too* long—especially when young—because we must learn to stand on our own two feet.

But if the world must be made of car crashes and unspeaking books, let there at least be no guilt in companionship, no matter how brief. To quote Valerie, everything is silly because *everything* is temporary.

I know exactly what I want to do as I watch all of my own emotions play across Nolan's face, an unfamiliar mirror. The urge is so strong, I don't even need to summon the whales for the courage to do it.

"In the interest of our years of friendship and maintaining what matters, I'm going to hug you," I announce, leaning across our beanbags for a sloppy two-armed affair that leaves my nose pressed into his sharp collarbone.

At first, he is as rigid as a board and as unforgiving as yesterday's storm that struck our little patch of mattering. But his right arm comes around me and cradles my head to his shoulder, his left squishing down into the beanbag to rest against my back, and we're locked in an embrace that heats me up from the inside with relief. In his arms, I can feel what he doesn't say, the guilt that he *could have saved them*. He is a co-sufferer, a co-rememberer.

When we break apart, Nolan looks at me like I'm the sun that can soak up all his puddles of grief.

"I'll tell you," he says. "I'll tell you what Jenna said . . . if you still want to know."

This is what I came for. The whole reason I flew to Michigan, leaving everything I know behind. And it's being handed to me . . . by Nolan Endsley, no less.

I can't make words come out of my mouth, but Nolan must see the answer in my eyes because he nods, inhaling all the air in the room.

"I was standing outside the Author Oasis," he says on an exhale. "It was only a couple of conference rooms away from the public, but it had food and was mostly quiet, so that's where I stayed while the other authors were on panels. Alex had gone to check on the sound system for my 'big announcement' session."

"Why weren't you scheduled for any panels?" I ask when he pauses to breathe. I swallow down the strange déjà vu at hearing myself ask what I'd wondered aloud to Jenna when I'd first seen the schedule.

"Alex made me do a panel once, at another event," Nolan says. "At the end, all the audience questions were for me, about Orman."

"So?" I ask.

"You say 'So,' until you remember there were five other very successful authors—all much older than me—on that same panel, who had to sit there and pretend not to mind."

We are quiet as I imagine Nolan's unease at being the most

sought-after person in the room. Looking at his downturned head and thoughtful eyes, I can't imagine him speaking in front of a group of people.

"So . . . Jenna?" It's a question, a plea to continue the conversation to its inevitable end, and though my voice doesn't shake, I fear the pit in my stomach will open and swallow me whole.

Maybe Nolan can sense this, or maybe he feels the chill coming through the cracks of the boathouse, but he scoots closer to me so that our bent knees touch at the sides.

"So Alex had left me alone, and I panicked. About the public speaking, about the 'big announcement' of the final Orman book's publication date, about . . . about a lot of things."

"But you didn't show up to the event," I say.

Nolan sighs. I think he has used more air sighing than breathing today.

"No, I didn't," he says. "Mostly thanks to Jenna. She found me, looking, as you put it, *troubled*."

He pauses, waiting to see if I will push to know the reason for his distress. Every part of my body is burning with curiosity, but asking Nolan what made him freak out would be a betrayal of our infinitesimal relationship and kill it stone dead. I sneak a look at him from the corner of my eye; his face is unattractively scrunched up as if waiting for a blow, which I guess he is.

"You were troubled, Jenna found you, and . . ." I prompt, trying to sound nonchalant as I ignore the question hanging between us.

Nolan turns his head from the water to me, eyes wide with relief and something else I can't identify.

"Yes," he echoes. "Jenna found me."

In a flash of movement, Nolan juts his arm out to mine and clasps our hands together. His grip is too forceful at first, inexperienced, but he loosens his fingers when he brings our joined hands to rest on his knee.

"Is this okay?" he asks. He's back to looking at the wall behind me, but keeps sneaking glances my way.

"It's okay," I say, which isn't true at all. *Okay* is far too blasé a word for the mix of elation and guilt that seeps through my veins. I didn't answer Nolan's question. I don't know how this will end, but I can feel the ticking time bomb of my departure and its added shrapnel of hurting Nolan.

I strain to hear Jenna's voice floating from somewhere over the backs of the whales, from a distant land where death is a memory and the past is misplaced history, but she is silent.

"She came out of nowhere," Nolan says. His thumb brushes the top of my hand. "I didn't see her come up to me; she was just there all of a sudden, with her hand on my arm. She pulled me to a window seat, told me her name, and started showing me pictures on her cell phone. I thought it was silly at first, but she was narrating each photo and I had no choice but to calm down and listen."

Jenna and her bloody plans have come full circle, and her snarky, know-it-all voice drifts across the spaces between us.

See?

My head swims with Nolan's words from that night. *"Because not so long ago somebody did the same thing I'm about to do for you. Sit."*

It's too much, too much, too much.

Nolan's thumb quickens, rubbing worried circles into my wrist.

"She showed me pictures of her family, of high school

dances, of bookstores she visited," he continues. "She showed me lots of pictures, Amelia, but the one I remember best was the picture she showed me of you."

I'm crying, silent tears that don't leave me gasping for breath or needing to rip books in half but that taste almost sweet in their saltiness. When did emotions start having emotions of their own, and how do I make it stop?

"Me?" I ask, to distract myself from the too-muchness.

Nolan is quiet again, this time for so long that I look to see if he heard me. He's staring at me head-on, no corners of eyes or self-conscious glances.

It suddenly occurs to me that the reason he stared so much my first night in the bookstore was because it was not, in fact, a one-sided knowing. He knew me, at least by sight, and he was probably just as shocked to see me as I was him.

Oh, Jenna. What have you planned?

"You were reading my first book," Nolan says, our eyes still locked. His voice has dropped in reverence, and I lean closer to hear over the sound of my heartbeat pumping in my ears. "You had crammed yourself into a chair at the library and were wearing headphones. You looked completely oblivious to everyone and everything."

"I guess I must have been," I say. My voice sounds far away, an echo in a cave that never quite settles in the ear. "I've never seen that picture. I didn't even know she had taken one like it."

An avalanche of words tumbles out of Nolan, like he can't stop. Like he, too, is still learning that his emotions are multifaceted and strange and that sometimes word-vomiting is the only acceptable catharsis. "She pulled up the picture on her phone and I asked her to stop scrolling. Your face was . . . I don't know. Your face looked so at peace, but also—" He pauses, his eyes finally dropping from mine to scan the carpet for hidden words. "You were so *alive* without moving. It made me proud of Orman. It made me want to write something else that would make you look like that."

My heart is still sputtering along, trying to hold Jenna and N. E. Endsley and Orman and Nolan's hand all at once.

"But what did she say?" I ask, and when that doesn't sound quite right, I try again. "How did she help you so much?"

Nolan looks at me, and his eyes are glassy, as if in every other universe besides this one he is crying.

"She told me that, right or wrong, I was allowed to make my own choices. That whatever was bothering me may not be completely in my control, but my reaction could be. She didn't ask specifics, either. She just . . . she just helped."

Nolan breathes out, and it sounds like a release of so much more than air.

"I've thought a lot about it since," he says. "And it's more what she showed me than what she said. With all those pictures, she showed me that the world still turns, with or without me. That other people have lives and they live independently of the people in my life. And that what I wrote mattered to an actual human being in a library in Texas. What I wrote made somebody light up from the inside and made her fearsome to behold without her having to move a muscle."

Nolan stops, breath spent from his frenzied explanation. I remain still, allowing him room to fill the silence.

"She told me that I had to take care of myself first," he says. "How I owe the world my best work, and the world would wait—eagerly, impatiently—but my readers, you included, would wait for me to finish what I started with Orman. The world would wait for me to be ready."

"God," I whisper. "She told you all that in the span of a few minutes?"

He laughs and says, "Yes. She left quite abruptly. She told me she had to go, that the girl in the photo would be returning soon and expect her to be there. She said, 'If I don't go now, Amelia will find us.' I asked her if Amelia was the girl in the picture and Jenna said yes. She told me your name, she told me you loved my books and that you were the most infuriatingly persistent person she had ever known. Jenna told me she had to go, because if you found Jenna with me, you would 'insist on being best friends, and with all due respect, Nolan, you have some decisions to make.'"

"She was probably right," I say, wiping tears from my cheeks. "You would have hated me."

"Probably," Nolan says. I glare at him, but he is smiling rue-fully, and I marvel again that the stern, no-nonsense author inhabits the same body as the boy with the writing fort and the beanbags.

I'm trying to think what it all means, piecing together everything that has happened since Jenna's death, making a new kind of road map that will show me where I ought to go, when my phone buzzes in my pocket.

I know without looking that it's Mark checking in on his lunch hour. Other than the occasional text message—*I'm alive. I'm safe. I'm alive.*—I haven't spoken to him or Trisha since my arrival.

"I have to take this," I tell Nolan as I rise, my pants sticking to my legs after sitting in the beanbag for so long. "Sorry. I'm going to step outside for some air."

"I'll be here," Nolan says. His face is neutral when I glance at him, but his tone suggests something more than just being *here* in the boathouse.

I answer my phone as I shut the front door behind me.

"Hi, Mark. Sorry I haven't called."

"Good to hear your voice, kiddo. How's Michigan treatin' ya?"

"Oh . . ." I look over my shoulder at the boathouse as I walk toward the lake, kicking my shoes off in the sand. "It's pretty cool, actually. Lots to do . . . lots to see."

"Glad to hear it. Have you figured out where that book came from?"

The water swirls around my ankles as I walk into the lake, the hem of my jeans becoming damp. The 101st copy is the farthest thing from my mind in the wake of Nolan telling me about his meeting with Jenna.

"I think so," I say. "Maybe."

"Well, good. Listen, hon. I called you because I have some news."

My voice rushes out of me, and I almost slip on the slick rock floor of the lake. "Is everything okay? Is Mrs. Willi—Trisha okay?"

"Oh, no, no, no. Nothing like that. This is good news! Trisha told me not to tell you yet, but the paperwork just came across my desk, and I can't resist. Trisha and I are funding a college scholarship in Jenna's name."

I trip on one of the larger rocks and almost fall into the water. His comment about school has come from the sky, a meteor given my exact coordinates so it can take me out. Is this Jenna's way of making sure I go through with the original plan?

"That's a great idea," my mouth says. I turn my head when I hear the boathouse door open. Nolan half raises his arm in an awkward wave and I can't help but smile. I point at my phone and hold up my index finger in the universal signal for *One more minute*—also the universal signal for *I'm hoping this will be over quickly, but it might last a millennium.*

"What do you think, Amelia?" Mr. Williams asks.

I've tuned out a moment too long. I turn back to the lake, hoping to piece together enough information so it's not totally obvious I haven't been listening. "I'm not sure," I say. "What do you think?"

There's a longish pause before he says, "Do you forget to think sometimes, too?"

Metallic guilt seeps into my mouth and fills my nostrils with its brutish scent. I know exactly what Mark is talking about—the curtain of hurt that can block out the sounds of whales and anger and everything in between—except, in this moment, I'm not obsessing over Jenna's absence. But Mark *is*, and I could at least pay attention.

"I'm sorry," I say. "Can you repeat that last bit?"

"The scholarship in Jenna's name? We would like you to be the first official recipient. We . . ." He pauses and I hear him blowing his nose. "This is what Jenna would want, for you to live out your dreams of pursuing a life in academia."

What Jenna would want.

I search for the clever wind, but it's nowhere to be found.

It feels like everything in the world is pressing in on me. The air is heavy and immovable, the pebbles and water convening to strangle my feet as Nolan's eyes burn holes into my back.

"Thank you," I tell Mark. "I don't know what to say."

An acceptance. I've just implicitly accepted his offer.

Another manacle ensnares my ankle. I tell myself it's good. I should be thanking my lucky stars that the Williamses are going to fund it all in Jenna's name.

"You don't have to say anything yet," Mark says. "We'll talk it over when you come home this weekend. Are you ready to come back? I don't want you to feel any financial pressures. We'll take care of it. We're just excited for you to start school."

My heart is thumping in my throat again, each beat bringing me closer and closer to years of inescapable expectations that I can't fully hate because the voice on the phone so desperately wants good things for me.

And that voice is all I have left of Jenna in this world.

"Mostly ready to come back," I say. And to add an ounce of truth into this conversation, I add, "But I'm enjoying my time here, too."

"Well, have a great time, Amelia. Trish and I can't wait to see your pictures!"

I haven't touched my camera since I got here, but I don't tell Mark.

When the call disconnects, my phone screen returns to its usual backdrop. I haven't really looked at it in a while. It's a picture I took of a tree bent over on itself, its long, thick branches scraping the ground near the trunk, forming a natural archway. I used to think it was beautiful, a portal to another world. But now I wonder if it can still be called a tree if it lives bent in two rather than stretching toward the sky. I shove the phone back into my pocket.

"I just. Want. To be," I say to the air.

"I understand," Nolan says, and I jump at his voice so close to my ear.

"Sorry," he says. "I saw you finish on the phone."

I nod, but I'm thinking about how whales will swim on and on through ice and blue and sky no matter what happens to me, but does that mean I should live how I want? Or does that mean it doesn't matter what I want and I should live up to everyone's expectations and make the best of it?

"Is everything okay?" Nolan asks. "I know that's a stupid question in general, but I meant for it to apply to this exact moment, to your call."

"Yeah," I say, still staring over the lake and begging the whales to make decisions for me. "I mean, yeah, I know what you meant, and I'm not sure if everything's okay or terrible. That was Jenna's dad. He wanted to let me know that he and Jenna's mom are going to pay my college tuition. With a scholarship. In her name."

"Wow," Nolan says. That's all he says.

"Wow?" I ask.

"That's a lot to turn down." Gentle, small waves lap at the silence. "You don't sound happy about it."

I groan, leaning to pick up a rock from the shallow water. Up close, I can see strange little sunbursts imprinted on one side.

"Coral fossils," Nolan says absently. "They're called Petoskey stones."

We both stare at the rock in my palm until my heart leaves my throat.

"Jenna . . . She had everything mapped out for us, and her parents act like it's their job to make sure the last one standing upholds the plan. It's not like I can say no. I have no excuse *to* say no."

Nolan looks out at the horizon when he asks, "Why wouldn't you say no? Because of the money?"

"I mean, partly, I guess," I say. "I—my mom—we can't

afford college. But . . . I don't know. I've never been sure of what I want to do, so I might as well do this, right?"

"No. Tell them thanks but no thanks and figure out what it is *you* want," Nolan says. Like it's obvious. Like it wouldn't be ripping out the Williamses' hearts and squashing them for sport.

"Oh, okay," I say, sarcasm and bitterness leaking into my voice. "And you can call your publisher and tell them you're ready to publish the third Orman book."

Nolan stands back like I've slapped him.

"That's different," he says. "It's not so simple."

"Why not?" I turn the stone over and over in my hand, and as it dries, the little sunbursts disappear.

"You *know* it's different."

"I *know* it's hard for you because you're not sure what you want to do yet. It's obvious you're not ready to move forward with Orman. Well, it's the same for me, Nolan. The exact same thing."

"But it's *not*," he says. "You are letting Jenna call the shots when you should be the one deciding."

"Jenna is dead," I say. The last word comes out hard. It's my turn to be hurt. "She can't tell me what to do anymore."

"That's a half-truth and you know it," Nolan says. "The dead can hold more sway than the living."

I flinch but don't answer. Agitated, he turns, sloshing back through the water to the shore and his discarded sneakers. I don't follow, even when he stops and crooks his arm, waiting for me to take it.

When I don't move, he turns his head.

"Come *on*, Amelia."

"I'm not Wally," I protest. "I don't come when called."

He rolls his eyes at me, smiling softly, with apology. The

line between us pulls from where it has been sagging in the water.

"Amelia, come with me. There's something I need to show you. Let me . . ." He takes a step toward me, extending his hand. "Let me take you to Orman."

I want to take his hand and follow him to whatever magical place inspired my favorite books, but what if it wrecks me? What if it makes the manacles feel even tighter than they already are? I have what I came for, his memory about Jenna. Maybe that should be enough. I shouldn't ask about Orman or the 101st copy. Maybe it was all just a means to get me here, Jenna pulling strings from . . . wherever she is. I should cut my losses before I grow even more attached to a person that I'm going to lose.

"I'm leaving soon," I tell him, hating myself for every word. "I have to go back to Texas. In the fall, I'll go to Montana. After that, graduate school. There's no room for you in their plan, Nolan. That is how *this*"—I gesture between us—"ends. It doesn't matter what movies we saw, what fake school we went to, what stupid pictures we drew. At the end of the week, I'm going away, and you'll stay here, and we should stop this before we get hurt."

Nolan watches me, his eyes falling to the erratic rise and fall of my chest, to my hands clenched at my sides. He crosses to me in three easy strides and waits for me to look up into his remarkably calm eyes before he speaks.

"We've already been hurt," he murmurs, slowly reaching out to take my hand, to lead me from the lake. "What's one more scar?"

I don't realize until we're halfway to town that his fear of water seemed to vanish when he was beside me.

chapter twelve

The high afternoon sun slows the town to a crawl. We walk past shop owners flipping BACK SOON signs and locking front doors, nap-ready children being tugged behind their parents, and other teens drifting into the quiet coffee shops with live musicians singing through scratchy speakers.

When I finally loop my arm through the crook of Nolan's elbow, he brings his hand up to cover mine. Even with our arms linked, I have trouble keeping up with him as we head to the other side of town, past Val's, farther than I've ever been in Lochbrook. When we come to a small hill covered with trees pressed tightly together, we are forced to drop arms to navigate them.

Eventually, we come to a low iron fence. It's as if the dead and their memories might walk out if some sort of barrier weren't erected to keep them in.

Orman is in a graveyard?

I used to like cemeteries. I liked the pristine grass, uniform and almost fake in its perfection. I liked the solemnness laced with serenity, perfect for reflection or brooding or simply remembering that life has its hard limits.

I hate them now. They make me think of cold and loss, and somehow each gravestone has become not one of many but an individual story with its own queue of mourners.

This is why I stop. Nolan has to give me a gentle tug on the arm to coax my feet back into movement.

"It's okay," he says. I'm not sure which of us he is trying to reassure. "Please?"

It's his *please* that pushes me through the low, open gate, and for once I am glad that Jenna—or what's left of her physical shell—is not here.

But who *is*?

We crunch through soggy leaves, wet from yesterday's rain, and past a mix of terribly old and bitterly new headstones. I read the names as we go and can't keep myself from saying a silent prayer for those left behind, even if the death date is a century before my time. The train station of my mind is filled with errant, disconnected engines that speed past the loading platform. Can you inherit grief like you inherit eye color? I wonder how many people came to these funerals. I wonder if there's anything left of the casket or the person in there. I wonder if there's anyone left who remembers Jane Smith or Daniel Folks.

Somewhere nearby, I hear a chorus of high, tinkling wind chimes. The sound grows louder as Nolan stops in front of another iron gate. It quarters off the far left corner of the cemetery. A mini forest of trees that have not been cut down to make room for more bodies stands within. This gate is locked and much higher than the low gate through which we entered. Nolan takes a key on a long silver chain from beneath his shirt and fits it into the padlock, the gate creeping open with a cheerful, almost welcoming whine.

We stand at the mouth of the gate, me confused and terrified about whose grave I'm about to see, while also trying not
to think of Jenna and her grave and her deadness. Nolan puts
the silver chain back over his head and reaches down, linking
his fingers through mine.

"Okay?" he asks.

I look down at our joined hands, turning them from side to
side with the movement of my wrist.

"It's okay," I say.

And somehow it is.

Through the heavy green trees, the branches just barely
grazing our arms, we walk side by side for the few steps it takes
to reach the small clearing. From here, I could almost imagine a wide forest spreading out around us, endless and dark
and enchanting. The chimes play their haunted melodies,
smiling at our joined hands.

My breath catches when I see the two smoothed hunks of
petrified wood nestled between twin cedar trees, each natural
headstone bearing a small metal plaque. They feel like Orman, blissfully new while unmistakably old. Their purpose
is enough to make my insides roll into a ball, but at Nolan's
urging, I release his hand and fall forward to my knees to read
the words aloud.

"Emily Jane Endsley and Avery Juniper Endsley. Together
in life and death."

The birth dates are separated by a handful of years, but the
date after each dash is the same.

Sisters. Nolan Endsley had younger sisters. And they
died on the same day. "Everyone thinks I came up with Orman in high school, which is partly true," Nolan begins.
"Most of it came from before, though, when my sisters and

I were little. I made up stories for them, worlds. Orman was their favorite."

I continue to rack my brain for any whisper of siblings in interviews or internet ramblings and find nothing. Nolan shakes his head at my expression.

"They're not mentioned anywhere," he says. "Anywhere. Dad made sure of that."

"But why?" I ask. My brain is scrambling for an answer. Maybe there is bad blood between him and his family, now that he has taken the stories he made for his dead sisters and turned them into gold.

Nolan sighs, and I recognize the slight shake in his breath for what it is: the piteous, defeated sound of grief.

"They're dead." It's all but a whisper. And then, impossibly quieter: "It's my fault."

Dead means something new when death has touched you. Before Jenna died, the death of other people seemed like a sad story that didn't ever quite reach my heart. Death was inevitable, natural in its unnaturalness.

Death was for other people.

But as I watch the first hint of a tear nestle in the corner of Nolan's eye, I feel the ground beneath us give way, my own tides of grief rising up to meet his.

I suddenly feel impossibly old. But I force myself to look at the stones, at Nolan, and the evidence of our artificial history, which we created to justify a relationship that feels much older than a couple of days, and I make myself stand in the waves.

"We summered here as a family," Nolan says, staring at the stones. His eyes are glazed, unseeing. "The blue house was our vacation home—I bought it from my mom with the money from my first book. Every year my mom, dad, me, Emily, and

Avery came here. Dad would fly back and forth to New York for meetings and Mom would spend time in town, so the three of us would be left alone a lot."

He pauses, his eyes refocusing and turning back to me. "It's safe here, obviously." He laughs a little huff of air, completely devoid of mirth. "I mean, the crime rate hovers somewhere around zero percent. I don't want to make it sound like they put us in danger. Besides, we loved it.

"Except, I was supposed to watch them," he says. "Every summer, we vacationed here. Every summer, I was supposed to keep an eye on them. But I was fourteen and stubborn and pimply and I liked the girl who worked at the ice cream shop, so I told Emily and Avery they were old enough to go to the water alone. I told them to go and to check back in later. They begged me to come, especially Emily, who was always afraid of everything. They never came back."

He moves to sit on the ground next to me, our hands finding each other through the fog of our thoughts and the ominous presence of Jenna and his sisters. He shivers and clenches his eyes shut.

"I looked everywhere," he says. "I went to the beach and to the house. I went to all our favorite spots in town, with Alex. He came to help me after I rushed into the store crying. When we couldn't find them, Alex got Val and we drove in her car and looked and looked. Val took me to the police station. They asked if I knew where the girls had last gone. I didn't, but I guessed that, maybe without anyone telling them not to, they went to the alcove and tried to swim there. We were never allowed, because of the riptides. And that's exactly what happened."

A long pause ensues. The wind chimes cry through the trees

and the leaves rustle their discontent. Behind Nolan's eyes, a pack of wolves descends on a lost squirrel. The squirrel does not struggle as it is ripped apart. It thinks this is the way of things. It thinks it deserves this fate.

"After, all Dad was worried about was keeping it out of the press. No articles in the paper, no nightly news coverage. I hated him for it—strolling around in his rumpled suit, yelling into his phone—but I think it was just something for him to do. I think he still does it, you know? That's why he never stops working, so he doesn't have to think about the girls or me." A pause. "It's my fault," Nolan repeats.

I want to say this isn't his fault, death waits for no person and comes whenever it pleases, but I don't contradict him. Sometimes the best way to absolve the guilty is to let them feel the weight of their culpability, no matter how untrue.

"When Jenna died," I say, voice quivering, "I thought that was my fault, too. She offered to take me. The Williamses wanted to pay for me to go to Ireland with her to study abroad. They're so generous, but I didn't want any more of their charity than I had already taken. It was too much, too perfect, and not meant for me. I said no and no and no until they stopped asking. And I can't help but think I could have changed something if I were there, like I could have thrown myself over her so we would both survive the crash. Or I could have stopped her from getting into the car in the first place by convincing her to try a different snack food from every place in town or something, instead. I could have changed the outcome."

"That's ridiculous," Nolan says. "You weren't even in the country. How could it be your fault?"

"Nolan, you are not a current," I say. "A sulking, determined force of nature, sure, but you are not the current that killed your sisters."

"But I am," he says. "I could have prevented it."

"You don't know that," I argue.

"Of course I do! I was supposed to be watching them, but I had better things to do, so they died." His voice flickers between outrage and fear, sadness and despair.

"We can't die in their stead," I say, tears muddling my voice. I'm on my hands and knees, facing him, pleading with him, with myself. "We *can't*. No matter how much we want to or how much easier it would be, we can't take their places. We have to learn to live like this, Nolan. For their sake. And for ours."

We're both breathing hard, our rising voices fusing with the sound of the chimes, a distressed, clanging noise that causes the whales to forget to rise to the surface for air.

Sorry doesn't help. And there is nothing you can say to someone who is hurting to make them feel better. Jenna is not here, and neither are Emily and Avery, and words—no matter how eloquent or pleading—will not bring them back.

Instead I say, "You sent them to Orman, didn't you?"

It clicks together like the easiest of children's puzzles, with a space for each distinct shape cut out in a slab of wood. Emily and Avery were transformed into Emmeline and Ainsley and swept off in a magic boat to Orman.

"I did," Nolan says, so quietly I almost can't hear him above the wind chimes.

"So when Jenna found you . . ." I trail off. I don't need to finish.

"It was the water," he says. "It's always the water. I looked out the window at the Pacific and could see them playing in the waves. It—" He stops, taking a deep breath. "It wasn't the first time I've seen them drown, but it doesn't ever get easier, that part of it. I saw them get pulled under and disappear. And, like my therapist told me to, I let myself see them rise up together, inside the magical canoe from Orman as it broke the waves, sailing out to sea. But this time the canoe broke beneath them and they drowned again. Twice in less than five minutes."

I rub his wrist with my thumb. There's nothing to say.

"The only thing I could think, standing at that window, was how I was about to give away the last parts of them I have, the last story, the last everything. I would have to say good-bye to Orman, but also good-bye to them. I couldn't visit them in the forests or castles again, couldn't drop in when I felt lonely or sad or . . . or . . ." He releases another huff of angry air. "God, aren't authors supposed to have all the words?" He tries to force a laugh, but it comes out more like a sob.

"Broken?" I offered. "You couldn't go to them when you felt broken anymore."

He nods, a short decisive tick. "Yes, Amelia. Broken."

We sit together in brokenness for a while. The wind chimes are tugging at my vocal cords, asking me to speak, and like all those years ago when Jenna found me outside of Downtown Books, I say the first thing that comes to mind.

"Jenna wanted me to be an English professor," I say. "She had it all planned. Like, on a poster board and everything. We would go to the same schools, take the same electives and basic classes together. . . . She labeled it 'The Master Plan' and kept it in her room, where anyone could see."

Nolan leans forward, running a hand along Emily's stone. "And you don't want to be a professor?"

I bunch my knees to my chest and lightly bang my forehead against them. "I don't know," I mumble. "I have no idea."

"So, don't," he says. "Be something else. Be whatever you want to be."

"But how am I supposed to know what that is? Everyone else seems to know already. They're premed or engineering majors or marine biologists or something with an actual title. I just want to read books or take pictures or find the world's best ham sandwich. . . . How can any of those things be made into a career?"

Nolan is silent, his free hand now stroking Avery's stone. "There are a hundred thousand ways to tell a story," he begins. "Medical students help people live longer and continue their own stories. Engineering majors tell a story of technology that goes back to cavemen with rocks and sticks. Marine biologists piece together shreds of plot until they know where whales sleep at night and where fish live in coral reefs. Everything is a story, not just writing. You need to find the story that means something to you, a story you like telling."

He falls silent again, the wind and chimes kicking up in a melancholy symphony that sounds like a heart breaking. I try to take my hand back to move windblown hair out of my eyes, but Nolan tightens his grip before quickly releasing it, like he doesn't want to let go.

"Sorry," he says. "Didn't mean to do that."

I leave my hand in his, using the other to rid my sight of hair.

I'm crying. I think I've cried more in the last month than I have the entire rest of my life. Maybe if Jenna were here, she would change her mind. Maybe if she knew I would be alone, she would tell me to forge my own path.

I am trying to hold it all in my head when Nolan says, "You're the only person outside of Lochbrook who knows about the girls. We managed to keep it from the press, even after the books became popular and reporters came to poke around, but only because Val has everyone scared shitless."

There is a question buried in his statement and how his hand tightens on mine. He wants to know that I won't say anything, that if the stars should fall from the sky and our fake and real friendships imploded into nothing, I wouldn't take this story to the press and sell it to the highest bidder.

He wants to know that he is safe.

And though it is dreadfully inappropriate, while sitting beside the graves of his sisters, with the manifested fog of my dead friend weaving its way around us, I kiss Nolan Endsley on the cheek.

He freezes, and I wonder if I've made a mistake, if I've misinterpreted the hand-holding and the sleeping in a pile on the bookstore floor. My face reddens with a blush of embarrassment and I make to pull back.

"Sorry," I mumble.

But his head whips toward me, his hand coming around to the back of my neck. For an unfathomable period of time, we stare at each other, the kind of staring where your eyes don't blink and your toes curl in your shoes the longer you look. The air between us is humming with a charge for which I have no name as the line between us tightens just short of breaking.

Behind his eyes, the trees in the once-dark forest are orange in the growing light. Wolves scamper off and gnash their teeth at the rising sun, and all manner of threatening, creepy shadows melt into nothing as I watch the world that is Nolan uncurl from its sleep.

When the light reaches his eyes and shines out, he tilts his head ever so slightly. I hold my breath as he both pulls me in and leans into me with a sigh that sounds like a crashing wave.

"Amelia," he whispers, and then his lips are on mine.

It's not my first kiss. There were boys I dated. But I forget their names and faces in this moment, as I press forward, trying to shrink the space between Nolan and me into nothing.

Nolan and me.

He kisses like he talks when he is passionate about something—thoroughly, completely, and with such precision you wonder if anyone else could ever compare.

We fall into a rhythm, quick, slow, quick, slow, but eventually the lack of breath catches up with me and I gently push him away.

"Need to breathe," I exhale.

He brings my lips back to his, but doesn't press them together.

"Breathe like this," he says against my lips, "but don't go."

A cruel reminder.

I take a deep breath. "I'm sorry I have to go back to Texas."

He leans back a fraction, sprawling his hand against my neck and rubbing his thumb up and down my cheekbone. "I'm sorry you feel trapped," he whispers.

I smile, but if his kiss was the sea, this smile is a puddle. "I'm sorry that you're sorry."

He tilts his head forward, stopping just short of our lips meeting again.

"Can we pretend," he says with his voice low, "that this is the part where you decide to stay in Lochbrook?"

My heart is steady in my chest, the butterflies at bay. It's an overlapping of universes, a burst in the space–time continuum.

For a second, I am Amelia, destined to stay in Michigan beside Nolan and his weird dog, confident in her lack of plans and laughing at the world. An Amelia who completely ignores Jenna's neat, orderly plans and instead makes her own blueprint. She collects one-shot photos, goes to community college, tries every program in the curriculum, and the clever wind is happy with her choice.

"I can't stay," I say, and under my breath I add, "I pinky promised." When Nolan's face falls, I continue, "But I am very, very good at pretend."

"Well." His smile is crooked, a little sad, but gleaming. "If that's the case . . ."

When our lips meet again, I feel the fire spread from his body to mine, burning any protests to ash. His hands tangle in my hair, and I don't think of Orman or Jenna. I don't think about mysterious packages, pinky promises, or how we are kissing in front of his sisters' graves.

Instead, I try to keep my heart from splitting in two as we build something we know is going to break.

When we return to the bookstore, the little meadow of grass surrounding Val's is bustling with activity. Wooden panels prop up temporary booths painted olive green, and people I half recognize from the store are attaching signs to the front of the vacant stalls. The book club man with the plaid tank top is wearing *another* plaid shirt, a short-sleeve button-down, and laughing, as a much younger man tries to straighten a sign that advertises fried hot dogs.

In the midst of it all is Alex, messenger bag tugging at his neck in a way that must be uncomfortable, phone in hand as he jogs from booth to booth. He looks frazzled, like the White Rabbit late for tea.

"What on *earth* . . ." I begin. None of this was here a few hours ago.

Nolan laughs at my expression. "The bazaar. It's a yearly thing Val puts on. Each year she picks a different cause and half the proceeds from all the stalls go to charity."

The flyer from the elevator pings into my head.

"It's for an elementary school this year, right?" I ask, as we near the bookstore's entrance. Distantly, I hear the clunky sound of a student playing piano.

"Yeah, the school library, I think."

"When's the bazaar?"

"Saturday."

"*Saturday?* As in 'day after tomorrow' Saturday? Shouldn't we be helping?"

Nolan gives me a beseeching look. "*No.*"

"Yes," Alex says, appearing behind us and throwing his arms over our shoulders. A strangely docile Wally sits at his heels. "*You* should be, Nolan. As our guest, Amelia is not honor bound, but it's the least she can do, if she's going to keep eating at the café for free."

"Hey, I tried to pay. Your mom won't let me."

Alex raises his hand off my shoulder and flutters his fingers. "Semantics. Do you two want to help me hang light strands in these trees or not?"

Nolan's response is a vulgar hand movement, while I gaze openmouthed at the trees surrounding the clearing.

"*Which* trees?" I ask. "You can't possibly mean all of them."

"Only the ones with leaves."

"Alex, they *all* have leaves," I say.

He must take this as a confirmation of our volunteering, because he's off, presumably to find the endless strands of lights we will need to light up the forest around us.

Nolan says nothing as we watch Alex hurry away, but he tries to murder me with his eyes.

"What?"

"You know what," he says. "We could be inside eating food or reading books or . . ." He trails off, cheeks red.

I grin. "Kissing?"

He glares as his face reddens further, but his voice is even when he says, "Yes, if you'd like."

My heart stumbles a little at the way his eyes are eating me whole, but I try to make my voice as normal as his and say, "But if we help Alex today, we can have all day tomorrow to ourselves."

"Or . . ." Nolan darts his eyes around the clearing before raising his hand to touch my still-blushing cheek. "We could say screw it and have both."

I'm about to agree, to squash down my need to please Alex and prove to him that I am a friend, not a fan, when Alex's arrival is trumpeted by a squeaky dolly. Nolan drops his hand from my face, but not quickly enough.

Alex makes his eyes comically wide. "Canoodling on the bazaar grounds, are we?"

Nolan rolls his eyes. "Mosquito," he says, and, as if to demonstrate, lightly slaps my cheek with the tips of his fingers. "There was a mosquito on her face. No canoodling here."

It's my turn to say something funny and witty, but I can't think of an appropriate response. My head is still swimming with thoughts of Nolan's sisters, of Jenna, of the distant haze that is my pinky-promised future. Instead, I wind my arm around Nolan's, pulling myself to his side.

"It's only temporary," I tell Alex. "I still have to go back to Texas."

"Temporary." Alex makes a sound like he doesn't believe me, but his eyes leap worriedly to Nolan's face.

"She pinky promised," Nolan says, and I'm proud of the steadiness in his voice. His fingers interlace through mine.

I look up at Nolan, he looks down at me, and for another split second I imagine staying. I allow the whales to swim tight circles around us as I play this game of pretend.

This alternate future unspools before me like a ribbon, and I marvel at its countless photographs, the sheer number of books waiting to be read, the new landscapes waiting to be discovered behind Nolan's eyes.

I ignore the consequences of staying—the disappointment of the Williamses, the weight of Jenna's expectations never easing, the sheer terror of deviating from a set path—and instead imagine long nights of Nolan reading me to sleep, afternoons of one-shot photography, and mornings of being rudely awakened by an ill-behaved mongrel.

"Are you okay with this?"

At first I think Alex is asking if I'm okay with my daydreams, if I'm willing to pay the price to have them spun into reality. But the whales swim away when he clasps Nolan's shoulder in that distinctly boy way as they lock eyes.

Friendship. Pure, sparkling friendship shines between them, and I wonder at the thickness of the thread that has bound them through years and tragedies.

Jenna prickles at my thoughts, and I half wonder whether

the thread that binds *us* is made stronger or weaker by her death. Or maybe it was cut in half the moment she died and now I'm untethered and desperately trying to do anything I can to reconnect us.

Nolan's hand tightens around mine, grounding me. "I'm okay with it," he says to Alex. "It's her choice. Whatever she wants."

We put our bleeding hearts away to begin lighting the trees. Alex keeps stealing looks at me when he thinks I'm too busy unwinding lights, but instead of looking away when our eyes meet, he just smiles down at me from where he and Nolan sit perched on the low branches of the same tree.

It goes quickly. Alex is surprisingly slapdash with his application and even tells Nolan not to be so "precious" about it.

"It's going to look cool even if you don't wrap every single knot."

Nolan doesn't look up from wrapping the world's tiniest twig. "I want it to be perfect," he says.

"I blame you for this, you know." Alex glares at me. "What have you done with my devil-may-care friend?"

I grin. "I canoodled him," I say simply.

Even if we were to string up enough lights to cover the forest of the lost golden-haired princess, it still wouldn't be as bright as Alex's and Nolan's laughter.

That night, when I leave my bed to go to the Orman room, I run the last few steps down the hallway, eager to see Nolan's face after an evening spent with him and Alex, exchanging stories about Jenna and Emily and Avery beside the fireplace downstairs.

We talked for hours, and the more Nolan spoke of Avery's precociousness and Emily's sweetness, the more Alex recounted stories of "those Endsley kids" causing trouble in the lighthouse room, the less dead they seemed. I said so to Nolan, after telling them how Jenna and I met, how she saved me from my own darkness and showed me a real family.

"Talking about her makes me feel like I haven't lost her."

"You haven't," Nolan said. "We haven't lost them. They're not gone; they're just somewhere else."

"Somewhere we aren't, though."

"Yeah," Alex said. "That's the part that's complete shit."

I thought talking about Jenna for so long would hurt, but I feel lighter than air, a helium balloon held to Nolan's fist by the line between us.

We said our good nights when the store closed, but I had only been in bed for an hour when I felt a tug on the thread, a low pulse.

Come away, come away.

He's in the Orman room, and there's no sign of Alex or Wally. And even though we don't fall asleep on the floor this time, we take turns reading from *The Forest Between the Sea and the Sky* until our voices slur with fatigue and all the stars—old and new—have winked out from the early morning sky.

chapter thirteen

When I come down to the store early Friday morning, Nolan is waiting for me. There is a newfound freedom between us, a kind of wild abandonment that can only be found on the other side of sharing dark truths and painful stories. And saliva.

It almost makes me forget that I leave in two days.

Almost.

"Let's buy a bunch of books and go read them at the beach," he says, by way of greeting.

Self-portrait: an hourglass, but instead of sand, it is filled with tiny books, and trick photography is used to make it appear like the subject—me—is trapped inside.

I am both repulsed by and drawn to the rows of books, my flesh recoiling as my soul lurches forward in a desperate attempt to fling itself from my body and wrap around a story. I've been avoiding stories and all their complications, but now that I'm ready to return to them, I'm worried it won't be the same, even after Nolan read to me two nights in a row.

I'm a mess.

I say as much to Nolan, who has selected the history room

as our first destination. A headless mannequin dressed in Regency garb greets us, and there are replicas of major historical documents on the wall.

"We're all messes," he says. "Isn't that the point?"

"Sucky point," I say.

"Sucky world," he answers.

The sentiment seems too harsh and I say so.

"Tell me something that doesn't suck," he says, head hunched over a book he holds open in one palm, with the last bite of an apple in the other.

"Sunsets," I say.

"Heightened by the pollution that is slowly killing our planet," he says.

"Puppies," I say.

"Which part? The one where they are used as meat in some countries or the one where there are more than the world wants so we destroy them?"

It's a stupid game, depressing, and I love it.

"The ocean," I say.

"It's too sandy." He snaps the book closed, puts it back on the shelf, before floating with purpose to the next. "People die in the ocean."

"People die everywhere," I retort, ignoring the slight jab at my heart.

"Exactly," Nolan says. He turns to face me. "Because everything sucks."

We stare at each other. Nolan—unbelievably, blessedly—cracks first. His mouth tilts upward and his eyes finally catch the mirth.

I laugh. "I guess everything has the potential to suck. It just has to be in context."

"Maybe we should do our best to stay out of context, then." It's a joke that, to anyone else, would sound, well, out of context. One of those sad smiles, the kind an author might describe as wan or wistful, settles into my jaw. Because sometimes it feels like you are living a nostalgic moment even while it is happening, like it is too fake or perfect or distant to be truly experienced, and this is one of them.

We move to the Victorian room, with its reading chairs covered in lace, fringed lamps, and ornate blush-pink bookcases. The light fixture is a chandelier dripping with pearls, and music well suited for an Austen heroine's monologue streams softly through speakers. Nolan is scanning the shelves, one finger dragging along spines until he finds what he's after.

"Have you read this?"

I can't make out the title, but the cover portrays a woman in a long gown, on horseback, and the book is almost as thick as a dictionary.

"No?" I say with uncertainty. Nolan drops it definitively into the handled basket at his feet, which already holds two books from the history room.

He's like a bee buzzing from flower to flower, darting around a room loosely organized by the emotions the books provoke. He is about to head to the next room when I spot a familiar royal blue cover with a Scottish word as the title. It makes my chest feel a bit hollow, Jenna's promise to bring me a kilted Highlander coming back to me.

"Have you read this one?" I ask, pushing past the ache.

Nolan lifts an eyebrow. "No. Should I?"

I'm about to explain that the plot is complicated and awesome and involves time travel, Scottish rebellions, and folklore, but I stop myself. I will sound like a crazed fan if I try to do the story justice, but also I don't want to cry about Jenna.

"You should," I say. "I think you'd like it."

Nolan tosses it into the basket. "Did you want to pick anything? Grab whatever you'd like; we'll take them all down to the lake."

I don't comment that he is taking both our hurts—water and books—and combining them into a golden afternoon.

It's so luxurious and extravagant. I shouldn't use Mark's card for such a frivolous purchase, but it's too alluring to resist, and he wouldn't mind. He'd probably be thrilled. I pick a couple of books from the mystery room and one from the adventure room and put them alongside the others.

When we go downstairs to pay, Nolan doesn't bother to ask Valerie to come over from the piano. He goes behind the counter himself and scans each book, stacking them neatly to the side and paying with his card.

"I can pay for mine," I protest.

"Of course you can," he says, putting the books in a canvas tote he extracts from under the counter. "But I can, too. It's not a big deal."

"I should pay for my own," I say, and I wonder why I'm being so insistent.

"Let me do this for you," Nolan says. "Please." And in a move that seems terribly bold, with the clusters of patrons loitering nearby, he reaches forward and touches my cheek. "Let me give you stories."

It's easily the sexiest thing anyone has ever said to me, and suddenly I understand the word *desire* on a whole new level.

We sneak out the back door—so Alex, in his bazaar prep

mayhem, doesn't recruit us to help unclog cotton candy machines—and take Nolan's car to his house so we only have to carry the books down the hill rather than through town. It's the first time I've sat in his car, the leather interior still new and so different from Alex's old truck, but already it feels like I belong.

I don't have time to decide whether this is weird or not.

It *all* feels strange—lying outstretched on the beach next to the fort, our bare toes digging into the sand as Nolan reads from the Scottish romance novel I picked for him, and I from the high fantasy novel he chose. Our other books spill from the tote in a warm scene that promises hours and hours of being lost in separate stories together, like this is something we do and will continue to do every day.

It's surreal, this feeling. It's brand new and bubbly and delicate, but it also feels like I'm remembering it instead of living it, like maybe in some long-ago life I was sitting on this same patch of beach with Nolan Endsley, his dark hair a silhouette against the water.

My internal camera lens must be overactive today. It suggests this would make a perfect photo—Nolan and me by the water as spectral shadow puppets.

In the Orman Chronicles, after the girls discover Emmeline is the new queen, they stumble across a room full of snow globes that contain tiny, confined worlds and real occupants who live inside of them. Emmeline finds this comforting, but to Ainsley it is constraining.

"It looks nice," Emmeline said. "You could have your books and family and whoever else you wanted and nobody else to bother you."

"That's stupid," Ainsley said. "What's the point of being alive if you're not going to be bothered into something better?"

"What's the point of being alive if you're too busy being bothered to do any living?" Emmeline retorted.

Most people agree with Ainsley. It's her quote that gets tattooed on arms, next to words like *wanderlust* and *traveler*, in calligraphy. Jenna was an Ainsley, always reaching for the next branch, the next success. I've always identified as an Emmeline, happy being spontaneous if that spontaneity is confined to a small space.

But my snow globe has been shaken up, and now I'm not so sure.

But if I must be confined, I wish this could be my snow globe forever, this moment with Nolan Endsley. The possibility is stuck in my throat in a small, hopeful lump.

I set my book down and stare out over the lake. A speedboat races across the horizon and the occasional distant shriek of water-skiers meets my ears. Gulls circle overhead, their greedy cries melting into the sound of lapping waves. I tilt my head back and imagine taking a photo of a seagull from beneath its flight, against the dazzling blue sky. *A Bird's Belly View*. It would be stupid and cheesy enough that even Jenna would have been tempted to laugh. She would have pinned it on her wall, too.

I try to return to my book, but after reading the same page twice, I throw it behind me with a groan.

"That bad?" Nolan asks, without looking up from his book. His expression is rapt, consumed by the story. "Did a character die?"

"No," I say. "I'm just . . . I'm lost."

There's a sharp jab in the fat of my right hip, and I roll over to see Nolan's prying finger retreating to turn a page.

"Found you," he says. "You can't be lost with somebody sitting right next you. . . . Do you ever find out if the ghost in this book is actually a ghost? And do the stones work for everyone or just her?"

The cynic in me wants to argue that togetherness does not cancel out lostness. Instead, the whales come back, even though I keep swearing I don't need them anymore, and I let myself sink back into the snow globe with Nolan.

Two hours pass before Nolan's phone begins to ring, an unsophisticated, robotic melody that is nothing like modern ringtones.

"Nineteen ninety-five is calling," I quip.

"We weren't even *alive* in nineteen ninety-five," Nolan says, before he shuts the ringer off and goes back to his book.

"Anyone important?" I ask.

Nolan half smiles at me over the book, settling onto his stomach in the warm sand. "Not particularly."

This is proven incorrect when, fifteen minutes later, a red pickup comes roaring into the driveway of the blue house on the hill above us.

Nolan and I sit up, brushing sand from our arms and stretching away the sunny laziness and our respective plots as Alex comes stomping down the hill, his face thunderous.

"Hi, Alex," I say, when his feet sink into the sand, but he ignores me and heads straight for Nolan, who looks like he would consider going for a swim in the lake rather than deal with his friend.

"Alex," he begins. "Dude, what's your—"

"My problem?" Alex has stopped a foot away from where

Nolan sits, one hand clenched around his cell phone, the other tugging at the collar of his shirt. "My problem, Nolan, is *somebody* forgot to confirm the inflatable waterslide last month, when they said they would, so the company rented it out to an end-of-summer bash in *Wisconsin!* And now, less than twenty-four hours before the bazaar that I finally, *finally* convinced Mom I can handle planning on my own, our biggest chance of direct donations is in the toilet, and I didn't even *know* about it because my best friend is an ass who didn't bother to tell me."

"I forgot." Nolan scrambles to his feet. "I forgot, and when I remembered, I figured *you* probably called to confirm, because that's how we work: You give me an assignment, I ignore the assignment, and you do it yourself. I'm an idiot, and you fix it."

There's a touch of exasperated humor in Nolan's tone, and I think Alex can hear it, because he leans forward like he might actually strangle Nolan.

"What's the big deal? What about the booths and stuff?" I ask.

Alex's look is cutting. "Amelia, I like you. *Nolan* likes you. It would pain me to dump you in the lake. Stay out of this."

"Lay off her, Alex," Nolan says. "Besides, she's right. You've got tons of booths. It'll be fine."

If Alex had magic powers that could summon storms, we'd all be killed in a fiery sharknado.

"The waterslide was *supposed* to be rented at a steep discount," he grits out. "And we were going to charge a dollar a slide, which means we could make *a whole lot of money.* It's the biggest earner at the festival. *Now* our best hope is that Mr. Larson's donated hand-knit scarves will sell."

"DIY and handmade stuff is in," Nolan pipes up hopefully.

Alex's anger breaks off long enough for him to give Nolan's uniform of jeans and an old T-shirt a withering look.

"Yes, Nolan, because you are *so* in tune with what is hip and cool."

"Look," I interrupt. "There has to be something else we can do that will be cheap and bring in money."

"Not on such short notice, we can't. I've already thought of everything," Alex says.

Nolan snorts. "I doubt that."

"Fine, Nolan, *you* think of something. And if you can't, I'm going to improvise a pie-throwing booth, and guess who I'll put in the hot seat for *that*?"

Loose tendrils of possibility collect into a little ball that I turn over and over in my head. It's a great idea—surefire—but Nolan might kill me if I suggest it.

"Out with it," Nolan says, reading my face. "Whatever it is, it better not have anything to do with pie."

"Well . . ." I begin. "Seeing as how it *is* your fault, Nolan . . ."

"What is it?" Alex asks.

I look at Nolan, watching his reaction as I mumble, "You could have a signing."

Nolan is already shaking his head, and Alex crows with laughter. "A book signing. Like, with people? Amelia, are we talking about the same person? You have a better shot at the pie booth."

I drop my gaze from Nolan, looking at my feet. "It could be ticketed. *No* cost. Every cent would go toward the library."

"And after, we can invite the fairies," Alex says blankly. "Right after Santa comes out with his reindeer and the Easter Bunny hides some eggs."

I'm growing hot with embarrassment when Nolan says, "Alex. *Lay off.* She's only trying to help."

"Yeah, well, I need actual help, not harebrained ideas."

"It's not harebrained," Nolan says. "I'm going to do it."

"It *is* harebrained. You're never going to . . ." Alex trails off, his eyes widening. "Wait. What did you just say?"

"It's not a bad idea," Nolan says nonchalantly. "She's right. It'll probably bring in more money than the waterslide."

Alex's arms are loose by his side, his phone almost slipping out of his hand. He looks between Nolan and me like he's watching a Ping-Pong match, his slackened jaw giving him a dorky expression.

"Where are we going to get enough Orman books on short notice?" Alex asks.

Nolan looks to me and I shrug. "People can bring them from home. They'll pay for the signatures."

"Anything else we can help you with, Alex?" Nolan's tone is practiced boredom. "I, for one, would like to get back to reading, if that's all right with you."

Alex shakes his head, still stunned. "You're really going to do it?"

Nolan lifts a corner of his mouth before answering, "Everything sucks anyway. I might as well be useful if I'm going to be miserable." When Alex stands there staring, Nolan raises his eyebrows. "Is that all?"

"Um . . ." Alex's voice is dazed. "Our, um, event photographer has been recruited to help with the sound system. He's the only one who knows how to work the portable speakers. I don't suppose you know how to fix that, too?"

If I had doubts that Jenna had anything to do with this,

they're carried away by the sudden gust of wind that blows among the three of us.

A slow grin melts across Nolan's face. I shake my head.

"No," I say. "No, I'm not any good. I'm not even a hobbyist. I *have* a camera; it doesn't mean I really know how to—"

"You have a camera?" Alex breathes out in relief. "Brilliant! You're hired. It only pays in cotton candy and fried hot dogs, I'm afraid, but you'll work perfectly. Consider it your rent for living with Mom for the week!"

I don't want to do this. I mean, I do, but I don't. This is not on plan. Worse, it's another brick in a wall I will eventually have to knock down.

This trip was supposed to be about figuring out the 101st edition mystery and going home, ready to face my future, but instead I'm sinking into the quicksand that is my love of photography, my hands itching to hold my camera.

"Okay?" Nolan asks.

He won't push, I realize. If I really don't want to, they'll figure out something else. But somewhere the whales are swimming, and they don't care what I do for one evening, so before I can second-guess it again, I tell Alex, "Yes. I'll take photos for you."

I'm surprised when Alex's arms wrap around my shoulders in a firm embrace.

"Thank you," he whispers.

And somehow I know he isn't thanking me for the photography.

chapter fourteen

The next evening, I am transfixed as the snow globe morphs from a lakeside retreat to a glowing festival of color and sound.

Alex was right about the trees. Even though the strands aren't tightly wound, the sheer volume of lights makes the air crackle with delight and whimsy. If Val's is an enchanted castle surrounded by a magical forest, then this bazaar is the bustling magical marketplace in stories, where the heroine goes to sell her wares to feed her family.

In the Orman books, Emmeline and Ainsley have a high-stakes chase through a night market. They run as quickly as they can but are constantly besieged by people selling their goods—magic potions, flowers that smell like fresh bread, quilts sewn with black thread that promise to keep them warm no matter how bitter the weather.

I'm beginning to see where Nolan got the idea. From where I stand, I count at least two dozen booths. Most sell handmade goods or food, but the booth closest to me sells succulents and air plants bedded inside glass ornaments. They hang, catching the lights from the trees.

It's like I've fallen into another time.

Two little boys run past me, almost knocking me over in their excitement as they clamber over to the woman selling cotton candy and popcorn. I snap a picture of them in motion, their bodies blurred against a solid background of oak-green wooden booths and the much taller legs of the adults standing behind them. I don't know what I'll call it yet, but it brings to mind wind chimes. I think of Emily and Avery. They probably ran through this bazaar, too. I think of Jenna. The whales waft happily between booths like great blue storm clouds.

The camera strap around my neck feels like a warm scarf against the slight chill in the air, and I wonder how long my hair will hold the scent of caramel popcorn and fried dough.

"Like it?"

I half assume it's Nolan at first, but Alex is the one smiling at me. His eyes are strained around the corners, and expectant, like what I think of the bazaar really matters.

"Alex, it's beautiful," I say. "Like, crazy good."

He nods, like this is bare-minimum praise. "So, not too bad?"

"I'm sure your mom is proud," I try again.

"You haven't been going to these every year for your whole life," Alex says. "It's . . . maybe just barely okay in comparison."

"It's the best I've seen," Nolan says. He comes up between Alex and me and bumps his shoulder against Alex's. "You re-designed the layout of the booths."

Alex shrugs. "I thought maybe if the food vendors were spread out instead of in one spot, it might increase foot traffic and encourage people to try more than one thing, and—"

"Alex," Nolan interrupts. "It's awesome. Really."

What a strange turn of events, Nolan bolstering Alex with

confidence and kindness. Even though he's nearly obsessed with the perfection of the bazaar, Alex must realize this, too, because the look he gives Nolan is a mix of pride and surprise.

I raise my camera and take a photo.

"Bromance," I say, cupping my hand around the screen to see the thumbnail. "Aww, it turned out cute."

"Cute," Alex says, right as Nolan says, "Delete that immediately."

Nolan goes for the camera, but I jerk it out of his reach, catching some of my hair in the neck strap and wincing.

"No way. It's your fault I'm playing photographer, and now you want to rain on my creativity? I don't think so."

Nolan shoots Alex a sardonic look.

"Is it too late to get a less manipulative photographer?"

"I'll call up Dr. Faust," Alex deadpans. "Maybe he'll have an idea."

I'm filled with a goofiness that surprises me, wiggling my fingers at them brazenly over my shoulder as I go to take photos of the booths.

It seems everyone in town and then some has shown up to shop and eat their fill. An untamed energy runs like a current from booth to booth, sweeping up couples walking hand in hand and kids begging smiling parents to *Look at this* or *Bring one of these home.*

I tell myself I'm only taking pictures because it is helping Alex and Nolan and an underfunded elementary school library, but my camera and I know I'm lying. I keep obsessively checking my photos, unexpected pride filling me when I see that I've managed to capture a candid smile or a whiff of this place's spirit through my lens.

I want the photos to be good and real *for me.*

Through the lens, I watch Mr. Larson dress up kids from the local elementary school as models for his knitted wares, lining them up in front of his booth with misshapen mittens crammed onto their small fingers and lopsided scarves fitted snugly around their necks. Wally sits obediently next to a girl in pigtails, sporting a blue knit collar and a rawhide bone.

Valerie's students are playing an upright piano on a low wooden stage that has been set up at the center of the bazaar. She watches fondly, absently fiddling with her looped necklaces and giving a quiet smile. I snap a photo and call it *The Sorcerer's Apprentice.*

The wind blows hair into my face and I whisper, "It's only one night. Nothing more," just in case it is clever.

The wind must have other concerns, though, because I feel a slight tug on the thread connecting me to the boy who spends his nights reading aloud on the Orman room floor.

Help.

When I find him, Nolan is sitting alone at a table in front of a huge line, trying to sign the books of three squealing tweens who keep jumbling around the table to take selfies with his downturned head.

"This is going to get *so. Many. Likes,*" one of the girls says.

"Do you think Justine is going to be jealous? She's going to be *so* jealous," her friend responds.

I make my way through the throng to Nolan's side. He's got the world's fakest smile plastered on his face and his eyes are wild.

"Where's Alex?" I ask. "I thought he was going to stay with you for crowd control?"

"Popcorn emergency," Nolan mutters. "Said he'd be back ten minutes ago."

Their books signed, the three girls walk off, after dropping a couple of bucks each into the glass jar labeled "Library Donations." It sits next to another jar that reads "3 tickets per signature." That one is already half full of blue tickets. It's been less than thirty minutes and Nolan has already seen half a jar's worth of people.

I have to help him.

Before the next fan can step to the table, I gesture widely with a smile.

"Hello, there! Thanks so much for waiting. We're only doing signatures this evening, but I will take photos of you at the table and post them to Val's website."

Nolan and I work as a well-oiled machine, me stepping into the role of crowd control, personal photographer, and name speller, all in one. Everyone seems okay with the stipulation of no personal photos, though some ask why they can't go behind the table. I tell them the truth.

"It's overwhelming," I say to one disgruntled middle-aged woman. "And if he's going to get through all these signatures, we need to keep the line moving."

Nolan overhears this and shoots me a grateful smile.

"Holding up?" I ask him, as the woman collects her *six* books.

"Just," he says. "Just."

The quaint lampposts Alex has managed to position on either side of the signing table cast Nolan's face in shadow, and I resist the urge to press the pad of my thumb against the scrunch between his eyebrows. I want to take him away, to tell him he will never have to sit behind a table and be stared at by people again.

Instead, I briefly squeeze his hand beneath the table, and

ask, "Does it help or hurt to know that all of these people are carrying around a version of Avery and Emily?"

As if conjured by my question, two young girls step eagerly to the table. It's obvious they're sisters, the younger a shorter carbon copy of the other. The little girl can't reach the top of the ticket jar, comically straining on tiptoe. Her sister plucks the tickets from her outstretched hand and deposits them with her own. With that taken care of, the little girl zooms around the table and wiggles between Nolan and me.

"Can I sit here?" She points at a frozen Nolan's lap. "I can't see over there." Her voice is a little too loud and much too brazen in a way only young children's can be. The look in her eye makes me think of the glint in Ainsley's when she first sees Orman.

The folding table we set up for the signing isn't tall, but she's right—it's just high enough that she can't get a clear view of Nolan, especially in the dim lighting. To her, it probably seems like a perfectly ordinary solution, born of a lifetime of being hoisted onto shoulders and bent knees.

I'm about to kindly let her down, to guide her back to where her sister stands, shifting foot to foot, embarrassed, when Nolan leans forward in his chair and addresses the little girl directly.

"Do you have a book for me to sign?"

His voice is so warm and gentle it makes me pause.

The girl points over the table to her sister. "We share," she says. "She reads. I listen. She says I read too slow."

"You'll get faster." Nolan laughs as he rises from his chair to slide onto folded knees next to the little girl. "Can you see now?"

She looks hard at his face and twists her mouth, pointing a chubby finger back at her sister. "Jennifer thinks you're cute."

Nolan blinks in a way that makes me think he wants to scoot this little girl back to her side of the table, but she plows on.

"What happens to Emmeline and Ainsley? Jennifer says if we were in Orman she would feed me to the sirens to get some quiet, but that doesn't happen, right?"

"Julie," the red-faced older sister warns as she hands Nolan a pristine copy of his second book. "Let Mr. Endsley sign our book so he can meet the other people, okay?"

But little Julie will not be deterred, and I'm starting to think this will end in a tantrum—Julie's or Nolan's—when Nolan cups his hand around Julie's ear.

As he whispers, Julie's face glows, the sun peeking through clouds after days of rain. They sit this way for at least a minute, and it takes a curious glance from Jennifer to remind me of my role as event photographer. I snap a picture of this pilfered moment in the grass.

Nolan and Julie melt away. Inside the lens, they shift, and Nolan whispers to another little girl, one that shares his dark waves and seafoam eyes, and he's an older brother revealing the location of the hidden holiday gifts.

Nolan doesn't see this little girl as Ainsley of Orman. To him, she is Avery Endsley.

There is a very good chance that this exact photo exists somewhere else in the world, with these players in these poses, but it's *this* context that makes it special. It's because it *is* Nolan and Julie in the damp grass while quiet Jennifer looks on that makes the photo worth taking at all.

As Nolan pulls away to sign the book, I break my rule and take three photos in quick succession. I can't resist capturing all the moments of Julie spelling her name aloud while Jennifer shyly gazes at Nolan. The photos are no less real or special for being one of many.

There's no time to ask Nolan what he whispered to Julie. The line of people is getting restless. He signs for what feels like hours more, and even though he's strained from interacting with this many people, he handles it well. Since the sisters left, the squint between his eyes has eased.

When I lower my camera from what must be at least the three hundredth photo, I find Alex at my side. His curly hair is sticking up in all directions and I smooth it into place as he pushes a cold water bottle into my other hand. Alex and I are now associates on the Care and Keeping of Nolan Endsley team and I am happy.

Something inside me sparkles at having a friend and a common cause, but I force my voice to be casual when I ask, "Rough night?"

Alex shrugs. "It's going surprisingly well. There were some popcorn issues and Wally was stealing hot dogs from an open cooler, but besides the guy that complained about Mr. Larson's coffee, most everyone seems to be having a good time."

"I saw your mom earlier," I say. "She was pretty happy about only being on piano duty."

I step forward to moderate a gaggle of young boys who want Nolan to sign their books at the same time. I take their photo, hand Nolan the rest of the water, and return to Alex.

"Rough night?" Alex asks me my own question. He hasn't looked away from the line still stretched out in front of the signing table.

I shrug and smile. "Surprisingly well. I don't feel comfortable leaving him, though. The crowd . . ." I trail off. There's no need to explain to my many-years-senior associate.

"I hated to leave him," Alex says. "But I hated it less, knowing you would turn up."

There's something odd about his tone, so I stay quiet, uncertain.

"You know," he says, "and I mean this with all sincerity, I'm not saying it to make you stay, but you're maybe the best thing that's happened to Nolan in a really, really long time."

Stay. No, no, no. I will not let the weight of my leaving crush this evening where Nolan Endsley is smiling at me and Alex is treating me like a real friend and my camera is not collecting dust but is helping me breathe again. I push away the closeness of tomorrow and make myself focus on the whales to keep the unwanted thoughts away.

I try to blow it off. "It could have been anybody. He just needed someone to see him as himself instead of as N. E."

Alex turns his head downward to look at me. "Yes, because I'm sure he would have told *any* random girl about his sisters after only three days."

My eyes leap to Nolan. The small furrow between his brows disappears completely when our eyes meet, and he smiles in my direction. I wave at him with one hand, a goofy smile covering my face before I can stop it.

Alex watches this exchange with his know-it-all smile and I want to punch him in the throat.

"It's not like that," I tell him. "We're friends."

Lies. Alex isn't buying it.

"Amelia, don't be an imbecile. Friends don't touch other

friends' faces and stare into their eyes like the sun is shining out of their every pore."

I loll my head toward him and try to ignore the pitter-pattering of my heart when I think of Nolan looking at me like that.

"That's beautiful, Alex. Have you considered taking up writing? Nolan could use the competition."

He grins. "Computers are more my thing. Much more straightforward. I have enough drama from keeping after Nolan. I don't need to invent more."

"Am I part of that drama?"

He taps a finger against his chin, pretending to consider. "You certainly were an unexpected addition, yes."

And even though everything has become so convoluted, because it's the last night and I still want to know, I ask, "Do you really not know who sent me the book? Who brought me here?"

He looks away, playfulness gone. "If you ask me, it's fate."

I frown. "*Fate* isn't real. It's for storybooks and Disney movies. I refuse to believe it's real."

"Fate doesn't need to be believed in for it to be true."

I roll my eyes. "Did I miss a chance to photograph the fortune cookie booth? Fate has nothing to do with any of this. I don't know how she did it, but Jenna arranged for me to get that book. I showed up, and—"

"It wasn't Jenna, Amelia. It was fate."

Alex and his stupid walls. Now I'm trapped in the festival behind his eyes and in the one he's created in real life, and it's as if he's determined to keep me inside and make me believe in things I've long since abandoned.

I gave up on fate when I learned that Jenna was dead.

I'm about to tell him so, to push Alex away with a few sharp words about what he can do with *fate*, when he says, "I hope you two didn't have any ideas about making out in the Orman room tonight, because I need your help. When the bazaar is over, meet me at the marina. Bring Nolan."

I'm grumpy, but too curious not to ask, "What's at the marina?"

Alex winks. "You'll see."

As he walks back toward the bazaar, I ask, "How do you know I'll come?"

Without turning, Alex calls, "It's your fate."

chapter fifteen

After the fireworks are over and the twinkle lights blink off, Nolan signs his last signature and slouches onto the table with a low groan.

I pat his shoulder half comfortingly, half jokingly, and his hand reaches up to cover mine, holding it in place. Neither of us says anything. The thread between us glows bright and I know what this means to him. A curse has been broken, and Alex, Valerie, and I are probably the only ones who understand what this night has cost Nolan.

We listen to plastic chests full of slushy melted ice and water being poured into flower beds, the sleepy mutterings of cotton candy machine operators, and—distantly—a barking Wally who has eaten his fill of discarded nachos and hot dog buns. Alex is still dancing along the periphery of the bazaar, collecting blue pouches of cash and tickets.

"You okay?" Nolan asks, his voice hoarse from talking to the entirety of Lochbrook and then some.

"I am," I say. My surprise at this truth warms my voice. "Are you?"

He looks up at me, his eyes crinkling at the corners when he says, "I guess not *everything* sucks."

When Nolan recuperates enough to rise from the table, we stand close together, the tips of his fingers nudging my side as we look up at the stars through the puffs of firework smoke lingering in the sky. I slip my hand firmly into his and ask, "What did you tell her? That little girl?"

He laughs. "What she wanted to know, of course."

I drop his hand without thinking and turn to face him, but his gaze stays focused on the heavens.

"You told her what happens to the girls in Orman? Really?"

He's quiet for a minute. "You never asked why I agreed to the signing," he says in answer.

"To help Alex," I say.

"No."

"To help Valerie?"

He drops his gaze to me, his mouth quirking. In this light, his cheekbones almost look as sharp as they do in his author photo.

"Because if I can do that"—he points at the signing area—"you can do anything." He reaches down and nudges the camera where it hangs below my chest. "Anything."

We're silent, Nolan staring at me until I drop my gaze to fiddle with the camera lens.

"It's not that simple," I say. I can't meet his eyes, so I speak to the camera. "It sounds cheesy, but it's true. If your sisters had asked you to do one thing before they died, something totally in your power, that wouldn't hurt you and might even *help* you . . . wouldn't you do it? For them?"

Nolan doesn't answer. It is answer enough.

"I have to go tomorrow," I say. "I can't stay, Nolan. You know that, right?"

224 • ashley schumacher

He reaches down and squeezes my hand.

"Nolan," I try again. "I need you to—"

"Shh," he says. "Pretend with me."

And with Nolan's warm fingers between mine, I do. I let the whales swoop in on a wind much cleverer than I, and I don't think of what it will cost me to leave this snow globe tomorrow.

It's a walkable distance to the marina, where boats of all shapes and sizes bob on gentle waves. Our footsteps echo across the wooden planks as Nolan guides me to a modest blue pontoon boat, his tight hold on my hand the only indication that he's bothered being near the water.

"Okay?" I ask.

He squeezes my hand. "I'll always be okay when I'm with you, Amelia."

When I look up at him, his dark hair blends into the night sky and his eyes become tiny constellations. I want to look at him forever, but tomorrow's departure is settling into my stomach like a stone and I'm having a hard time forgetting.

"You'll have to be okay after I'm gone, you know," I say.

He tilts his head to look at the sky. "I know," he says quietly. A pause. "I talked to my editor this morning."

I suddenly become very interested in our linked hands.

"And?" I whisper.

He nudges my chin up and I try to trace the patterns of the stars in his eyes.

"It does help." His voice is soft. "It helps that others can know shadows of who Avery and Emily were by reading about Orman. It helps."

There's a significant pause.

"I'm sending them the final book."

"Nolan." I breathe. "Are you sure? Really?"

His smile is lopsided, and he looks down at our feet, embarrassed. "I am. It's not perfect, but it doesn't have to be. It's . . . for them."

I throw my arms around his neck and I'm kissing him. Not a drowning kiss, not a final-good-bye kiss, but a kiss of wonder and surprise.

It's another too perfect moment, made all the less real by my leaving tomorrow. It makes me hesitate and I draw back, but before Nolan can ask what's wrong, Alex is thumping his way down the dock.

Wally gets to us first, licking our knees before crashing onto the pontoon boat, standing on the worn plush seats and barking at nothing and then rushing busily to the back of the boat and out of sight.

Alex's face is that mixture of exhaustion and relief that comes at the end of a particularly long day. His hair is askew again, and when he sees me looking, he leans down so I can brush it back into place. He straightens and claps his hands together.

"You're probably wondering why I summoned you to the dock. The bad news is we are sadly bereft of a floating vessel. The good news is Mr. Larson agreed to loan us his for the evening."

"But what about Nolan's—"

Alex cuts me off with a wave.

"We don't have to leave the dock. But I figured it would be nice to have dinner under the stars instead of in the store."

Nolan's hand tightens in mine. "We can take it out," he says.

When he sees our doubtful faces, he adds, "Really. It might be fun."

I can tell Alex doesn't want to risk upsetting Nolan, but I ask, "Will it help you or hurt you if we are out on the water?"

His hand lets go of mine, and he pulls me softly to his side. Alex studiously ignores us, looking down at his phone.

"I think it'll help," Nolan whispers. "Maybe we'll wash up on an island somewhere and you'll have to stay."

"Or we'll get stranded on Orman," I say, because this is the best kind of pretend.

"God, I hope not." Alex laughs, giving up the pretense that he isn't listening in. "Wally wouldn't last five minutes against a tree knight."

"*You* wouldn't last five minutes against a tree knight," Nolan says.

The two of them keep bickering as Alex unties us from the dock and starts the engine. Lights flicker on around the edge of the boat, but even so, Alex says we can't go too far at night.

True to his word, he kills the engine when the shore is still well within sight. It would be swimmable, if need be, but it's far enough away from Lochbrook and Val's to make us feel we're somewhere else entirely.

We're all staring up at the stars when Nolan says, "This is perfect."

"Nothing's perfect," Alex says.

I smile. "This is."

Perfection lasts about two minutes before Alex announces that Wally has peed on the cooler, contaminating our elaborate dinner of wine, cheese, crackers, and little rolls of lunch meat.

"Alex, there was hardly enough food in here to feed a rabbit anyway," Nolan says, peering into the urine-soaked cooler.

"It was supposed to be a charcuterie plate. Besides, rabbits are herbivores."

"Hardly the point." Nolan sighs. "I'm starving."

Wally, sensing the change in mood, is sitting shamefaced behind the wheel of the boat. I suspect if he had opposable thumbs, he would have steered us back to the dock.

I lean around Nolan to gaze upon the damage wrought by what must be the world's most idiotic dog. "Is *charcuterie* French for 'after-school snack'? Because that's what this looks like."

"I mean, most of it is packaged in plastic," Alex says, fishing out a baggie of cheese cubes. "Maybe it's okay to eat?"

A glistening drop of pee trembles on the edge of the bag, and Nolan and I both lean backwards.

"*Fine,*" Alex says. "Fine. We won't risk the food. But look!" He holds a shiny bottle triumphantly above his head. "The wine is one hundred percent okay to drink."

Nolan eyes the glistening bottle, damp from ice or pee, and nods. "Fine, but you're pouring."

The sky is the kind of pitch-black dark that makes you feel too small, where you can only just make out hazy puffs that might be clouds or distant galaxies.

I go home tomorrow, but here the whales can take a night swim and splash me into forgetting about everything except my growling stomach and the way Nolan's back looks solid and strong even though he's hunched over with his elbows on his knees, the wine bottle dangling from a hand. It had to be wiped clean because Alex forgot the paper cups, though he blamed their absence on Wally, too.

Nolan passes the bottle to me, and without thinking too much about it, I take a swig. Jenna's disapproval at our three-way underage drinking radiates from wherever she is, and I try to appease her. *Alex is almost as responsible as you*, I tell her in my head.

"Pregnant," Alex announces. He's lying outstretched on one of the cushioned benches. Wally sits at his feet, occasionally licking the bit of exposed ankle between pant leg and shoe in apology.

He's had a long day, I add.

"Wally is regrettably bereft of the necessary organs to support a pregnancy, Alexander. Try again." Nolan stands with a little wobble, his posture made looser by the proximity to the water or the wine or both, and then arranges himself on the bench to mirror Alex, his head in my lap.

Alex throws the cork at Nolan, but he misses and it plunks into the water. Wally jolts up to bark but then thinks better of exhibiting any more bad behavior and sinks back down onto Alex's ankles.

"I was talking about things I hate in books," Alex says, like it's totally obvious. "I hate when anything other than a person carrying a fetus is described as 'pregnant.' How can a moment be pregnant with silence? Is it going to give birth to silence? Won't that be loud?"

Without being asked, I hand the bottle to Alex. He unsuccessfully attempts to take a sip while lying down and spills at least a quarter of the bottle onto his shirt.

I wince. *Okay*, I tell Jenna. *This is a really bad example, but I swear he's usually very sensible.*

"Alexander's brain is fried," Nolan announces.

"Is not," Alex says. "It's relieved the bazaar is over, and slightly intoxicated. There's a difference."

"You've barely had two sips of wine," I argue. "You can't be feeling it yet."

"You know what I *am* feeling?" Alex straightens up and hands the bottle to Nolan. "That my head is fuzzy from too many nights of too little sleep, and probably hunger-induced delusion. Let's all share a stupid story. Go."

Nolan and I look dumbly at each other and then at Alex.

"Fine," Alex says. "I'll start for you. Nolan took fencing in college."

"You went to school?" I had assumed he hadn't gone.

He sighs. "One semester."

"That's it?"

"That's it."

I can tell he would rather not talk about it, but it's the last night and I've had enough wine to warm my insides, so I ask, "What was your major?"

"I didn't really have one. I just took classes I thought might be interesting."

"They were all English classes, except for fencing," Alex pipes up helpfully.

I look down into Nolan's face. "And you didn't like the English stuff?"

Nolan drops my gaze. "No. I didn't like how author names were suddenly trading cards, a kind of academic currency. They didn't have any real meaning. And everybody loved to argue over which one was the rarest, the most valuable, but nobody wanted to . . ." He falters and throws his arms up haphazardly, trying to make his frustration tangible.

"Read?" I ask.

He nods and then, eager to switch subjects, adds, "Besides, Alex will end up doing enough school for both of us combined. He's going to live and die in academia."

Alex, who appears to be doing his best impression of being drunk on less than one glass of wine, will not let Nolan's college experience go.

"Oh! Speaking of fencing, tell her about the sword thing."

Nolan blushes so hard I'm worried the boat might catch fire.

"Don't you want to know why he carries around that ridiculous phone?" Alex asks.

"If he wants to tell me." I keep my voice neutral. If I sound too excited, Nolan will balk. He sighs and rolls off my lap and into a sitting position, his face grumpy.

A pause. "It was because of a review."

"Like that explains everything," Alex mutters, and I shush him.

Nolan glares at Alex before turning to me. "Long story short, I read a bad early review on my phone. It pissed me off. I broke the phone. End of story."

Now Alex is sitting up, dislodging his legs from Wally's girth.

"Oh no it isn't. You *stabbed* your brand-new phone with a literal bejeweled *sword*."

I can't bite back my laughter at the ridiculous image in my head. Nolan poised above his cell phone, the hilt of a sword clutched between two hands as if he had just pulled it from a stone. It's ridiculous enough to be one of my fantastical photos.

"You stabbed your phone?" I repeat. "And where did you get a sword?"

Nolan opens his mouth to answer, but Alex beats him to it. "He *bought* it. Custom-made, too. It was like, literally the first thing he bought when his advance check came in. I know, because he sent me a picture of it. This was of course before he had a phone camera that was complete crap."

"Who doesn't want a sword?" Nolan asks indignantly.

Alex immediately raises his hand. He looks to me and waits expectantly. When I don't move, he scoffs.

"You must really have it bad for him if you're willing to pretend you would spend actual real-life dollars on a sword."

"I think it would be neat," I say. I don't mention that, after years of traveling through wardrobes and sailing to foreign lands, I've already thought of what name I would give my weapon. (Pen. Because it's mightier than the sword.) "A lot of people have swords."

"Yeah," Alex says. "But most people don't use them to stab their phones until they are so broken even the manufacturer's help desk says it's beyond repair."

Nolan looks at me, shamefaced. "It was a really bad review. *And* I was only fifteen."

"But that doesn't explain the clunker phone from the eighteen hundreds," I say.

Alex bursts into loud hearty laughter so contagious that even Nolan joins in.

"He did it *twice*," Alex wheezes. "He got a new phone and read another review and stabbed it *again*."

"I was *fifteen*," Nolan reminds us through his laughter. "No impulse control. It was easier to get a crappy phone to stab instead of banking on my ability to walk away."

"He keeps saying he'll get a new phone, but he never does," Alex tells the floor of the boat. He's bent over to put his head

232 • ashley schumacher

between his knees, taking in deep gulps of air around more peals of laughter.

"It hasn't broken yet. No reason to get something new," Nolan says. "And the best part is that I don't have the review app on here, so I haven't even wanted to stab it."

When our laughing fit passes, it grows quiet, and we lounge and look at the stars. It's late enough that I feel the dark weaving the old kind of magic that has bound friends together through decades of sleepovers and accidental late-night talks on porches and doorsteps. There's something about the absence of light mixed with near-exhaustion that loosens tongues and strengthens relationships.

I don't fight the memory of Jenna when it comes for me. It's less a single remembrance and more a cobbled-together picture of admitting deep truths to each other, stretched out over dozens of nights.

Some nights I would let my anger and confusion about my parents boil over. I would rail against how absent they felt, the unfairness that the two people who once argued playfully over the placement of glow-in-the-dark stars on my ceiling could fall so out of love with each other, and with me.

But on the good nights, we would talk about things that secretly delighted us, our hopes and dreams for futures we didn't quite believe were real.

Remembering those—and that there won't be more with Jenna—puts a lump in my throat. I swallow around it.

"Resurrection," I say, breaking the silence.

"Huh?" Alex says.

I can't see Nolan's face—we're lying with our heads side by side and our bodies stretched out to opposite ends of the bench—but his cheek lifts against mine.

"The thing she hates in books," he says.

"Why?"

"It's . . ." I stop, collecting my thoughts before they scatter to the stars. "I used to not mind it, but now the idea of somebody dying and being brought back just makes me angry that I wasn't born into a world that can *do* that. It's so far outside of my experience with death, I can't even entertain it anymore."

They're quiet for so long, I wonder if I've broken the mood. Wally slinks over to curl up on my feet and rest his huge head on my kneecaps. He looks at me with large brown eyes that seem to understand the tangle of emotions in my chest. I rub behind his ears and wish on a star that if I am ever sent to a place where animals are magically bound to human companions, I'll get a dog like Wally. Accident prone and all.

In my head, I take a photo of me standing triumphantly on a hill, hands on hips, feet parted, my fearless horse-sized dog at my side, his head tilted up into the wind and tongue lolling. *Disaster Duo,* I call it. It's up to the viewer to choose whether they are fixing disasters or causing them.

"Death sucks," Alex whispers.

"Everything sucks," Nolan answers. I laugh low in my throat at our inside joke, and Nolan trails his fingertips across my lips like he might catch it.

We spend the evening outstretched like this, unmoored from the shore and sensible conversation. We talk about death and how it sucks and where do we go when it happens. (Nolan: Heaven. Alex: Not sure. Me: Somewhere else, but not nowhere.) Alex shares his favorite memories of summers with the Endsley kids, most of which involved filched ice cream and forts made out of books. (They once got in trouble for the forts because they damaged an entire shipment of brand-new hardbacks that, after, had to be sold at a discount.) Nolan tells me about how he and Alex spent the first month after Nolan bought his family's summer home painting over the green walls with light gray paint, managing to mess it up so badly that Nolan had to hire professionals to redo everything.

I tell them about Jenna. How her lipstick saved me, about Moot and family dinners where I never felt like an extra puzzle piece that didn't fit. We laugh as I recount the time I pushed her into the Williamses' pool fully clothed and she hauled me in after her and I ended up with a black eye when my face met her knee. We laugh harder when I tell them it was the day before a dance and Jenna was furious because she had labored over finding makeup to match the dress she made me wear. She had not accounted for greenish-yellow skin as a base for eye shadow.

Our laughter dies off, lulled by the soft waves grazing the boat, the distant sounds of Lochbrook going to sleep for the night.

"If Nolan's right and we all end up in a heaven somewhere," Alex says, "I want Jenna to train Wally. I think she's the only one who can do it. I really do."

Nolan walks me to the door of Val's, and I almost ask him to stay with me in the Orman room. But he looks too tired to endure another night of sleeping against bookcases, so I say, "See you tomorrow, right?"

"Tomorrow," he promises. I think he's going to kiss me good night, but he doesn't.

Behind his eyes, I watch the forest start to darken, as if the sky around us is sucking out his light. "You never asked my least favorite thing about books," he says.

I don't ask. I don't want to. I want to go on pretending that this night is the first of many bazaars I will photograph, the first of many nights I'll go to bed hungry because Wally ruined a planned dinner.

But Nolan tells me anyway.

"I hate endings," he says. "Hate them. If the story is good, it's never going to be long enough."

The words are out of my mouth before I can hold the sentence in my head. "But we keep reading."

Nolan's smile is lazy and slow and my toes curl in my shoes. He leans down and his breath brushes my forehead, my cheeks, and he pulls away.

"Good night, Amelia."

The trains of thought zip through without stopping as I climb the stairs to my weird little guest room with the sink in the corner, but I don't try to find out where they are going. I am on every single train and they are all taking me back to Texas and away from Nolan.

My last conscious thought before sleep is a flash of a photo that doesn't exist. I'm on a train platform and Nolan is on one train and Jenna is on another. They are going in opposite directions. They stick their hands out the windows, beckoning me to come with them.

I fall asleep before I can see the photo that shows me which train I choose.

chapter sixteen

The next morning, Nolan is waiting for me when I get off the elevator, and relief courses through my veins. I half worried he wouldn't be here, that he would want an Irish good-bye. I wouldn't blame him if he did.

"There's one last thing I want to show you," he says. "Before you go."

He sounds unsure, and I wonder what could be so big as to cause him to hesitate when he has already shown me his sisters' graves.

"What is it?" I ask with forced brightness. "Do you collect weird taxidermy in glass jars?"

He snorts. "*No.*"

"Do you have an embarrassing stack of failed internet memes that you tried to make before you launched your illustrious writing career?"

I make up all sorts of nonsensical things over breakfast at the café, each more ridiculous than the last.

"Christmas movie scripts," I decide. "N. E. Endsley has

authored some of the world's most *heartwarming* kisses on berry farms."

Nolan isn't listening to me as we rise from the table. But instead of going to the stairs, he heads to the Orman room and stops halfway there. He looks down the long hallway and pokes his head into the last two rooms at the end, a paranoid meerkat scouting for predators.

"We have to be quick," he says with great urgency, and my mind goes blank as he falls to the floor and *moves* a square piece of the carpet, exposing a slatted door with a leather strap. He pulls on the strap, the door puckering open like a folding window shutter, revealing a short ladder that extends into the darkness of this . . . hole in the bookstore.

"Wait, what?" I hear myself ask. Is this the part where I'm finally murdered by the crazy, reclusive author? Maybe it's research for a murder mystery he wants to write and he needs to know whether anyone can hear me scream in his creepy bookstore dungeon.

"Come *on*," Nolan moans, slipping down the ladder. And because he can read my mind he says, "Amelia, get that look off your face. Nobody's going to kill you. Get in before someone sees."

I am unceremoniously pulled after him by my calves, our bodies much too large to both occupy the ladder at the same time.

As soon as my head is clear of the opening, Nolan scoots the carpet back into place and raises the door back up with a soft *click*, effectively leaving us in total darkness.

I'm thinking about testing my scream theory when he clicks on the light.

As if this world weren't charming enough, N. E. Endsley has carved out a second office space within the walls of A Measure of Prose's first floor. I thought my brain had its fill of awe and wonder, but I was wrong. I'm having a hard time keeping my mouth closed and my hands at my sides.

It is maybe a square foot or so smaller than the fort, but you wouldn't be able to tell, if it weren't for the low ceiling. There is another desk pressed into the corner—this one made of metal, not wood—that takes up most of the space, aside from the lines of modern plastic shelves filled to the brim with journals: leather bound, Moleskines, and spirals. Slim wooden boxes with intricate carvings are stacked atop one another, with tiny typed labels that display dates from four or five years ago to the present. There are piles of elegant pen cases worth almost as much as the fountain pens they protect, and bottles of ink that look like they belong in Flourish and Blotts, not in a cellar-like wing of Val's bookstore.

But they do belong. This space feels like a reflection of him—both Old World and New, modern and inexplicably traditional in its melancholy and its contradictory contents.

Nolan is watchful, unspeaking. His gaze says he is showing me something vitally important to him, as important as the cemetery where his sisters are buried, and he desperately wants to know what I think.

His eyes want to know if it's enough to make me stop pretending, to make me stay.

But I can't think clearly. I feel like Belle examining the Beast's massive library or Cinderella when the slipper fits. Every heroine from every story I've ever read is bursting from her bindings to come flutter in my chest and assure me that this is okay, this feeling of bigness and rightness and wrongness all mixed together. It's more than okay that I am experiencing something other than grief. It's okay that I'm not entirely sure if the feeling is a good one or a bad one.

"I've never shown this to anyone," Nolan says, breaking the silence. "Except Alex, but he doesn't count. He just wants to use the Wi-Fi, since we're right above the router. We think the space was built to hold electronics, like speaker system equipment and stuff. Or at least that's our best guess, since it's ventilated. See?" He points at a vent beside one of the shelves, its little plastic slats fluttering open on a silent wind.

Nolan chuckles uncertainly. He is waiting for me to say something, but the space in my chest is only getting bigger and shows no signs of stopping. I have the strangest thought that, if I wanted to, I could bring this whole bookstore crumbling to the ground by touching my index finger to the boarded wall of this room and releasing all the energy stored in my body.

I turn to Nolan and say the truest thing I can articulate. "It's you."

What I should have said is that I feel like I am standing inside of his heart.

If this were a different kind of story, if we were shelved in the romance room, or even the adventure room, my statement would mean Nolan closing the space between us and kissing me fervently on the lips, and the music would swirl and the birds would come down with showers of glitter and ribbons to make me a dress, and together we would ride off into the sunset, with Wally trotting happily behind—but it's not that kind of story.

This is the kind of story where Nolan nods as if to say he agrees, that he is a co-acknowledger of this too-big feeling, and leans forward to gently place his palm against my cheek.

"I want you to know everything," he says. "Everything and anything you want. You can open anything, ask anything. I'll answer, I swear. These"—he moves his hand from my cheek to gesture at the shelves—"contain the outlines for Orman, and stories from when I was in junior high and didn't know what I was doing. Diaries and notes and things that probably don't even make sense to me anymore." He's talking so quickly that I'm having a hard time believing he knows exactly what he's saying.

And I realize he has probably wanted somebody to know everything for a very long time, craved an intimacy with somebody new, somebody who is not Alex or Valerie, who might understand a fraction of his new existence.

I decide to start at the beginning, because even though beginnings can be intimidating, I've begun to rather like them. I gently pry the first journal out of the first shelf and sit on the hardwood floor to read. Nolan paces back and forth like a dog circling his bed and finally sits across from me, leaning against the blank wall, a front row seat to my examinations.

The journal I hold is one of many bound in leather, this one decorated with a large tree with intricate limbs stretching toward a brown leather sky. Roots curl downward from the trunk and wrap themselves around the silver clasp that binds the book closed. I flick it open with my thumb and turn to the first thick page. At first, it seems terribly underwhelming: a long list of names in different languages in an adolescent scrawl, their meanings scribbled at the sides. School notes, or glorified doodles. But the word *Orman* catches my eye and I gasp.

"Orman." I breathe the word like it is precious, and I suppose to me it is.

"The very first time I wrote it," he says, "I was probably about ten. Avery was begging for a story about the trees that grow around here—she swore they whispered her name—and Emily wanted 'something pretty' to play pretend. I was already dabbling in writing stupid short stories, so I thought I'd try and write something big to impress them."

"I guess it worked." I laugh.

There is only a tinge of sadness to his smile. "I guess it did."

"You loved them a lot, didn't you?" I ask.

"Of course. I do. They are my sisters."

Neither of us acknowledges his choice of present tense. I bend my head back over the journal, trying to appear casual while flipping through the first inklings of what would some-day become the phenomenon of Orman.

"Did you really know about the tree knights so early on?" I ask.

"I knew what they did, but they weren't all female until later on, when I started to develop the world—building to fit an actual story structure rather than just a bunch of made-up games and plots we acted out. They were always meant to be guardians, though. That much I knew."

When I finish skimming the first journal, I move on to the next, which proves to be completely unrelated to Orman and is rather the half-scribbled thoughts of a young boy with too many hormones.

"Please say you did not tell this Rebecca Wise girl that you thought her breasts were more beautiful than mountain peaks," I say. "Please. I need to know this information before I can continue to live."

Nolan has the decency to blush a shade of red that rivals my own.

"We never spoke," he said. "Unless you count the time she handed me my pencil when I dropped it by her locker in the hallway."

"According to page three, you *do* count it, because it's written about here in great detail."

"Oh, God," Nolan says into his hands. "I take it back. You don't have to read everything."

"Oh, but I do! It's my duty as the first person allowed in here. It's for posterity, Nolan. Somebody deserves to know what the great N. E. Endsley thought about Rebecca Wise and . . ." I pause, my finger scanning down the page. "Jessica Rabbit?"

Despite his red hue, Nolan stares me down. "You have to admit, Jessica Rabbit is hot."

"I do not. I mean, if *you're* into unrealistic animated hourglass portrayals of women . . . rabbits? Was she supposed to be a rabbit?"

"She married Roger Rabbit; she's a human," Nolan says defensively.

"Like that makes it better."

"Whatever. Can't you just skip to the next journal?"

"Fine, but only because we can't possibly read every single one of these. Do you have any you would recommend? Like maybe one that is a little less wet dream and a little more substance?"

Nolan stands in front of the case, fingers tapping against his full bottom lip, and now I'm thinking of kissing him. Will there be more before I leave? And is it fair to him or me that I *want* there to be another?

My first kiss was with Greg Peterson, during homeroom our fifth-grade year, on a dare, and we both got sent to the nurse's office for a lecture because whooping cough was going around. It was a dare I had taken willingly, because I had a crush on Greg, but I was more disappointed in the kiss than in the whooping cough I got a week later.

I thought maybe I was going to be someone who would rather read than kiss.

But just as I didn't really understand death until Jenna, I never fully appreciated the appeal of kissing until Nolan roused a longing in me that I couldn't name. I used to think that love interests falling into each other's arms in stories sounded disorderly and . . . kind of boring.

But there's nothing boring about kissing Nolan Endsley.

When he turns back to me with a journal—a regular black spiral—I try not to look like I was checking him out the way he checked out poor Rebecca Wise of the mountainous boobs, or that I am disappointed in the plainness of the journal.

"This one," Nolan says.

It's another diary, from an older Nolan Endsley. Each entry is meticulously headed with the date and the time it was written, and the handwriting is so sharp and orderly that I imagine it would prick my finger to touch.

"The first bits aren't important," he says. "It's around July thirty-first that you'll want to start reading."

I know what I'm going to find, but I'm still not fully prepared when I read the first line: "They are dead."

I jerk my head up, but Nolan is looking down at his hands, lacing his fingers together and apart unseeingly.

"Are you sure?" I ask.

He looks at me. "I am," he says.

So I read.

They are dead. Avery and Emily are dead. They are dead. Dead. Dead. Everything hurts. My heart actually literally hurts. I thought it was a heart attack, but Val says it's not physical pain like that, and it feels like it, but it's not. It's not like the cut on my arm from where Mom clawed at me when she heard. Her hands were manicured. She was getting a manicure and I was supposed to watch them. She told me she was getting a manicure and told me before we left the house, "Look after them, Nolan." Like I haven't always looked after them. Like I needed to be told.

Oh God, oh God, oh God. They're dead. I saw them. I wasn't supposed to. Alex tried to hold me back, but he's smaller than I am and I'm big and stupid, so I went and looked when they pulled them out of the water. They looked like drowned corpses in a horror movie, cold and blue and cold. But how? They were here a few hours ago?

Dead. Dead. Dead. Dead. My fault. Dead.

It hurts. I want them to be here and I want them to come into my room and tell me it's a joke. I want them to jump on Alex and wake him up.

Alex is sleeping on the floor. He says he's not leaving me. He says it's not my fault.

Dad got home an hour ago. He was still wearing his tie and suit from the meeting and I came downstairs to see him. I don't know why, but I wanted to know what he would say. He told me everything was okay, that it wasn't my fault, that we would be okay. But I heard him and Mom shouting at each other and then I ran back up to my room.

Dead.

Emily asked me today if I would take her to the bookstore, if I would read to her again. I told her no, that I had something to do, that she should go play with Avery and I would see them tonight.

But it's tonight. They're not here.

Help, help, help.

Help. Dead.

I wish I were dead.

The last word is streaked across the page, the pen going in a straight line to nowhere as if the hand of the writer were jerked. I look up, crying, and Nolan looks like he is remembering how crying feels, without actually doing it.

"Alexander," he says simply. "He woke up and saw what I was writing and took the pen from my hand and told me it wasn't my fault. That even if it was, I owed it to my sisters to live."

I wipe my nose on my arm. "And you listened."

"Sort of. I took it to mean that it was my curse to keep on living, my punishment." He snorts. "At least he made it feel that way. Especially when he crawled into the twin bed with me because I 'couldn't be trusted alone.'"

And because I'm sitting inside his heart and he wants me

246 • ashley schumacher

to know, I feel compelled to ask, even if I'm not sure I want to know the answer, "Do you still feel that way? Like it's a punishment?"

"No." His eyes drop to my lips. "It's a privilege."

I put the journal back in its place and move to find another. "Show me something else," I say.

I read entry after entry about his parents. His father had left what remained of his family after Avery and Emily were gone, but Nolan saw more of him because the court ordered they spend time together every other weekend. Nolan didn't care for the stuffy business suit he saw. Nolan's mother, unlike mine, flourished in her independence and spent hours each week on excessive grooming, socializing, and—thanks to a hefty divorce settlement—shopping. She is painted with Nolan's words as an unsympathetic, flat character from a fairy tale, a wicked mother who cares little for the heir to the family throne. But she comes up so often, his every interaction with her recorded, that I wonder if he knows he has written his longing into the sentences that claim he does not miss or need her.

An entry from a little under a year ago details their interaction when he turned eighteen and bought the Endsleys' summer home in Lochbrook.

Mom sent a sealed note via her realtor. Why the woman hasn't learned how to text or email, I don't know. "If you want to purchase the furnishings, I can send my assistant over to determine a reasonable price." I bet the money from Dad has run out already and she'll force me to haggle with some nameless assistant for my childhood bedspread, Emily's picture books, and Avery's soccer ball.

"Show me something happy," I say, when I can bear the weight no longer. "Something good."

"Something that doesn't suck?" He smiles. As I've read, he's been thumbing through journals on his own, and he looks no worse for wear. I wonder if it's easier for him to relive fragments of memory with me nearby. I hope so.

He hands me another leather-bound journal, this one with a dangling cord wrapped tightly around its middle.

"What is this?" I ask.

"Something good," he says.

The handwriting inside is legible, but only just. I begin to read the first entry, which is undated and sideways on the page in another childish scrawl.

Today we went to Orman. Orman is Turkish for forest. I read it in a book. I also read a book about a mouse and his mouse friends. It was weird and the mouse had a weird name. Em and A liked Orman. I made it up. They want to go again tomorrow. For lunch I ate sandwiches but Em cried because she wanted my ham sandwich instead of her cheese sandwich so we traded. Avery was mad because I found out aviary means bird cage. I read it in a book. She said she doesn't want to be in a cage. Em cried because she thought Avery would be in a cage but then she forgot and finished her sandwich.

I'm giggling, and the feeling is so foreign that it makes my stomach feel as if I've drunk an entire carbonated beverage in one gulp.

"That's not the good part." Nolan leans over to flip a few pages. "Start on the top of this one."

*Mrs. S says I can call her Valerie. Mrs. S owns the
bookstore. Mama doesn't care if we go to the bookstore
by ourselves. We have to hold hands when we go alone.
Mama drops us off and says she'll be back in an hour.
Valerie feeds us green potato chips that she says are
vegetable chips but they are really just potato chips. She
makes us wipe our hands so we don't get crumbs on the
books. The room with the lighthouse and the mountain
is my favorite. Em and A said it is where Orman lives.
I told them they were right. They think I am the King of
Orman. I think they are right.*

"Wait," I say. "The Orman room was there before Orman?"
Nolan nods, smiling as he reads his childhood writing up-
side down. "Yeah. Orman wouldn't be what it is if not for Val
and this store."

"Or Avery and Emily," I say.

He nods, a sad but not too sad smile on his lips. "Yes."

I delight in this moment in Nolan Endsley's heart, with the
history of Orman and him open in my hands. I let it overlap
with thoughts of Jenna and her insistence on buying perfectly
formed books. I think about how my dad used to read to me
every night before I fell asleep. I marvel at two little girls and
a barely older boy playing pretend on sandy beaches beneath
a shimmering sun and in the cool shelter of an extraordinary
bookstore. And I slowly start to populate the bleak world with
things that make life worth living.

When I'm done rebuilding the world, it is made up of love,
the loss of it and the finding of it. It is the *finding*, the possibility of discovering more that I love in this lifetime and not

wasting time on things I don't, that makes me grapple for my cell phone before I can change my mind.

When Nolan looks at me questioningly, I say, "Can you give me a minute alone? There's something I need to do."

He scrutinizes me, my phone lit up and ready to call Mark, and smiles.

"I'll go make sure Wally isn't causing mass destruction. Don't forget to put the carpet back when you leave."

He stops halfway up the ladder, the thread between us pulling my gaze to his.

"Amelia?"

"Yeah?"

"Good luck."

He waits perched at the top of the ladder, his head tilted as he listens intently, before he decides the coast is clear and scuttles to open the door and push the rug out of the way in a single practiced move. There is absolutely no way he's never been caught.

I wait until I hear him slide the carpet back over the door and then I swiftly call Mark, before I can overthink it or a clever wind can intervene.

Mark answers on the first ring.

"Amelia, is everything all right? Can you get to the airport okay? Are you hurt?"

I wish the compass rug were here to fiddle with. I pleat the denim of my jeans between my fingers instead.

"No, I'm fine. I just . . . I wanted to see if you could talk."

"I'm a little busy right now. Can we chat tonight, when we pick you up from the airport? I've got a client here and—"

"I don't want the scholarship," I blurt out, scrunching up

my eyes. "I . . . I mean, I don't want to be a professor. At least, not of English. I think. I don't know what I want to do at all."

I hear muffled voices, Mark apologizing to whatever client is in the room with him, and the sound of a heavy door closing.

He'll understand. Mark will be warm and concerned. He'll help me find a way to explain to Trisha.

"Amelia, what is the meaning of this?"

His voice is a hiss, a serpent in my new garden, and my stomach drops. I've never heard Mr. Williams's voice rise above mild irritation. It seems silly, but I thought him incapable of anger, like it wasn't in his chemical makeup.

I was wrong.

"I'm sorry," I whisper. This time I'm not apologizing for Jenna's death but for my own perplexities, my inability to choose a path that is smart and safe and secure. I need to explain why I've changed my mind, but how do you explain clever winds and invisible whales to lawyers in suits?

"It's not what I want," I say.

"You want to major in something different?"

"I don't know," I whisper. "I don't know if I want to go to Montana at all."

Silence.

"Jenna would want you in school as planned. This is nonsensical. Amelia, what *else* can you do?" His voice rises until it fills up all the phone lines between Dallas and Lochbrook. It is a large lump of sound working its way through wires, startling birds and small children gazing out car windows, even though I know cell phones don't use wires.

"I don't know," I say again, my earlier resolve vanishing. "I don't . . . I'm not sure. Maybe photography? I was thinking maybe I could start out at a community college. Figure out what it is I want to do."

"That is *not* a suitable course of action. That will not help you get into the finest graduate schools in the country. Community college is a place for retirees to take computer lessons and for kids who weren't accepted into schools like the one you *will be* attending. Is that what you want? To waste all of your intellect and precious time?"

I'm floundering in his sea of words, hands clawing at the waves and trying to find air to breathe. "No," I say. "That's not what I want."

I want to say he's wrong about community college and ask what's so wrong with figuring out what I want to do and what I'm good at before I spend thousands of his dollars on a degree I might not even like.

I want to tell him that I don't know what I'm doing, that Jenna was the smart, efficient one, not me.

My lungs are out of air, but Mark's aren't.

"Amelia," he says, keeping his voice calm and level, if strained. "You have suffered a terrible tragedy at a very young age. You are understandably distraught. Trisha and I understand better than anyone how close you two were." Jenna's dad has started crying, and I'm left to drown in his tears as well as his words. I want to tug the thread between Nolan and me as hard as I can, but Mark keeps talking. "Go to school like you planned, like Jenna wanted. You should have everything you need to lead a successful life. We will help you. Do you understand?"

I don't understand anything anymore, but I want this conversation to be over, so I say, "Yes, I understand."

"You must give yourself a chance to adjust. You must give

yourself a chance at a prosperous life, Amelia. It's what Jenna would want."

His voice breaks when he says her name, and now he's sobbing into the phone.

"I'll go," I say. Anything to stop the crying and the net of anxiety that has dropped over my head. "I'll go to school in Montana. I'll do it."

I hear him blowing his nose away from the phone and I wonder if he's standing in a hallway surrounded by colleagues watching him blubber.

"Amelia, hon, I only want you to be happy."

"I understand," I say again. "I'm sorry."

"I only want you to be happy," he repeats. "There's no reason to throw everything away, okay? Not everything has to change all at once, Amelia. We're going to help you. It's going to be okay, Amelia. It's all going to be okay."

When the line cuts off, I want to scream. I want to take every journal from Nolan's secret office and drop them into the lake to watch the pages darken and disintegrate. I want to watch the lost princess lose herself in the forest, and again in the water, until all that's left of her is a disembodied strand of long, pale hair. I want to watch Orman crumple and drown beneath the waves of expectations and adulthood and right and wrong that eat away at my life, my choices. I want to take my library back from the clutches of Nolan Endsley's wildfire, along with his searing kiss, and douse it in lake water until he's too scared to ever approach me again.

I want to go back to a time when he was no more than a picture on the back flap of one of my favorite books.

I want to have never met him.

It's N. E. Endsley's fault, and every author that came before and will come after him, for making me believe that I have a choice, that magic could be real.

But Nolan's right. Magic isn't real. The books *lie*.

I'm tired of pretending they don't.

chapter seventeen

Nolan isn't waiting for me when I come out of his secret heart, so I walk downstairs to tell Valerie I'm leaving for the airport.

She doesn't stop bustling around the register when I tell her. The cash drawer keeps popping out, no matter how hard she shoves it. I count at least three sighs of exasperation before she gives up, slipping the glasses on the end of her nose to the top of her head.

"So soon? You're welcome to stay as long as you wish," she says casually. "Should you find the company too engaging or the store too pleasant, I'm sure I could find some work hours lying around, if you need some petty cash to convince you to extend your visit."

She says this like I planned to come here, like it has always been a summer getaway. I stop absently polishing the counter with my sleeve long enough to entertain the possibility of this place being my snow globe. I could *live* here, among characters and beloved plots and people with stories in their hearts and at their fingertips. Lazy days could be spent photographing the tourists, the locals, learning their favorite stories and trying to catch the gleam in their eyes through a lens. I could tell the tale of stories themselves and watch words on a page mold the people who read them.

I could stay with Nolan.

This thought is the most dangerous of all. I'm still living out the consequences of aligning my life so carefully with another, so I shut Nolan's name out of my mind with the avalanche of Mark's words and make myself say, "Thanks for everything, Valerie. But I really have to get back to Dallas. I have a college prep seminar to attend."

"You're really going back?"

Alex appears from the office behind the counter, his eyes watching me even as he bends beneath the stubborn drawer for two seconds and extracts a calcified piece of dog kibble before slamming it shut. The register pings happily and Valerie mumbles something under her breath that sounds an awful lot like a curse, while Alex stares me down.

When I don't answer right away, Alex turns to Valerie and says, "Is she really going back?"

"I'm *right here*," I say.

"Why can't she stay for the summer?" Alex asks, ignoring me. "Everyone else does."

"I can't stay here," I say. "Jenna . . . her parents . . . they want me in Dallas. It's where I belong."

The words sound like tin cans kicked across gravel, hollow and repetitive.

"You have to stay," Alex says. His eyes are pleading with mine, drowning on behalf of another. "At least a little longer. If you care about him at all you'll—"

The door jingles open as Nolan ducks in behind an eager

Wally, who does not pause to greet us as he races up the stairs. I can hear Mr. Larson cooing in Wally-speak from here.

Alex, Valerie, and I stare at Nolan silently, all of us waiting for the other to speak first.

"What's going on?" Nolan asks. I pretend not to notice the way his face lights up when he sees me.

"I have to go," I tell him without preamble. A single pebble rolls down a mountain and the earth shudders, knowing more will follow. "I can't stay."

The light behind his eyes immediately shutters as his smile falls flat. It's like I've shoved him, taken all of my strength and pushed him into another dimension, where I've drowned every whale beneath the waves just because I could, just because I wanted to watch him suffer.

"I thought maybe you were changing your mind." His voice is steady, a bridge over a barely contained river. "You were calling to tell them—"

"I wasn't," I lie. "I mean, I can't." I beg him with my eyes to understand. "I *have* to go."

His face flickers from disbelief to anger to pain to anger again. Even now I can't help but wonder how I ever thought he was anything less than gorgeous just because he looks nothing like his author photo. I drag my eyes from the top of his head to the long fingers that I can as easily imagine tangling in my hair as typing Orman. They are not clenched but hang limply at his sides, forgotten.

He appears to be burning from within, and he is beautiful, but I tell myself not to notice, because otherwise I will not leave.

"After I told you about the girls," he says. "And this morning. After the bazaar and the photos? After everything I told you, you've decided that you're just going to keep doing what you're *supposed to*?"

Customers are starting to float in and out the door in search of lunch. We must make quite a sight, Nolan and Alex and Valerie and me, standing in a square of angry whispers and misunderstood feelings that move between us like poisonous vapors.

Valerie exchanges a look with Alex, but I can't read it because Nolan is refusing to break eye contact.

I wasn't wrong to think the forest behind his eyes was dark. I wasn't wrong to think he was hiding. But as we look at each other, I see what I couldn't make out a few days ago. He isn't only hiding himself from the world; he has used the branches to protect his sisters, to protect his family from the prying eyes of those who would mishandle their memory and poke holes in Orman for sport. He has grown himself a wall of thorns to hide any shred of vulnerability, but last night he flicked his fingers and the thorns receded to let me into his inner sanctum. This morning, he gave me access to his very heart.

And now I'm betraying him by shoving it back into his chest.

He won't be able to forgive me, so I give him one more reason to hate me as I break our connection, turning to Valerie. "I need to go upstairs and pack my things."

"I will assist you," she says, her voice unreadable.

I don't look at Nolan.

When we're in the elevator, I am shocked by how Valerie says nothing. She was my top choice for supernatural guardian, the helpful, wizened godmother with a staff made of books and sheet music that would steer me toward my fate. But at a time when she might issue counsel, she is silent, focused on the layering of her long necklaces. I find the piano music coming through the elevator speakers intensely annoying.

As she unlocks the door to her apartments, I hear my mouth say, "You aren't going to say anything?"

Valerie inclines her head and looks at me, key paused midturn.

"What would you like me to say?"

This makes me angry. Supernatural guardians are supposed to have the answers, not ask the questions.

When I don't speak, Valerie says, "I believe you are at a crossroads, dear. And there is not a soul in this world or the next that can make your decision for you."

"That's it? That's your sage advice? I've got two choices and you won't help me?"

She turns the lock and opens the door and we're in the guest room and my shaking hands are unzipping my bag and only then does she say, "I was married at the age of twenty-one, in my third year in college. We met when I accompanied one of his opera performances as a final for my piano courses. He was wonderful and went on to sell albums and give performances all over the world." She sighs, her eyes closed in a way that I recognize as trying to drag concrete memories from the unreliable past we carry in our heads. "We traveled the world, he and I. We ate every kind of food imaginable. He used to say it was because opera singers weren't supposed to be so skinny."

This makes my stomach hurt, because I am desperate to travel the world with Nolan like this but I must be lava and wind and fire. I must be immovable, so I concentrate very hard on folding clothes into my bulging duffel.

"I was a widow by thirty-two," Valerie says, like it's a history lesson and it doesn't hurt her to think of it. "He died in his sleep. A brain aneurism that led to a stroke. It was all very quick and there wasn't much to be done about it. Highly unusual for his age, but there you have it, dear. We are all victims of unlikely statistics at least once in our lives. We had a great deal of money stored up by then, enough for me to spend the rest of my days holed up in our too-large home in the big city with our only baby, Alexander, for company. I'm an orphan, you know, and George's family did not care much for my lack of high breeding."

This I find completely absurd, but I say nothing.

"I could have hidden, Amelia, and really, that's what the world lets you do if you wish it. It lets you hide from anything that hurts or might remind you of your pain. It's too big and too unwieldy to expose you at every turn if you truly want to conceal yourself. But I wanted to face the hurt and discover new hurts and rupture old ones. I wanted my George to know that I lived in his stead in a way that he could not have foreseen when he was alive, one that would have delighted him if he could see me. I opened a store that sold our two greatest passions, music and books, and I continued to give others the gift of playing music. It has not always been easy, but I did not want an easy, acquiescing life, the life many expected I would choose after George's death. I couldn't stomach it."

Again, I say nothing. My bag is packed, so I sling the handle over my shoulder. I am stone. I am lava. I will not be deterred.

Valerie is looking at me levelly, like she knows what I'm going to do and won't try to stop me. But she isn't going to stand silently by, either.

"You must choose, Amelia, what you want your life to be.

Only you can provide the courage necessary to tirelessly pursue your choices, and therefore it *must* be you who decides the path before you."

If this were a different story, I would drop my bag and hug Valerie. I would announce my intention to stay and would race downstairs to kiss Nolan Endsley until he forgot about my ever leaving.

But this is the story of Amelia Griffin, who must now learn how to live in the wake of her best friend's death. She must decide what she wants her forever life to be, not just her immediate life or the life she has pretended to possess for the past few days. She must be brave and strong and determined.

No matter how alluring, no matter how much my heart aches at leaving Nolan, I can't impulsively upend my future to pursue something so uncertain. Maybe *this* was Jenna's plan, to have me realize she was right all along. She and her parents have only ever wanted the best for me.

I breathe in, out, and will my eyes to remain empty pools. "Thank you for everything, Valerie," I say. "I have to go."

If she's surprised, she doesn't show it. I make myself ignore the disappointment I see in her eyes and walk to the elevator, leaving her standing in the abandoned guest room.

I don't need a godmother anymore.

When the elevator opens to the first floor, Alex and Nolan are sitting on the mismatched chairs, the mood of the room humid and too close, like the air is angry with me, too. Alex looks up, but Nolan stares resolutely at the water bottle he holds between loose hands.

I ignore Alex and come to stand before Nolan. I owe him this much. I owe him a good-bye.

"I have to go," I say. "I'm sorry. I know you don't understand, but this is something that I *have* to do. I was wrong. I need to go back to school and become what I'm supposed to be."

He refuses to look up or speak. I talk to the downward curve of his neck and am furious with myself for the tears that come bubbling up to cool my hardened heart.

"I don't expect to hear from you," I say. And because I will never be truly volcanic in my resolve, I add, "This has all mattered to me. *You've* mattered to me. Truly."

Still he says nothing and doesn't look at me.

"Good-bye, Nolan," I say.

Some historic version of Amelia would ask him to call or write or visit or *something*, but New Amelia knows it is best to leave everything where it belongs—here, in Lochbrook, by the waves of the lake that never was and never will be an ocean.

I give a halfhearted wave to Alex and Valerie. I should offer gratitude for their kindness but I am out of explanations and good-byes for today. I walk mechanically out of the bookstore, the bells above the door mournfully chirping their good-bye.

I'm halfway down the path to the parking lot where my rental sits when he calls my name, and though the lava inside me says to bolt, my legs refuse to move. He has anchored me to the spot with the Old Magic of only my name, and I am frozen.

"Amelia," he says. He stops a few yards away from me. "Amelia."

It's just my name, so why does it sound like everything I ever wanted to hear?

"Nolan," I say. What else *can* I say? I have to go.

"This isn't you," he says. "This isn't what Jenna would want."

"But it is," I say. "I have to go back."

He is panting from the run, from distress—I don't know. It's no longer my business to know. He's dragging his hands through his hair and pacing in front of my car—drowning on land—and I make the ground between us crack and splinter to keep him and his misery at a distance.

"There's a photo," he says suddenly, eyes shining. "There is a photo of a girl curled in a chair. She isn't looking at the camera and she has headphones on. She's—" His voice cracks and he pauses. "She's the most beautiful girl in existence. She makes everything brighter around her because she is filled with stories, and even when she thinks she can't take any more, she lets in another chapter and another. Because it's who she is."

I make myself open the hatchback and throw in my bag.

"She sees whales in the sky and has stories to tell, too. She's not exactly sure how she wants to tell them, but she will."

I slam the trunk closed.

"I love her," Nolan whispers, and my heart stops. "I know it's too soon, and unrealistic, and stupid, but I love Amelia Griffin, and if she will let me love her—in whatever way she wants to—we could tell each other stories forever. Of pictures and whales and . . . anything you want, Amelia."

I ignore the wonder in his voice, the hope. If I were stronger I would kiss him good-bye, but I'm not strong. The sooner I go, the sooner we can forget. The sooner everything can go back to normal.

I leave Nolan Endsley standing thunderstruck and more broken than I found him, his face growing smaller and smaller in my rearview mirror. I wait to feel the thread between us sever and wonder if it will be like a rubber band snapping back to leave an angry welt on my arm, one final retaliation.

But it doesn't.

I shouldn't have come here.

There are no whales in the lake when I drive past. There is nothing hiding in the trees, promising adventure or peril. It's just a lake. It's just some trees.

chapter eighteen

Everything is back to normal. Well, the new, Jennaless normal.

It's my new mantra, what I tell myself every morning when I wake up to the sticky Texas heat and the sound of my mom watching TV.

Everything is back to normal.

I go to the college seminar and take careful notes. It's actually useful, full of experts in life coaching and nutrition, teaching us things like how to make a cheap salad taste good and how to have a part-time job and still be social while taking a full course load.

When it's over and I'm packing up my stuff, one of the instructors thanks me for coming and asks where I'm going to school.

"Missoula," I say.

"That's such a great school." She beams. Her smile is huge and genuine, as if I told her I won the lottery twice in a row and want to split the winnings with her. "You're going to love it. Do you know what you want to study?"

My mind is busy collecting my pens and notebook and

checking to make sure I have my cell phone and I wait too long to answer, so I blurt out the first thing that lands on my tongue.

"Photography," I say.

Lies, lies, lies.

"Oh!" She leans forward and grabs my arm excitedly. "Make sure you check out the Missoula Art Museum. You'll just *die*."

I spend the rest of the day telling myself to be normal, as punishment for my slip. I tell myself it won't happen again.

When the press release announcing the extension of N. E. Endsley's Orman Chronicles breaks the internet, I find out along with everyone else that there will now be five books instead of three. N. E. Endsley does not call me to tell me the third novel will come out next June, and I do not call him.

I eat dinner at the Williamses' twice a week. We sign the paperwork for my scholarship, discuss my first semester, and I don't go to Jenna's bedroom to say good-bye at the end of each visit, because what's left to talk about?

Everything is back to normal.

Except for photography.

A few days after the seminar, I squash my brain's plea of normalcy long enough to walk to Downtown Books and inform them I am going to be their event photographer for what's left of summer. It has nothing to do with the clever wind—I left that in Lochbrook—but I need a guilty pleasure to get me through the rest of my time here. And maybe it will help release some of this absurd photography energy so I can get on with my life.

It's only a month.

"We can't pay you," Becky's boss—decidedly un-Valerie-like

in his sweatpants and book shirt—tells me. "We don't have the budget."

"I'm just in it for the experience," I say.

Lies. Lies. Lies.

It has meant taking more than one picture at a time—another new normal meant to absolve part of my guilt—and with at least two author events a week, the photo library I post to the Downtown Books blog is almost doubling each week.

"You're good," an author I recognize from CCBF says, as she looks over my shoulder after her event. I've captured her midlaugh, signing a book for an eager fan. "You should go professional."

I tell her thank you and try to ignore the compliment as it plinks down the empty well inside me.

My walk home tonight feels particularly grueling. I'm exhausted. There were two back-to-back events at the store, my feet are sore, and all day I've been stewing over the roommate survey the college sent me.

It's supposed to set me up with my ideal match, to give us time to interact and get to know each other before the semester starts. The thought has trailed after me like my own personal rain cloud all day, and since the clever wind didn't follow me home, I've had to tug it behind me lest it rain on innocent patrons.

When I get home, I drop my camera on my bedspread, too tired to put it away, and allow myself a brief game of pretend. Even though the new normal has meant forgoing all imagination beyond reading, I take the little rain cloud with me when I go shower. I watch as it floats beneath the spigot, growing dark as it fills with water and then drains itself over my head.

Serves me right.

The bathroom steam curls behind me as, wrapped in a towel, I return to my bedroom, where I will edit a few photos before I go to sleep.

I'm thinking I really *should* fill out that survey, too, when my eyes focus on my mother. She's sitting on my bed in her new grocery store polo, my camera in her hand.

"Mom?"

Her head jerks, blonde hair flying up in surprise as she quickly sets the camera aside.

"Sorry," she says guiltily, like she was reading my diary.

She looks older, her shoulders frail and arms thin. Her nails look brittle and dull.

Adjusting my towel tighter, I sit next to her on the bed, reaching across her to grab my camera. It's still on, the thumbnails from tonight's event in their neat, orderly rows.

I should be mad at her for snooping, but I'm not.

She's looking at me from the side of her eyes and the TV is blaring an electric toothbrush commercial from the living room, but something about sitting next to her—my crustacean mother, who never found another shell to live in after my father left us—makes me pity her.

It also makes me think of Nolan and flip phones and Orman.

Nolan.

A whale peeps out hopefully from the waves, the first I've seen since Lochbrook, but I shove it under the water and sail on in my carefully steered, carefully constructed vessel of efficiency and adulthood.

"I've been taking photos at the bookstore," I tell her. "Author signings and stuff."

I tilt the camera's viewer to her, where a photo of an older white guy with his mouth open, an overly thick book in front of him, awaits. "This is John Rinker. He writes really boring books that everyone loves."

I click through a few more thumbnails, pausing on one from an event last week. A woman grins hugely at the camera, holding her middle-grade book above her head like a Super Bowl trophy.

"This is a new author. She was so excited to have her book published that she didn't care only six people came to her event. She said you can't control what happens to your book once it's published but she loved writing it, and loved that other people—no matter how few—were reading it."

My mom doesn't say anything, but she hasn't returned to her shows, either.

I keep scrolling back, trying to find something to interest her, but it's mostly a lot of people excited about a lot of books—until I stop at the first photo.

She's of great interest to me.

Jenna's head is bent. She's looking at the CCBF schedule, her mouth quirked in concentration and mild amusement at my off-camera excitement. Her hair slides around the curve of her cheek, coming to rest in a small tangle of curls under her chin.

She's beautiful. It makes my heart stop.

"Jenna," I tell my mother thickly. "Before . . ."

I stop, not letting the tears tumble out with my words.

Mom gently takes the camera from my hands. If she was anyone else's mother, she would hug me, but she only clicks through the photos, hitting the little arrow to leave Jenna behind.

"I watch a show on channel nine," she says. "It's called *The*

Talent Seekers. Have you heard of it? Anyway, they have an episode on photography. I've seen it twice."

Click. Click.

"These are good, Ames. Really good."

She angles the viewer to show me a photo she's settled on, lightly tracing a chipped nail along the image of a customer leaning against the wall, her head thrown back in laughter at something an author said.

I like this photo, too. Her eyes are closed, but painted above her head, on the wall behind her, are the ever-watching eyes of Dr. Eckleburg from *The Great Gatsby.* If I were to call it anything, it'd be *Dreaming with Your Eyes Shut.*

"It doesn't matter," I tell Mom. "It's not something I can turn into a career. I wouldn't even know how to go about it."

Mom clicks through a few more thumbnails and says, "I think you just have to do it, kid. And keep doing it." She hands the camera back to me. "The bookshop isn't a bad place to start."

This is all very, very abnormal.

"But I have plans," I say. "The Williamses . . . they want me to go to college for something different, something safer."

I want her to tell me I'm making the right choice. Or even the wrong choice. But because my mother is my mother and not anyone else, she has reached the end of her bandwidth.

"Suit yourself," she says, rising from the bed.

I click back to the picture of Jenna and stare at it until my hair dries, tracing every pore and detail of her that I can.

I want to see her. I want to tell her about Orman, about Nolan and Wally and Val's. I want to make her laugh with stories about Mr. Larson's coffee and to share her tears over Avery and Emily.

But Jenna's not here.

The wind blows through the crack in my window. It's not a clever wind, just a Texas breeze. But it makes me think of wind chimes and cemeteries, and suddenly I know where I need to go.

A memory: Jenna and me in the back of her parents' car. Her dad is driving with one hand on the steering wheel, the other interlaced with Mrs. Williams's on the middle console. Jenna is ignoring them completely, but my eyes keep wandering to the way their hands fit together so neatly.

"How much longer?" Jenna's eyes are glued to the internet browser on her phone screen and her thumb is hovering over the Refresh icon.

I jerk my eyes to my phone, open to the clock app that shows the time down to the second.

"Two minutes. Will you chill out? It's not going to sell out that fast."

Jenna doesn't glare at me, but she would if she wasn't afraid to look away from her phone.

"I'm not taking chances," she says.

"I'm Not Taking Chances: A Memoir by Jenna Williams," I say in my best droll voice.

"Amelia, it's not funny. This is my lucky lipstick we're talking about."

"What is it you're worried about, Jenna love?" Mrs. Williams asks from the front seat.

Jenna sighs. "ColorCentral is known for selling out of lipstick. It's a miracle they're restocking a color to begin with, and it's the only berry colored matte I've found that doesn't make me look like I'm wearing clown makeup."

"And it's apparently lucky," I add. "One minute, Jenna."

"What makes it lucky?" her dad asks.

A pause.

"I was wearing it when I first properly met Amelia," Jenna says matter-of-factly. "I saw her in the window because I was looking at my reflection to check my new lipstick."

I have never heard this story.

"Amelia, time."

"Jenna?"

She narrows her eyes but doesn't look up. "*Time*, Amelia. I need the time."

"*Jenna.*"

She looks up. "What?"

"You're ridiculous," I say. And because I suddenly feel the need to tell her, I add, "I love you, but you're ridiculous."

"I'm not ridiculous," she says, looking back down at her phone. "It was the first time I had worn it and, A, I looked fabulous and, B, it made us friends. So excuse me for trying to do everything in my power to ensure our friendship lasts forever."

"Four seconds," I say.

She buys ten tubes of the same lipstick. When she announces this triumphantly to the car, her dad says, "You don't need makeup to look beautiful, sugar, but if it makes you happy, I'm happy." Her mom calls it a waste of money but is appeased when Jenna offers to give her one of the tubes.

"Ridiculous," I repeat, but I smile when I say it, because she thinks meeting me is worth deeming lipstick lucky.

Her answering smile is dazzling, the gleaming one that

272 • ashley schumacher

makes me believe she really could be a celestial being trapped in human skin.

"May our friendship last longer than ColorCentral's restocks," she says.

"Duh," I say.

I haven't been to her grave since the funeral. When the headstone came in, Mark offered to take me to see it, but I didn't want to.

I *still* don't want to, not really, but I have nowhere else to go where I can reach her. I know she's not really there, but it seems like the place to go for the confession I have weighing on my chest.

It's too dark to see without my phone's flashlight, and it takes wandering up and down aisle after aisle of the dead before I find Jenna's grave.

There is a bouquet of fake yellow flowers stuffed into the permanent metal vase attached to the stone. They're garish, even at night, and I absently rearrange them with one hand, the other pointed downward at the stone I don't want to read.

Reading it is the final step. It means she's not coming back, that I'm the one responsible for making decisions *and* for living with them.

I turn my phone light off and sit on the thin sidewalk in the dark.

Cricket and locust songs fill the air around me, an uproar of insect melodies that hides my voice when I say, "Hello, Jenna."

There is no answer. No wind. But I have some things to say and somebody—Jenna, this headstone, these bugs—might as well hear them.

I mean to start with photography, but what comes out is, "I know you sent me a book." I laugh. "And I went all the way to Lochbrook to see if I could find out more about it . . . about you. I guess I sort of did."

A car engine roars in the distance and I pause to listen until it fades into the night.

"I talked to Nolan. About you and his sisters and Orman. He told me you saved him at the festival. I'm pretty sure he's the one who sent the book. Or maybe Val somehow? I don't know. But that's not what I wanted to tell you."

I take a breath. I tell myself everything is normal, that it's perfectly ordinary for a girl to sit alone, weeping onto the unread headstone of her best friend, in the dark.

"I wanted to tell you that I'm sorry. I'm sorry I wasn't there to save you, to pull you from the car, or at least be there when you died. I'm sorry I didn't hug you as hard as I should have at the airport. I should have crushed you. I should have meant it.

"I should have *known* when you died, and I didn't, and I'm so, so sorry."

I'm crying, and I don't stop when the ground shakes beneath my legs and erupts, ginormous blue whales tearing from the earth, their huge bodies rising around me like fast-growing trees. Dorsal fins and barnacles and rubbery skin covered in tiny hairs brush against me, scraping my elbows and upsweeping my hair as I dissolve into fractured sobs that drown out all the locusts and lake storms in the world.

I pour out my every regret, my every good and sparkling memory mixed with every bitter memory of her death. I let them seep into the ground as whales twist themselves from the soil and take to the sky, floating on a clever wind that has come howling in from the far reaches of Michigan to greet them.

"I'm sorry about the photography. I don't even know *why* I love it. I just do. It's part of me and I've been carrying it around like this insidious, awful thing, but Jenna, I think it's the best part of me and . . . and . . .

"I can't be you," I say. "I have to choose and I don't choose your plan and I hope you understand." I'm crying anew, and my tears taste like the ocean as I am purged by water rather than flame. I force my head to look at her headstone, to trace the lines of her name with my fingertips.

"How am I going to tell your parents, Jenna? I don't want to hurt them. What am I going to do? Tell me what I should do." My voice cracks.

I'm still drowning on land when a hand rests on the back of my head. I nearly jump out of my skin, my eyes not quite taking in the long, pale legs before me.

"Mrs. Williams?"

The noise stops—even the crickets—as Trisha Williams strokes the hair back from my damp face, her perfectly manicured nails combing my scalp.

"I can go if you want," she says. "I stop by sometimes after a long workday, but I can always come back tomorrow if you want some time alone."

"No." I wipe my face with my sleeve, hurrying to stand. "No, stay."

My ears are ringing in the absence of the whale rumpus and tears. All I can hear is the wind, twisting and winding between us and the grave below.

Tell her, Amelia. Jenna's voice is soft, triumphant. *Tell her.*

Who am I to argue with the wind? With Jenna?

I'm purged once more as I tell Trisha Williams about Lochbrook, about Jenna rescuing N. E. Endsley, and about Nolan. I sniffle my way through my discussion with Mark in Nolan's heart, but I can't stop giggling when I tell her about the stick figure drawings we drew in the fort and about Wally's caffeine habit.

I don't mention Avery and Emily, or Nolan's journals.

Unlike the wind, Trisha nods and murmurs in response to my story, and by the time I'm finished, we are both sitting on the ground and she is crying, too. Quiet, steady tears for a quiet, steady woman.

"I don't want to go to Montana," I tell her. "And I don't know what I want to do yet, but it's not that. It's not being a professor."

I shudder as the confession I've kept buried under stacks of books and blueprints comes ripping out of me. I'm fully expecting Trisha to be like Mark, angry and hurt. Instead, she digs out a pack of tissues from her purse and mops my face like I'm four. Snot smears against my cheek, but the movement is so loving and affectionate that I don't mind.

She grabs my chin firmly between her fingers, her nails barely grazing my cheeks, and says, "Amelia Griffin, Jenna doesn't want you to live her life, she wants you to live *yours. I* want you to live yours. It's all you can do, baby. That's all any of us can do."

Together we sit on Trisha's unfolded blazer, the clever wind caressing us as the insects take up their instinctual hum and the whales move north toward the horizon.

I sleep better than I ever have, after Trisha drops me off at my house.

276 • ashley schumacher

"I'll talk to Mark," she says in the driveway. She promises me over and over that he'll come around and won't be mad.

"We'll support you no matter what you do, Amelia. That's what family is for." She smiles Jenna's smile at me in the darkness of her car. "I'm a custody lawyer. I know these things."

It's a bad joke, but I'm so relieved to have finally made the right decision that I crack up anyway.

chapter nineteen

The next day's afternoon event at Downtown Books floats by in a haze. I snooze through two alarms after my graveside confessional with Trisha, managing to wake up only with time enough to make myself look vaguely professional, then I scoot off to the store to photograph a local author tea for two hours.

Along with my alarm clock, I wake to a text message from Mark, three lines typed late last night after I'd already fallen into a slumber overrun with whales and photographs.

I'm sorry, hon. I love you. Dinner tonight?

Just thinking of how I get to have my freedom *and* Mark and Trisha makes me feel rebellious and silly. There's a definite bounce in my step after the event, and when I see Becky approaching I suspect she's going to ask what kind of drugs I'm on.

Instead, Becky does the impossible: She hands me a small, sturdy box with a familiar sticker on its side, and my blood freezes. It's a calligraphy *V* in the middle of an open book.

Val's.

My heart is pumping too fast.

"Another package for you, Amelia. You really should give them your home address. We're not a post office, you know."

"Sure," I say. My mouth is on autopilot as my brain tries to summon whales to carry away the memories of Nolan Endsley that are leaking into my bloodstream, making me feel hopelessly warm. The whales don't come, so for a moment I sit and let them wash over me: Nolan laughing and choking on wine as Alex talks of swords and phones. Nolan insisting I draw stick figures like it's the most important thing in the world. Nolan kissing me in the Orman room. Nolan reading to me. Nolan, exhausted but triumphant, promising me that if he can conquer his fear, I can conquer mine.

"Amelia? Are you okay?"

I don't bother trying to sound normal as I shoulder my camera bag, holding the box between my hands like it's a life raft and these memories are a raging ocean.

"Sure, Becky. Thanks."

I don't even make it a foot out the bookstore door before I walk between buildings to a small square of brown grass with a wilting tree that the bookstore employees use as a break room. Dirt gets under my fingernails as I hastily sweep away cigarette butts and bottle caps and sit with my back against the trunk.

The box tape is sturdy, but it's no match for my curiosity. It takes me only a couple of seconds to rip the flaps open, but I sit for a full minute staring at the contents.

On top of crumpled packing paper is an envelope beside a plain black photo album with a plastic frame on the front. The photo in the frame is grainy. Alex must have taken it on his phone before we boarded the doomed dinner voyage.

It's already my new favorite picture.

Nolan's arm is wrapped around me and I can barely make out the pieces of my long hair stuck in his. We're not kissing, not even about to, but the trash condition of the photo can't hide the look of pure awe on our faces as we stare at each other.

My lips are open in laughter, eyes squinted over my rounded cheeks, but Nolan's warmth is contained in his eyes. He's looking at me, to quote Alex, like I'm the sun and I'm shining only for him.

I reluctantly stop staring at Nolan's face to open the album and suddenly I am back at the bazaar: Mr. Larson sitting in a folding lawn chair, an ankle resting on his knee, as he knits. Valerie smiling after Alex as he bustles by on some mission. A younger teenage boy sneezing into his funnel cake, powdered sugar rushing toward his face. He's lit just right by the twinkling tree lights.

I linger on the photo of Alex and Nolan's bromance, and the one of Nolan signing little Julie's book while her sister blushes in the background. Even with the rush of confused feelings boiling in my stomach, I'm stunned by the quality of my own work, especially since I spent more time at Nolan's signing table than taking photos.

These are actually good.

I flip through the entire album once more before turning to the letter. The envelope feels plump in my hands as I work my finger beneath the flap and tear it open. I tell myself to go slow, but years of reading have made me a hare, not a tortoise, and my eyes are gulping words whole before I can stop them:

Amelia,

*When I overheard the great N. E. Endsley being soothed by
a girl in sparkling tights at CCBF, I caught her as she was
leaving and offered to send her a signed copy of an Orman
book. I figured I owed her for not taking advantage of
Nolan in such a vulnerable state. She asked if I could send
it to her best friend instead, the one who introduced her to
the books. She gave me the address of the local bookstore (she
wasn't keen on handing out a home address to a complete
stranger) and said she'd make sure her friend received it.*

*I should have told you I was the one who sent the book when
you called the store or when you left to go back to Dallas.
I didn't tell you because I felt guilty for bringing you—
unintentionally, but still responsible—to Lochbrook, like I had
accidentally summoned a fangirl demon to haunt my friend.*

*He had been even less himself since the festival (I think he
felt defeated) but sometimes I would catch him staring out
the window and I knew his mind was somewhere else and
I couldn't go there to fetch him back.*

*But you could, Amelia. You gathered up your army of
kindness and empathy and marched through his darkness
to bring back my friend when I could not.*

*Jenna would be proud of you. So very proud. I know,
because I am so proud of Nolan, even if he sometimes acts
like an idiot.*

I thought you should have these—your photographs are just like you: They capture something only you know how to retrieve.

Whatever you decide, should you wish it, there will always be a job and—my mother said to mention—a bedroom with its very own sink waiting for you in Lochbrook. I have taken the liberty of enclosing a few photography programs in the area.

Forgive me for not telling you the whole truth, Amelia.

Forgive him for not writing to tell you he misses you himself.

Astra inclinant, sed non obligant,
Alex

P. S. Please read the packing paper. But don't ever, ever tell him I took them from his secret room, or he'll ban me from using the WiFi. Or stab me with a ridiculous bejeweled sword.

I smooth out a piece of crumpled paper I assumed was only there to protect the box's contents. I don't expect to see line after line of Nolan's messy, frustrated scrawl.

~~Amelia, I miss~~

~~Dearest Amelia~~

~~My dear Amelia~~

~~Amelia~~

~~This wasn't in our sketchbook~~

~~Dear Amelia,~~

~~Wally misses you.~~

~~I can't see the whales when you're not here~~

I lay the wrinkled pages faceup, corners overlapping so that it resembles a paper bouquet from above, place the photo album gently in the middle, and stand. One photo, I tell myself. I call it *Nonsense and Nonsensibility*, pack the contents back into their box, and head home to get ready for dinner with the Williamses.

A train slows down enough for me to catch it. I have a plan.

Mark and Trisha agree to stay at the hotel while I go to the bookstore alone.

They have come with me under the guise of needing a vacation, but I know they're coming to check out Lochbrook and Val's and . . .

Nolan.

The Michigan sun is setting and everything is golden, like I'm exploring some fictional world. The burgundy door with its cool metal handle is part of an elaborately crafted book.

The tinkle of the bell that sounds overhead as I step into Val's signals that magic is near.

But it's not magic that comes barking down the stairs, toenails scraping for purchase on the tile before hitting carpet and flinging itself at me in a furry whirlwind of excited keening.

I manage to get out a single unthreatening "No!" before he hits me, and I find myself in the unfortunate position of being flat on my back in Val's entryway once more.

Alex doesn't come to my rescue this time, but his mom does, standing imperiously over me like a Roman goddess and extending a graceful hand.

"You are late," she says.

I rub the back of my head to inspect for knots. "Late?"

She raises an eyebrow. "Amelia, what did I say about fools?"

"I'm not sure what you're talking about."

She raises the other eyebrow. "What can I do for you, Miss Griffin?"

I try to summon the whales, but maybe they're jet-lagged from flying alongside the plane.

"Where's Nolan?" I ask.

Valerie looks at me hard before raising her eyes to narrow them at something over my shoulder.

"It's Wednesday," another familiar voice says.

I twirl to see Alex beaming at me, arms open for a hug, which I gladly run into.

"Fort day?" I grin.

"I'll take you," he says. "If it's okay with you, Mom. I'll need to close the café."

Valerie appraises us, and I feel my joy slipping beneath her stern countenance. She hasn't smiled at me once since I got here.

Her tone is commanding when she asks, "Will you be available to take photos of our Christmas party?"

She wants to know if I'm staying. My face lights up.

"Put me down for the next two Christmas parties," I tell her.

She still doesn't smile, but her eyes are kind when she looks to her son and says, "All right. Take her to see the boy. And take that mongrel with you."

"I have to get back to the café," Alex says, when I don't open the truck door. "I mean, not *really*, but if you two are going to touch faces, I'd rather see you later." Wally has already leaped out the back and is running past the blue house and down toward the fort and out of sight.

"Amelia?"

"Hmm?"

Alex's eyes are kind when he takes my hand. "He'll be thrilled to see you."

My heart is beating in my throat and I can't imagine what it will do when I knock on the door of the boathouse.

I have to stall.

"But I haven't thanked you for the box and the album, and we haven't even talked about what Jenna told *you* at the festival, and—"

Alex's finger doesn't touch my lips to quiet me, but his intention is clear.

"We have time for that later, okay?"

My heart slows a little, and glows. What a luxury time is, what a gift.

I look out the passenger window.

"How can you be sure he doesn't hate me, since I didn't call or anything?"

I hear rather than see Alex's smile. "Fate. Now get out of my truck. There's less than three hundred forty days until the next bazaar and I'm a very busy man."

Nolan is not in the fort.

I see him as I descend the slight hill that slopes into the sand of the beach. He's standing knee-deep in the water, looking out at the pearl pink sunset.

Wally sees me first, and his welcoming bark startles a few gulls. The clamor of their wings and Wally's incessant yelps as he takes off after them cover the sound of my feet splashing into the water, shoes and all.

His spine is straight, his hands in the pockets of his jeans, and I want to know what he's thinking. I'm desperate to read his face, to trace the lines on his palm, to see if his lips are as soft as I remember, and I'm beginning to wonder if I'll have to tap him on the shoulder. Then I feel the thread go tight between us.

His shoulders tense, his hands easing out of his pockets, he slowly turns to face me.

Nolan Endsley does not say a word, but I can feel our connection humming with energy. I have to say something, *anything*, to break this terrible, terrible silence. All the words I rehearsed, all the scenarios I played out in my head, disappear.

"You're in the water," I say.

Nolan says nothing. I regroup. I try to put words to the tingling sensation in my fingers, the loud thrum of my heart.

"There's a photo," I say, "of two people, and they're looking at each other."

Nolan says nothing.

I'm already crying. I swallow thickly and press on. "They . . . it's stupid, and it doesn't make any sense, because they've only known each other for a few days, and everyone will make fun of them when they say it out loud, but I think they might be the kind of forever you read about in books."

His eyes blaze in the sunset's orange light.

"But more than that," I say, "they love each other's secrets. She loves his journals and he loves her photos. She tolerates his brain-damaged dog and he lets her sit closer than he's used to letting people near him."

Nolan takes a step forward, hand outstretched.

I lunge for it, trip over a rock in the lake, and right myself against his chest. I don't care how cheesy it is. Neither does he.

"There's a photo," I say, as he lowers his lips to my forehead, his eyes fluttering closed, "of a girl wearing headphones, and her favorite book balanced on her knees, and she loves you. She doesn't know it yet, but she's going to meet you, and it's going to be the very best of beginnings."

He stares at me and I realize he is looking at me to pull courage, like *I* am *his* whale. It's a burden and a privilege I will gladly bear, and I try to tell him that with my smile, my eyes, the thread pulsing between us.

He kisses me then, because of course he understands. And later there will be time, time for hungry *missed you* kisses and *I'm never leaving you again* kisses and everything in between, but for now it's enough to stand by the lake that is not the sea and let the clever wind ruffle our hair and be.

epilogue

If my life were a book, I would start the next part here, standing behind the camera tripod, taking pictures of Alex and Nolan maneuvering my boxes around the sink in my newly permanent residence in Val's spare room.

But this isn't a book; it's our story. Nolan and me.

And, for now, that means community college in Michigan—taking photography classes and fencing classes and even an intro to microbiology course because why not—and working at Val's. It means weekly video chats with the Williamses and the occasional phone call to my mother, who never turns off the TV when I call, but at least she answers.

It means long nights in the Orman room, reading side by side with Nolan, who frequently puts his book down to lean over and touch my wrist to make sure I'm staying, to which my heart says, *I am. I am. I am.*

Later, it might mean holding hands at our wedding on the lower level of Val's, with Alex officiating and Mark walking me down an aisle lined with our favorite books and people. It might mean endless nights spent alternating between Nolan signing his latest book for legions of fans and photo galleries with my name printed beneath every whimsical frame.

It could mean soft sobs from me and resolute tears from Nolan as we say good-bye to Wally, who dies at the ripe old age of sixteen and—Nolan says—years of deserved brain trauma. It might mean the same resolute tears and soft sobs, but reversed, when Val dies of cancer a few years later, her last words spent telling us to not be idiots and that she's quite overdue for a visit with George.

It could mean a strange existence where we take over running the bookstore and rent a room to a piano player named Michael, who is very odd but can absolutely be trusted to keep up Val's piano studio. It might mean framed photographs of Val, of Jenna, of Avery and Emily, on the bookstore's fireplace mantel.

It could mean a meaningful glance between Nolan and me, one stormy afternoon, when a young woman blows in the front door on the back of a gusty wind and marches up to Nolan and asks if we have any job openings because she's tried everywhere and doesn't know what else to do.

Everyone has a story about when they first read the Orman Chronicles, and this is mine.

I don't want to read ahead.

acknowledgments

First, all the thanks to Thao Le, the greatest agent in all the land and my fiercest champion. I'm still pinching myself that we get to work together. Your enthusiasm, immense publishing knowledge, and extensive guidance for this newbie is such a gift. Thank you for everything.

Thank you to Vicki Lame who believed in my characters (and defended Wally) from the beginning and who also didn't make fun of my *Game of Thrones* theories as the last season unfolded. Unlike that season, this story has benefitted from your keen editing and expertise, and I am forever grateful.

Endless gratitude to the Wednesday Books team: Jennie Conway, Jessica Katz, Anna Gorovoy, and Jeremy Haiting. Special thanks to Kerri Resnick for designing the whaletastic cover of my dreams and to Beatriz Naranjalidad for her illustrations. I'm still in awe. Many thanks also to Lexi Neuville and Brant Janeway for their marketing expertise and Sarah Bonamino for her publicity wrangling. I'm so happy to have y'all on my team and I'm forever thrilled to be part of the Wednesday family alongside so many wonderful authors.

Thank you to Alaysia for her insightful comments, and to my multitude of most-excellent writing friends: Lindsey, Karina, Ash, Amy, Kim, Meg, Clara, and Kiara. Thank you for all the writerly and moral support. You kept me sane. Extra special thanks to Jenna N., who let me borrow her name, even if she's still salty about her namesake's fate. (Sorry, Jenna.)

Many thanks and laughs to Cristin, Beth, Lynn, and all my Wordsmith Workshop friends for their endless love and willingness to answer hundreds of questions: Y'all are the absolute best, even if our time together is 99 percent chicken cutlets and weirdo documentaries and 1 percent writing. I wouldn't have it any other way.

Shout-out to the professors who made my time at UNT a touchstone for my craft and my life. Particular thanks to Dr. Armintor for being the world's best McNair mentor and letting me research young adult literature, Dr. Elrod for believing in me from the beginning, Amos Magliocco for teaching me to tell it slant, Dr. Rodman for encouraging me to write to my passions, Dr. Skinnell for making the study of rhetoric more fun than it ought to be, and Dr. Upchurch for his medieval maps and encouragement to pursue my writing.

Cassie, you get a paragraph all your own. Thank you, thank you, thank you for the long phone calls where one or both of us are eating in the other's ear, dubious fortune-teller card readings (whale and horse forever), chocolate shop visits when things are good, and flowers waiting on the doorstep when things are less good. You are the critique partner and friend of dreams and someday we'll live geographically close to each other and our productivity will be doomed. Your fingerprints are all over this story, and it's the better for it.

To my family, thank you for believing in me when I could

not believe in myself. Extra special thanks to Mom, who took me to the library every week of every summer and always believed she would hold my book in her hands, to Dad, who wouldn't tattle on me to Mom when I read under the covers past my bedtime, and to Amber, who endured years of my storytelling on the swing set and when we played pet shop. Also, all the love and thanks to the Ramos family, Cathy, and Scott. There's a reason y'all are in the family paragraph. I wouldn't have you anywhere else.

And finally, to Eddie. Somewhere in my youth or childhood, I must have done something good to end up on such a jolly holiday with you down this yellow brick road. (Also, maybe we should watch less TV. But maybe not.)